FIRESIDE

Visit us at www.boldstrokesbooks.com

By the Author

Tristaine: The Clinic

Battle for Tristaine

Tristaine Rises

Queens of Tristaine

Fireside

Acclaim for Culpepper's Tristaine Series

"When Brenna begins work as a medic at a clinic where political prisoners are held and interrogated, she's not supposed to feel anything for the miscreants she doctors. Despite cultural and political expectations, however, Brenna can't help but feel for her patients. In particular, one named Jess piques her curiosity....The first of what is so far a three-part series (*Battle For Tristaine: Book II, Tristaine Rises: Book III*), *The Clinic* sets the tone for what promises to be a terrific series. Culpepper's writing style is spare and evocative, her plotting precise. You can't help but feel strongly for the Amazon warrior women and their plight, and this book is a must-read for all those who enjoy light fantasy coupled with a powerful story of survival and adventure. Highly recommended." — *Midwest Book Review*

"...this smartly edited and tightly written 2nd edition [of *The Clinic*] takes hold of the reader immediately. It is engaging and thought provoking, and we are left pondering its lessons long after we read the last pages....Culpepper is an exceptional storyteller who has taken on a very difficult subject, the subjugation of one people over another, and turned it into a spellbinding novel. As an author, she understands well that fiction can teach us our own history without the force and harshness of nonfiction. Yet *The Clinic* is just as powerful in its telling." — *L-Word.com literature*

FIRESIDE

by

Cate Culpepper

2009

CREDITS
EDITORS:CINDY CRESAP AND STACIA SEAMAN
PRODUCTION DESIGN: STACIA SEAMAN
COVER DESIGN BY SHERI (GRAPHICARTIST2020@HOTMAIL.COM)

Acknowledgments

As always, warm appreciation to my editor, Cindy Cresap. Sheri created a wonderful cover image for this book. Radclyffe and the women of Bold Strokes Books continue to provide invaluable nurturing and support to writers of lesbian fiction, this one included.

I can't thank my friend and beta reader Connie Ward enough for her great feedback and sage medical advice. I'm also grateful for the support and creative input of my sister Bold Strokes bard Gill McKnight. Gill wanted me to jack up the action in this novel and rename it *BONFIRE!*, but she had many good ideas too.

And long years of appreciation to the women of the Tristaine discussion list. Thank you for your willingness to follow me from the wild plains of Tristaine to the peace of *Fireside*. The women in this story are Amazons too, at least in spirit—as are all of you.

Dedication

To the women who founded Seattle's Advocates for Abused
and Battered Lesbians, 1987
(Now the Northwest Network of Bi, Trans, Lesbian and Gay
Survivors of Abuse)
*Ginny NiCarthy, Merrill Cousin, Christa Irwin, Kathleen
Mangan*

And to the staff and residents of YouthCare's ISIS House
Seattle, Washington
A daily inspiration

CHAPTER ONE

Mac coughed the last of the bus exhaust from her lungs and filled them with frigid air, the kind conjured by January nights in Virginia. Razor cold. She shifted the strap of her duffel out of what seemed a permanent groove in her shoulder, wincing as an ominous twinge went off in her lower back.

To pass the time as she walked, she mentally checked off her bitching points for the evening—excuses for self-pity, should she feel so inclined. Weary and hamstrung after four days on a Greyhound. Dressed too lightly—her denim jacket was scant protection from the frosty night. Ancient back injury still asserting itself. And she was probably lost.

Mac didn't care. After crossing the country sleeping under the steel canopy of a bus, she was ravenous for stars, and the night sky was glorious with them. Their faint light glittered off the white swells of snow blanketing the rural road. She kicked slowly through ankle-deep drifts, grateful for the fresh powder. This hike would be much less fun if the snow was hard packed. Thick trees studded either side of the road, and the scent of pine and spruce cleared her sinuses and revived her energies. The silver globe of a full moon was just cresting a forested ridge, adding its welcome illumination to her path.

That this was indeed a path of sorts, Mac was almost certain. She wedged two fingers into the hip pocket of her jeans, drew out a folded sheet, and snapped it open. The bus had dropped her at its last stop, just outside Fredericksburg's city limits, and the shelter was supposed to be about a mile farther down this country road. The directions sketched in her neat script confirmed she was on the right path. As instructed, she had turned off the main road at the old billboard reading *Virginia Is For Lovers*—though someone had spray-painted out most of the words, in favor of a more succinct message—*Virginia Sucks*. In all fairness, Mac could not agree with this derogatory conclusion. Virginia suited her fine so far. She trudged on, enjoying the light crunch of her boots in the powder.

New Mexico had suited her fine too. So had Arizona. And Wyoming. And Colorado and Washington. Mac had greeted each of her new homes with optimism and hope, in the last fifteen years of her nomadic existence. She had found beauty to savor and friends to love, everywhere she went. She didn't doubt she would find those things here too.

But perhaps Virginia would be different. Maybe this time, her boots wouldn't start to hum after several months with the restless urge to move on. Maybe the loamy soil of a new state would finally prove deep and rich enough to allow her to take root.

Mac's step faltered and she turned her head, listening intently. She heard it again. There was no need to turn and look because there was nothing there. Mac looked back anyway. The path behind her was deserted and still, and there were no footprints save her own in the carpet of snow.

Whoever followed Mac still chose not to show himself. Or herself. She doubted now that they ever would—several years of coaxing and visiting quack spiritualists hadn't helped. These invisible footsteps had stalked her, off and on, as long as she could remember. It seemed her tiresome ghost had followed her even here, three thousand miles across the country.

Scowling, she defied her aching back and bent to scoop up a handful of snow. She balled it hard, then lobbed it back down the path. "Stop sneaking up on me," she snapped.

Then she straightened in surprise as her snowball careened off the very landmark the sheet of directions told her to watch for. A tasteful cedar sign bordered the side of the trail, marking an opening through the trees that would have been indistinguishable otherwise. Mac brushed dripping slush from the carved block lettering and FI—IDE became FIRESIDE.

Officially, the program was known as the Spillsbury County Transitional Shelter for Women and Children, but a confidential shelter couldn't trumpet its status on a roadside billboard, however secluded. Mac traced the grain of the wood, her fingers numb with cold. A fireside's benevolent image seemed more fitting. Faint gold light spilled around a bend in the narrow road ahead. No buildings were visible from here, but she'd found her way in.

Mac drew herself to her full height, in spite of loaded bag and aching back, and kicked through the drifts blocking the drive. She started up the steep incline, whistling, one hand jammed in her pocket to warm its stinging chill. It started to snow again, lightly, a dusting of lace.

❖

The woman was mad at her again. She could never figure out why the woman got so mad at her, but boy was she a big mean grouch. She threw that snowball right at her, and what if it had hit her? It could have hit her right in the eye! Not that it wouldn't have just passed right through her, but she would never throw a snowball at the woman, because she had good manners, unlike the woman. She stuck her tongue out at her again. A snowflake fell through her tongue, and that was fun. Then she realized the woman was disappearing up that little hill toward the light. She squeaked in dismay and hurried after her.

❖

The grounds revealed themselves to Mac slowly. First a long low building, angled off to her left, too distant and shadowed to offer much detail. Another far to Mac's right, a few meager lights burning behind curtained windows. The two buildings were like railroad cars forming the slanted sides of a triangle, a wide gap at its apex; but it was the house at the base of the triangle that drew Mac's eyes.

It was beautiful. She hadn't expected beautiful. She'd expected big, and it was that too. Beautiful and big. White columns, shingled roof, wooden shutters and two stories of *welcome*. Lord, this house glowed welcome like a beacon.

Smoke curled skyward from one of four narrow chimneys. The edge of the high roof was laced with strands of shining icicles. Mellow gold light bathed the worn cedar planks of the front porch.

Mac paused, panting slightly, and closed her eyes. She relaxed her shoulders and imagined herself another woman. A woman who'd just stepped from a taxi, perhaps, on a cold night like this, a sleeping toddler on one hip and a heavy suitcase weighting her arm. Mac looked at the house through that woman's eyes, close enough now to hear the soft music behind the wide front doors. *If I were that woman, I might hope healing could begin in such a place.*

But still she hesitated. Feathered snowflakes fell on Mac's eyelashes and she blinked them away, her weariness quieting the pleased wonder of this first greeting. She had knocked on so many doors for the first time, to a variety of welcomes, always hoping that the next door, in another house, a new city, would open to a more lasting peace.

Mac was thirty now, and she was getting tired. Her feet were cold and her back hurt. She had to trust that this house, and these women, would be gentle with her. She hitched her duffel higher and strode for the porch.

Fingers that had just pitched a snowball, Mac decided, should not then be asked to rap gloveless on an oak door. Mac sucked her smarting knuckles while she waited, hoping Fireside would live up to its name; she could use an hour's thaw in front of a roaring hearth. The music continued inside, the Spring passage of Vivaldi's *Four Seasons*.

Someone coughed within. Mac stilled her fist before it could knock a third time, hoping Vivian would answer. Vivian Childs, the program director of this outfit and now her supervisor, was the only staff member Mac had met in person. The warmth of Vivian's kilowatt smile would go far to ease the aches of long travel.

A small box two feet from Mac's ear exploded with static, and she flinched. It was an intercom, apparently, and it had just been coughed into. Mac pressed a hand to her heart.

"Yep," the box said. A woman's voice.

"Hello there," Mac said. "I'm Mac. You're expecting me, I think."

"Yep."

Long pause.

"Mac Laurie?" Mac tried again. "I left a message earlier, said I'd be in tonight. Vivian wasn't expecting me until tomorrow..."

Nothing. Mac stepped closer to the door and peered through the small glass oval she assumed was a peephole. She hoped the woman wouldn't cough again. The intercom made it sound like gunfire.

"All I see is an eyeball," the box said. "Reverse gears, please."

"Whoops." Mac backed up a step. She stared at the door full-face, then turned in a slow circle, and faced the door again. She jumped in spite of herself when the woman coughed.

"Mac Laurie," the box said. "You're the new shrink."

"Yep," Mac replied.

"Are you a smoking shrink?"

"I'm sorry?"

A heavy clank, and the door swung open. A black woman regarded Mac through a cloud of cigarette smoke, her fist perched on one hip and one booted foot toed neatly over the other. "Are you a shrink who smokes?"

"Ah." Mac smiled. "No. But I cohabitate comfortably with those who do."

"A rare species." The woman's blunt nails ticked on the door's edge as she eyed Mac up and down. She was husky, probably in her early forties, with ebony skin and keen eyes, her hair razored short. Her cigarette was clenched between strong white teeth, and laugh lines radiated around her full lips.

"Had to turn off the alarm thing." The woman moved quickly for her size, and her wave was a brisk snap toward a stairway. "Bedrooms are upstairs. She'll show you, hang on. *Abby.*" Cough, cough.

Then she was gone, rapid footfalls fading down the hall, a door closing with a slam of finality.

A resident? Mac didn't think so. According to Vivian, clients' units were in the two buildings out back. The main house contained offices and living space for staff. Therefore, Mac concluded, this smoking, snarling sentry was one of her new colleagues, her sister in social service. Mac remembered the laugh lines bracketing the woman's mouth, and relaxed a little.

She followed her nose down the hall and through the arched entry her greeter had indicated. It opened to a cavernous, high-ceilinged living room. Mac stared. Her last three apartments hadn't been this big.

She shrugged the duffel from her shoulder, wincing, and let it drop, the metal clasps clattering on the wood floor. She unzipped her jacket and rolled her shoulders, glad to be free of the dragging weight, then slid her hands in her back pockets.

Stepping down the two stairs leading into the room, Mac began a cautious walking tour. Big, she confirmed to herself. *Hello-ello-ello, bet it echoes in here.*

It might have been a gracious room once, and the cream walls and tall cherrywood bookcases still lent the space an air of hoop-skirted elegance. The slapdash furnishings were designed more for comfort than style. That suited Mac. A long wraparound sofa gave the room a cozy air, as did the two sprung armchairs, a rocking chair, and frayed broadloom throw rugs, all probably culled from a variety of donors.

Mac's boot heels clicked slowly on the hardwood as she circled the room. Then she discovered two treasures and stopped short in delight. A grandfather clock's whispered ticking held reign in the shadows of one corner. And at the far end of the room was the largest fieldstone fireplace she'd ever seen. Mac thought she could stand erect in there, and she topped out just shy of six feet. The grate was piled high with fragrant logs awaiting a match.

"Marshmallows," Mac whispered, holding her hands to the dark hearth. "Weenie dogs. Toasting my slippers here to warm my toes…"

The fireplace explained the pleasant, lingering scent of wood smoke. Mac clasped her hands behind her and turned, smiling. She rocked on her heels, listening to the ticking clock and the Vivaldi drifting softly from another room. It wasn't too late, Granddad said it was just cresting ten. They could still light a fire. Mac might suggest it if Cough ever came back.

One of the side doors opened, and Mac stopped rocking abruptly. A woman backed through the swinging door, which apparently led to the kitchen. She was drying her hands on a white towel. She turned and regarded Mac with a polite smile.

The woman's face was too severe to be pretty, but light blue eyes softened her. So did hair the shade of honey curling to the nape of her neck. Her frame was fine-boned and slender, but the hands working the towel looked strong.

"I understand you're Mac." The woman's voice held the faintest British inflection, an alluring sound.

"Mac Laurie." She nodded. "I know Vivian lives in town, not on-site. She said if she couldn't be here, I should present myself to Abby."

"Abby Glenn, resident medic." The woman flipped the towel

over her shoulder, a graceful movement. "Have you met Cleo, our legal muscle?"

"I believe so. The woman who shrieked for you, that was Cleo?"

"The shrieker, yes." Abby laughed softly and extended her hand. "We're pleased to have you, Mac. We were lucky to find someone with your experience on short notice."

Mac returned the formal handclasp, and Abby frowned down at her fingers.

"Was Cleo's welcome that chilly? I meant to reach the door first, honestly."

Mac grinned. "I walked here from the bus station. It's a little brisk out."

"Brisk? I wish you'd called for a ride. We could have spared you a cold hike."

"I enjoyed the walk." Mac shrugged. "It's beautiful out here."

"Well, that it is." Abby smiled again, and Mac caught a light scent of apples as she moved past her. "We'll have you warm soon. Cleo laid a fire this morning, and I've been looking forward to it all day. We've been brewing cider. It'll be ready by the time you defrost."

Mac savored the lilt in Abby's voice as she followed her to the large screened grate before the hearth. Mac went to the other side to help lift, but Abby shook her head.

"Better not. These sidings are fairly heavy, and your back's troubling you as it is. I can manage."

Mac stared at Abby as she slid the hinged screen to one side. "You shook my hand and knew my back hurts?"

"I watched you move and knew your back hurts," Abby corrected. Her smile turned shy. "I'm sorry, I'm showing off. I've been a doctor long enough to—"

She was interrupted by a loud metallic buzzing from the entry.

Abby sighed. "Not again."

The kitchen door slapped open and Cleo emerged, crunching an apple. She jerked her chin at Mac. "She broke something and set off our alarm?"

"She's innocent," Abby said, "I've watched her every move."

"Hokay." Cleo speared the apple in her teeth and jogged toward the entry.

Abby turned back to Mac. "We've just installed a new alarm system, and there are bugs to work out. This is the second time it's been triggered by ghosts, somehow."

The strident buzzing cut off, and Mac's awakened nerves tried to settle again.

"Hey? These are real specific ghosts." Cleo came to the doorway, frowning. "The panel says a switch was thrown manually by someone in the east wing."

"Hm." Abby tapped her thighs. "This isn't good. Ginny's in East Four, and one of her children is diabetic. If she's been careless with his meds again…"

"I'll get coats." Cleo disappeared down the hall.

"We need to check, Mac." Abby moved to a door in the far wall and returned seconds later carrying a small satchel. "Please make yourself comfortable. We should be back soon."

For a moment Mac was mightily tempted. She looked with longing toward the laid hearth and smelled the tantalizing spice of cider beginning to waft from the kitchen, and then she felt Cleo's measuring gaze.

"I wanted a tour of the grounds." Mac zipped her jacket shut. "Might as well start with the east wing."

"Well, at least you're already frozen." Abby shrugged into the coat Cleo held ready for her. "You're welcome to join us. Cleo, get a scarf, your cough is bad tonight." She opened the front door as Cleo snagged a muffler from the closet.

"Abby, don't lock it," Cleo growled. "You lock us out again, Abigail, my right hand to God, Vivian will make you shimmy down the chimney—"

"Instead of letting Cleo break a window," Abby told Mac as they stepped off the front porch. "Which set off the alarm the first time."

"Ah." Mac nodded.

Cold blasted Mac as they moved quickly out of the glow of the porch light—or as quickly as they could, wading through snow drifts—around the side of the house and into the darkness beyond. The wind rose, blowing the light snowfall into dizzying spirals.

Cleo broke ground for them, her short, powerful legs kicking a path clear toward the long building ahead. Hooded lights burned over the four apartment doors of the east wing, but they did little to push back the murk.

"The west and east wings both have four units, Mac." Abby's shoulders were hunched against the chill. "One, two, and three bedrooms. There's space enough for fairly large families, as well as single women. We're full most of the time, of course, though we have one vacancy now."

"Can't we brief her later?" Cleo was breathing hard, sending out clouds of vapor. "Show her a nice brochure or something?"

"The average stay is sixteen months," Abby continued serenely, "but we can contract up to two years. We prioritize women from outside the county, whose abusers are so persistent they need to put plenty of space—"

"Abby, she's going to quit in the morning anyway," Cleo growled, putting out a quick hand to steady Abby when she slipped. "After you amputate her frostbitten feet."

Mac trotted beside Abby, grinning. She liked Cleo.

Abby stepped up to the boarded walkway fronting the four east wing units. Mac glanced to her right, then stopped the other two with a low whistle. She waved them to her and spoke softly.

"The alarm might have been hit by a mother worried about a sick kid." Mac lowered her voice another notch. "It might also have been thrown by that skinny man over there who's trying to pry open a back window with a crowbar."

Abby straightened. "A man? Where?"

"Hush, Abby." Cleo frowned at Mac. "What did you see?"

"There's a guy behind the first unit. I saw him as we stepped on the porch." Mac spoke calmly, but her heart punched in her chest. "He's jimmying the window with a crowbar. I didn't see any other weapons, but I only caught a glimpse." She touched Abby's arm. "Hold it, you can hear him."

The man's hoarse grunts were clearly audible, even over the growl of the wind. He was weeping.

Cleo threw a look down the stretch of doorways. "Degale and Waymon are in One. They're here. Everyone's in tonight, except Terry, in Three. She took her little girl to see her cousins. They're signed out till morning." She slapped at her pockets. "My damn cell, of course, is charging on my desk."

"All right." Abby rubbed her forehead. "Ideally, we'd get everyone out, but I don't want the kids milling around in this mess. They're better off behind locked doors, at least until we know what this man's up to. Agreed?"

"Yep," Cleo said. Mac nodded.

"Cleo, go back to the house and call the police."

Cleo glanced at Mac. "Abby—"

"We're off the 911 grid, Cleo. We haven't time to tell Mac where the phone is, much less how to direct them to us, if need be. Go on, now."

Cleo blew out air explosively. "Okay, but no heroics here." She pointed at Mac. "You try to impress this girl with some grandstand play and get her hurt in the process, newbie, I'll skewer you on a stick. You two be careful." She jumped off the porch and loped back toward the house, muffling a coughing fit in her scarf.

Mac cleared her throat. "Take my jacket, Abby. If you sneeze tomorrow, I'm a dead woman."

Abby pressed a hand to her mouth. "Please don't make me laugh now, I'm in the midst of my first prowler. If we botch this, Cleo will lord it over us forever. I'd just as soon both of us went back with her, but we can't very well stroll off if this guy's trying to break in. We'll do what we can, all right?"

Mac nodded. "I'll follow your lead."

Abby drew a deep breath and stepped off the porch. She reached back and touched Mac as they approached the rear of the building, keeping well away from its corner. Mac stayed close behind her, in crisis mode now. She knew how to use an adrenaline rush.

Before she even saw the man, his muttering told her he was drunk. The rotgut fumes wafting toward them as they rounded the corner confirmed it. His language, what little Mac could understand through his slurring, told her he was enraged as well.

"Bitch lied. Right to my face. You lied right to my face…"

Abby stopped several yards from him and Mac took stock. There was a single arc lamp mounted high on a pole in the corner of the yard, but its stark illumination faded before reaching the end of the building. Mac saw well enough to know they might be in trouble.

The man was skinny but tall, and his long arms were wired with muscle. He was in shirtsleeves in this weather, further evidence of his state of mind. He knelt in two feet of snow, his chin covered with dark stubble, his eyes glowing red. Tears streaked his face, either from distress or cold. He gripped a long iron crowbar, trying to fit its forked end under a windowsill. He wasn't steady enough to hold his target, and the grate of steel jerking across wood set Mac's teeth on edge.

"You gonna talk to me, Terry!" The iron thudded back into the sill. He was blitzed, but still coherent. Mac wished he'd downed a few more shots; then they'd only have a sodden mumbler to deal with.

"Good evening," Abby called pleasantly. "My name is Abby, and I work here. I need to speak with you. Would you please put that iron down for a moment?"

The man hardly registered their presence, turning his head briefly before focusing again on the window. "Bitch lied. Walked out. Walked fucking out. I told her I'd kick her ass she do me like that…"

"Terry isn't here." Abby held her medical bag loose at her side, and Mac wondered if there was anything in it heavy enough to make a decent club. "Do you understand me? Terry's not here, but if you'll put the iron down, we'll try to help you."

"Screwed me up!" The man swept the bar in a sharp arc toward them, and Mac and Abby stepped back in tandem. The bar never came close, but the momentum of the swing knocked the man off balance. He smacked back against the building and sat sprawled in the snow. "Screwed me up," he roared again.

"Then don't get screwed now." Mac mirrored Abby's conversational tone. She kept her voice kind but firm. She moved a few cautious steps sideways, into the man's field of vision. "You'll be screwed again if you're arrested for breaking that window. You'll have to find some other way to handle this."

He blinked at Mac, panting.

Mac thrust her hands in her pockets. "If you break that window, the cops will cart you off to jail. You can't see Terry and your little girl if they lock you up. You need to see them, right?"

She caught Abby's slight nod out of the corner of her eye, and returned it. Willing her shoulders to relax, Mac waited until Abby stepped quietly into the shadow of the building. All they needed was time.

"Lied to me, I'm gonna break her head."

"It's lousy she lied, but you know this won't work." Mac eyed the bar still clenched in the man's hand and kept her distance, but his eyes were focusing now. He was listening. "It's freezing out here, man. You don't have any gloves. Your hands have to be killing you."

"Cold," the man moaned. He scrubbed his free arm across his face. "Bitch won't listen. I told her a hunnerd times, I told her I wouldn't do nothing. She don't listen. She took my kid."

"Terry's not here now, but I'll see her tomorrow." Mac lifted her chin. "You want me to talk to her for you, Jim?"

"Jim?" The intruder blinked at Mac. "Thass not my name. Ray's my name. She don't listen. She got law. Fuckin' cops." Tears coursed down his ravaged face, but he remained seated, and the bar stayed on the ground by his side. "Fuckin cops gimme papers."

Mac's gaze darted to Abby. Great, at least there was a restraining order on this guy. "What do the papers say about your daughter, Ray?" She slapped her pockets. "Damn, I forgot my smokes. You have any smokes, Ray?"

"Ain't got nothing. Ain't got no woman. Ain't got no kid."

Ain't got no crowbar, Mac thought. Ray dropped it in the snow to rub his face with both hands. She took a slow step forward and hunkered down on her heels, her hands dangling between her knees. She could still move quickly in this position, but her relaxed stance made her look harmless. Her voice became a low drawl. "You know Terry better than me. What do you want me to tell her tomorrow?"

"You tell her to talk to me!" he bawled. "She took my kid. Cops gimme papers. I come home, she's gone. No one say where. Shit, I ask 'em. Took my kid. I couldn't find nothing. I got nothing, but I told her I break her head, she run from me."

Easily the dullest conversation Mac had had in months, but at least it was two-way now. She wanted to keep him talking, to turn him toward function and away from feeling when she could. Her back was killing her, but she wasn't about to sit in the slush with this guy; it would be too hard to get up fast, and her height might seem threatening if she towered over him. He wasn't processing anything she said, but he was talking, responding, and the iron stayed on the ground at his side.

Mac saw the first flash of blue and red light splash across the ground. The police had followed procedure for a silent approach. She tensed to rise quickly if she had to, but either the wind covered the sound of the patrol car, or the man was far enough gone to be indifferent. "We can tell them you stopped when we asked you to," Mac told him. "You be cool, Ray, and we'll tell them that."

"I dint do nothing."

Mac sighed, then looked up sharply at the sound of a new voice.

"The cops are here, Abby!"

A thin woman leaned against the far corner of the building, hidden in shadow. The man's head twisted toward her.

"Gonna talk to you, Ter—"

Damn, Mac thought.

The man was scrabbling to his feet so she rose too, keenly aware of the crowbar. He left it on the ground. She heard Abby's indrawn breath somewhere near and the man was sliding, flailing in the snow as he tried to stand erect. Mac took his arm, either to restrain him or steady him, trying to distract his fixed attention from the woman at the far corner.

The clinical part of Mac's mind registered that he didn't attack her, that the push was instinctive, he just wanted her out of the way. She would have recognized deliberate violence, she'd known it before, but then the difference was academic, because both his huge hands were on her chest, and he gave one powerful shove.

Mac was airborne and then she landed, slam, flat on her back in the snow. She slid a good ten feet before coming to rest, snow gritting beneath the collar of her jacket.

There was a thwacking sound, and a guttural groan. Mac thought of Abby, and alarm sluiced through her. She lifted her head and saw the man huddled on his side against the wall, his hands cupping his groin, and Abby just lowering her boot.

Then there was a blur of navy blue windbreakers and shouting, and Mac heard a child crying. Cleo was back, and the two officers with her were doing a dandy job of cuffing the guy, so Mac rested her head in the snow again and looked up into the trees.

"Maybe Virginia does suck," she mumbled.

"What was that?" Abby crouched beside her. "Mac, how are you?"

"I'm fine. He didn't hurt me."

"You're sure? How's your back?"

"Stiff," Mac admitted. She tried a tentative flex. "But nothing's newly wrenched."

"All right, then. Grab an arm. Carefully, please."

Mac took hold of Abby's braced forearm and climbed to her feet. Her back griped but it didn't scream. She was okay. Abby patted her down thoroughly, brushing off clumps of wet snow. She was Mac's hero in that moment, this diminutive doctor and her flashing boot.

"Thanks, Doc," Mac said.

Abby's face lost its grim cast and she smiled up at her. "Think nothing of it, Counselor."

"Well? Well? Well?" Cleo was plowing toward them, and it seemed the only word she could bark in her urgency. She gripped their arms.

"We're fine, Cleo," Abby assured her. "You dropped your scarf," she added.

"Anyone hurt over there?" Both police officers knelt by the man huddled on the ground, and one trained a flashlight on their faces.

"We're okay." Mac nodded at their captive, who was groaning softly, his face in the snow. "How about him?"

"He'll be frisky again in a few hours." The cop snapped off his flashlight and slid it into his belt. "Looks like he got kicked in an anatomically sensitive location."

"I am a doctor," Abby said. "Thanks for coming so quickly, gentlemen."

"Our dispatch said we got a real rude summons from y'all." The other officer rose and adjusted the bill of his cap, grinning. "Some shrieking harpy called in something like, 'Get your ass out here now now now,' screamed over and over."

"It worked." Cleo pulled a sheaf of papers out of her pocket and passed them to him. "Here's a copy of his wife's restraining order."

They watched the two officers lift the dazed man from the snow and half carry him to the patrol car parked yards away.

"Well, ladies, we got a clipboard to fill out." The cop looked at Cleo. "Want to do the honors?"

"Sure, I can give you the basics." Cleo wrapped her jacket tighter around her waist, but not before Mac saw the gleaming grip of a handgun lodged in the belt of her jeans. "Abby, you and the newbie want to do something about our breathless audience over there?"

Mac turned and saw a huddled group standing in the shadows at the far end of the building, three women and assorted kids. The revolving dome light of the cruiser reached them faintly, highlighting their fixed stares.

"Oh Lord," Abby murmured, then slipped her arm through Mac's. "You did ask for a tour, Mac. Care to meet a few of our guests?"

"I'd be pleased." Mac's pulse had resumed a bearable rhythm, and she figured she could make a suitably composed first impression. She braced herself to absorb a fusillade of new names and faces.

They kicked through the snow to the back of the far apartment, and the group loosened and straggled as they approached. Mac sidestepped two kids tumbling in the slush and turned to meet an explosion of babble.

"Who was it? Was it Benny? It didn't look like Benny." A small woman had one toddler perched on her hip, and another clenched her hand.

"It wasn't Benny, Ginny, and he's been taken care of nicely." Abby's tone was soothing. "Apparently, he's Terry's husband."

"She's not here, but okay, how did he find us? This place is supposed to be secret, you said, so how did he find us? Did someone tell him where—"

"Lordy, Ginny, can't you cork it?" The black woman next to Ginny grinned at Abby. "These girls handled him fine."

Abby tapped the baseball bat perched on the woman's broad

shoulder. "Degale, dear, pray tell, what were you planning to do with that?"

"I was planning to whap a skinny white man upside the head," Degale said. "If Legs here couldn't sweet-talk him out of busting my window." She turned friendly eyes on Mac. "She did pretty good, though. I didn't get to."

"That she did," Abby said. "This is Mac Laurie, ladies. She's our new counselor."

Degale enfolded Mac's cold fingers in her large palm. "Nice to meet you, Mac Laurie."

"Same to you, Degale." Mac shook her hand.

"Where you hail from, Mac?"

"New Mexico and points west."

"They stack 'em high in New Mexico," Degale observed.

"That they do." Mac smiled.

"And this is Ginny and her two youngest," Abby went on. "And back there is Jo."

"Hell, Abby, don't point me out." The hunched woman in the back came forward, scowling. Her brown eyes darted a side look at Mac. "Yeah, hi, I'm the asshole who sounded off. You had that creep all peaceful until I piped up. He thought I was Terry, ho, she'd be so insulted. Me and Tina heard him outside. I'm the one who hit the alarm. You hate me now, already."

"Why?" Mac asked. "For backing us up when you could have stayed safe and toasty inside? Pleased to meet you, Jo."

"But how'd he find us?" Ginny still sounded shrill, and the child in her arms squirmed and whined.

"It's a good question, Ginny, and we need to find out." Abby gave her wrist a reassuring pat. "The police will question him, and we'll fill you all in on whatever we hear. For now, what do you say we get in out of this cold? Half of these kids don't have jackets."

But one of those kids wound strong little arms around Mac's leg with a gleeful howl.

"Hey, bucko, you're going to dump me on my kiester again."

Mac hopped to keep her balance, then lifted the boy into her arms.

"Son, you introduce yourself," Degale said.

"Waymon!" the boy shouted. "I got a truck!"

"Waymon's got a truck," Mac said. She smiled at his doe-soft eyes and pudgy cheeks. "I'm in love," she told Degale.

"Four years old, and he's got females falling at his tennies." Degale held out her hand. "You come with your grandma, little man, 'fore her feet freeze solid."

"Feet," Waymon repeated. "I got a truck." He slithered down Mac and jumped to grab his grandmother's fingers.

"So you're gonna tell us what happened?" Ginny asked Abby softly. "As soon as you know?"

"Just as soon as we know," Abby said. "Come on, let's round up the kids. It's way past their bedtime. I'll come with you and help get them settled."

"Tina and I will take care of her, Abby." Jo picked up the little girl clinging to Ginny's hand. "Tina will pour some cocoa down her, and we'll sit with her awhile. We'll be fine. You guys put in a long night already. Don't worry about us."

"Thanks, Jo." Mac laid her hand on Waymon's head. "Can I meet Tina in the morning?"

"We're in Two." Jo smiled. "And we're sleeping in, I warn you now."

"Good night, women." Abby steered a stray child after Ginny and Jo.

"Abby?" Degale turned back to them, Waymon curled on one arm. She lifted the bat slightly. "We wouldn't have let him mess with you two, honey."

Abby nodded. "Good rest, dear."

Mac lowered her voice. "Should we do a quick walk-through? These guys look fine, but others inside might be pretty shook."

Abby smiled. "Good idea, Counselor."

What they found pleased Mac. Women were gathering into

small groups in a few of the units, and she heard spatters of the kind of raucous, relieved laughter that follows a crisis settled without bloodshed. Fireside's residents turned to each other for support, as well as staff, and that spoke well for the diverse culture of the house. Abby and Cleo had established an atmosphere of mutual respect and caring that didn't always exist in the stressful climate of shelters.

When Mac and Abby emerged from the last unit, Cleo and the policeman were putting final touches on the incident report. Mac snuck a quick look inside the cruiser, which still pulsed blue and red light across the dark, snowy yard. Terry's husband appeared to have passed out in the backseat, but the other cop kept a wary eye on him from behind the wheel.

The cruiser pulled out, and they tromped back to the house, silent now in the buzz of post-crisis nerves. They gained the front porch and Abby reached for the door latch.

Locked.

"I've done it again," Abby said to the door. "I've done it again," she said to Cleo. She leaned her forehead against the door and sagged. "I do not bloody believe this…"

Cleo smiled smugly and twirled a ring of keys behind Abby's back, and Mac hooted. Cleo reached up and tousled Mac's dark hair.

"Welcome to Fireside, Counselor."

CHAPTER TWO

M ac." Cleo closed one eye and studied Mac. "Short for MacKenzie?"

Abby drummed her fingers on the arm of her rocking chair. Her jangled nerves were only now beginning to calm down after the night's excitement. She and Cleo and Mac had settled around the roaring fireplace mere minutes ago, but the interrogation was on. She could only hope their new colleague was up for it.

"Melissa? Missy?" Cleo dug her slippered feet under the thick cushion of the couch and pursed her full lips. "Melisande?"

"It's Macawai." Mac was sprawled on her back in front of the crackling fire, her long legs crossed on the flagstone floor.

Cleo's brow arched. "Macky what?"

Mac's smile was drowsy. "Macawai Kaya Laurie."

"What a unique name, Mac." Abby was pleased to see her relaxed and comfortable at last, after such a rocky introduction to her new home. "Is it Native American?"

Mac nodded. "Macawai is Sioux for 'generous.' Guess they didn't have a word for 'glutton.'"

Cleo coughed into her fist. "And Kaya?"

"Hopi, for 'older sister.' My folks wanted a large family, but turns out I was it." Mac winced and turned gingerly on her side. Her rich green eyes were warm with friendly interest. "What about you, Doc? Are you an Abigail?"

"I are, yes." Abby folded her legs onto the cushion of her hickory rocking chair. "It means 'father rejoices,' from the English. I spent several years in London as a child. My dad was quite the Anglophile." She dropped her eyes. She missed him more with every passing year. The pain of missing him was only slightly harder than her regret for failing him.

When she looked up again, Mac was regarding her with quiet sympathy. Her rugged features were unusually expressive, Abby noted, useful in a counselor's calling. In a single glance, Mac had sensed and acknowledged a loss Abby hadn't even had to explain.

"And the name of our African queen has the same meaning." Abby smiled at Cleo. "Doesn't it? Cleopatra, 'glory of the father'?"

"It's just Cleo. My *patra* had nothing to do with my glory." Cleo sipped steaming cider from the large mug balanced on her breast. "So, Macky-wai, sounds like you were born in the desert Southwest. But Viv tells us she found you up in Seattle?"

"Seattle, *sí*," Mac said. "By way of Tempe, Denver, Cheyenne, and Portland."

Cleo let out a low whistle. "That's a lot of U-Hauling for your tender years."

"It sure is." Mac watched the flames, and Abby thought she saw a wistfulness in her expression. "I met Vivian when she came to Seattle to visit her sister, Ruth, at Christmas. Ruth was my boss at the shelter there. We all loved what Vivian told us about Fireside."

"Well, we have a rather unusual setup here." Mac turned stiffly onto her back. Abby lifted a small pillow from the nearby sofa and tossed it to her. "Put this under your knees, Mac. It might help."

"Help her what?" Cleo asked.

"Mac's back is hurting her tonight."

"Aw, that crash onto your butt must have been fun." A hint of real sympathy softened Cleo's tone. "You need some aspirin?"

"Took some, thanks." Mac adjusted the pillow under her knees and lay down again, folding her hands contentedly over her waist. Her broad shoulders stretched the soft cotton fabric of a well-worn gray T-shirt, and denim cut-offs revealed muscled legs. Mac seemed easily comfortable in their company, an ability Abby envied. It took her long weeks to truly relax around new people. Cleo had terrified her for the first month she lived at Fireside, but then Cleo would terrify a seasoned Amazon warrior.

"I've never worked in a program with live-in staff." Mac groped for her mug of cider on the low table beside her. "Small group homes, maybe, but not a residential model like this."

"That's on account of Viv is psychotic." Cleo rotated her head slowly, to a series of muted snaps. "No way this *model* will work."

"True, it goes against everything we know about healthy professional boundaries." Abby was unfazed by Cleo's scowl. She knew Cleo was fiercely loyal to both Vivian and Fireside, and believed in their work with all her heart. "Social service workers are taught from day one that it's crucial to separate their jobs and home lives. Living on-site presents some personal challenges."

"Vivian said the upper floor of this main house is reserved for staff." Mac nodded toward the carpeted staircase. "That's more personal space than I've ever had."

Cleo jerked her chin at Abby. "Yeah, but you're sharing it with a maniac who will sneak into your room at night and drug you in your sleep."

Abby consulted the heavens. "Cleo, I happened to leave *one* smoking cessation brochure on your bedside table, that hardly constitutes—"

"Staff's got to be single." Cleo eyed Mac again. "No wives-slash-husbands, no dependent kids."

"Check and check," Mac replied. "Not inclined to acquire either anytime soon."

Cleo rubbed the back of her neck. "Your license up to date?"

"It is in Washington state. Vivian's started the paperwork for Virginia."

"Much experience in DV?"

"Cleo, honestly." Abby slid to the edge of the rocking chair. She tapped her knees. "Speaking of pains in the neck, get over here."

"Really?" Cleo's dark eyes lit up. "Hot doggy."

She churned her legs and drew her feet from under the sofa cushion, then scrambled across the floor on her hands and knees to Abby's chair. Abby noted with some amusement that along with her faded red sweats, Cleo was wearing the enormous bear-claw slippers that were her habitual nightly attire. They rather detracted from her butch ambience.

Cleo settled on the floor between Abby's knees and extended her short legs, which put one of her shaggy slippers directly in Mac's face. Mac snorted laughter and scratched the claws as if greeting a puppy.

"This here is Abby's only redeeming feature." Cleo closed her eyes as Abby's fingers probed gently at the base of her neck. "She gives primo massage."

"I might need a sledgehammer to break this up." Abby frowned, hoping the tension in Cleo's shoulders wasn't signaling the onset of one of her disabling headaches. She had grown very fond of Cleo in the ten months they had worked together. She just wished she could convince her to take better care of herself.

Abby glanced down at Mac. "I'm glad you're not easily intimidated by interrogation, Mac."

"I was expecting the questions, Abby. Vivian was real clear that the two of you get final say on my hire. We're giving it a month to see if it's a good match."

"Hell, you've got to be better than the twinkie." Cleo's brows lowered over her closed eyes.

A chuckle escaped Abby before she could suppress it.

"The twinkie?" Mac asked.

"Your predecessor." Abby smoothed the heel of her hand

at the base of Cleo's neck. "I'm afraid the first counselor Vivian hired didn't work out very well."

"She was a twinkie," Cleo muttered. "Jazz Hemlock, her name was, my right hand to God. She told us, many times, that she was drawn to Fireside to nurture our feministic awarement."

Mac sputtered gently into her mug. "Really?"

"She lasted three weeks. She lasted that long only because Abby kept me on a spiked collar whenever we were in the same room." Cleo purred like a cat as the muscles beneath Abby's hands began to relax. "That's nice, Ab."

"What did you think of her, Abby?" Mac asked.

Abby thought for a moment, feeling Mac's gaze. "She was just very young, emotionally, for this kind of work. It was too important to Jazz that the residents here accept the solutions she offered. She had a hard time grasping that we're not really about directing women's lives for them." She shrugged. "She was just overwhelmed, finally."

They were silent for a while, the soft Vivaldi lending a pleasant accompaniment to the crackling flames.

"You're gay, right?"

"Cleo!"

"Mmph!" Cleo slapped at the fingers Abby clasped over her mouth. "We kind of have to know, *Abigail*."

"You simply don't *ask* such things three hours after meeting—"

"Hey, some of the women we serve are gay. We need dykes on the staff. I've been Fireside's token lesbian for—"

"Fine, but could we let the poor woman spend the night before we quiz her on her sexual history?" Abby offered Mac an apologetic look, but Mac was listening cheerfully, apparently enjoying the debate. Abby tapped Cleo's head gently. "Don't make me get the spiked collar out again."

Cleo nudged Mac's shoulder with her furry slipper. "Sorry."

"That's okay. It's no secret where I fall on the GLBTQ

continuum." Mac smiled reassurance at Abby. "I'm a B, for bachelor. Were I not a bachelor, I'd have a lady on my arm."

"See, she'd have a lady on her arm." Cleo twisted and smiled smugly up at Abby. "Now we know, and how hard was that?"

"What's going to happen to—is it Terry?" Mac's expression sobered. "The woman whose husband visited tonight. Can the cops hold him long?"

"Depends." Cleo rotated her head slowly. "He has a few priors. I'll check on his chances for bail tomorrow."

"We know he'll be out eventually." Abby gave Cleo's shoulders a finishing pat, remembering the fear in Terry's voice. She had reached her at her sister's house to inform her of the intrusion, and she knew the news had awakened a hundred nightmares for the young mother. "I'm afraid she'll need an exit strategy, Cleo."

Cleo released a grunt of exasperation that became an explosive cough. "Robin just got settled in kindergarten, Abby. She loves it."

"I know she does."

"And Terry's halfway through that culinary arts training."

"Cleo, her husband knows where they live." Abby settled back into the rocker and rested her head against the hickory wood. "If he violated a restraining order once, he might do it again. They're not safe here any longer."

"So we ship them off to another shelter." Muddy anger was rising in Cleo's eyes. "Rip them out of another home. Damn, why do we tell women they need to come to us for their own protection, if that's the best we can do?"

Abby was silent. She hated this as much as Cleo did, and she could offer no defense. Mac was watching the flames quietly.

"I need a smoke." Cleo lumbered to her feet and stalked toward the wide staircase at the end of the cavernous living room. She paused and turned back, and her grudging smile was genuine. "You two get some good sleep."

"You too, honey. Take those vitamins in the morning." Abby

watched Cleo trudge up the stairs, despondence in every line of her body.

"She cares a lot about this place." Mac's low voice drew Abby back.

"Passionately." Abby nodded. "Cleo is passionate about many good things."

She wondered if Mac had seen the pistol Cleo quickly concealed in her jacket earlier tonight. Vivian had doubtless given Mac the basics about the present staff. Eventually, their new counselor might fairly wonder why an attorney who could be making huge sums of money had settled for the meager salaries of social service. Mac might fairly wonder why a board-certified doctor had made the same choice.

"Ah, listen," Mac whispered suddenly.

Abby had hardly registered the faint chiming of the grandfather clock in the corner, but now the musical midnight sequence reached her. She was struck by the childlike pleasure in Mac's eyes as she drank in the notes. Mac could have been any age at that moment, suspended in a simple enjoyment that banished thoughts of violent abusers and pistols and anyone's past.

The chimes faded. Abby rose from the rocking chair and extended a hand to Mac, and for the second time that evening, helped her to her feet. "You'll still be here in the morning, Mac, won't you? We haven't chased you off entirely?"

Mac smiled down at her. A dimple appeared in her cheek, incongruous given her obvious physical strength, and rather endearing. "I'll be here, ma'am. I'd like to think I'm made of stern enough stuff to weather a little opening night drama. Want to hear my first impressions?"

"I would, yes."

"I think you and Cleo and Vivian have founded an excellent program here, Abby. I'm going to work hard to do well by this place."

Abby realized she was still holding Mac's hand, and she

released it with a friendly pat. "Well, you've made an impressive first impression tonight yourself, Counselor. May I show you to your room?"

"I'd be pleased."

"Let me help with your bag. Your back's had enough excitement for one evening." Abby hefted the strap of Mac's duffel bag over her shoulder. She decided to leave the still-glowing coals alive in the hearth, liking the notion of their low flickering keeping watch over the sleeping house. Abby's own sleep had been fitful lately, but she was weary enough tonight to relish the thought of her cool sheets.

Mac followed her up the stairs, her boots whispering over the carpeted tread. Abby stumbled, trying to balance the heavy duffel, and Mac steadied her with one quick hand beneath her arm.

"Nice catch, Counselor."

"Think nothing of it, Doc."

Abby was beginning to feel a welcome confidence that in this new hire, it was Fireside that had scored a nice catch.

❖

She didn't like to go inside places, so she stayed outside most the time. She never got cold or hot, so outside was good. She looked through the window and saw the woman disappear upstairs, with the other lady. The woman looked sleepy and so she frowned, worried. She always tried to fall asleep before the woman did. She didn't like to be awake while the woman was asleep, because what if something happened and she didn't know what to do. And also it was too lonely when the woman was asleep.

She paced up and down the wooden deck of the front porch of the new house. The rocking swing thing would be good. She curled into one corner and cupped her hands beneath her cheek.

She wondered how long they would stay this time. She was

almost five, and she was getting tired. She always hoped the next house, in the next town, would be the one where they stayed and stayed. Fat chance with that dumb woman in there, though, she was such a big grouch. She fell asleep.

CHAPTER THREE

Mac's sneakers slapped a lazy cadence against the hard-packed earth, her breath frosting the air in easy bursts. She was not a particular devotee of power running, and her pace rarely edged out of jogging range. Mac ran because being outdoors was one of her favorite ways to greet a morning. She had run across arid desert plains, peaceful farmlands, and lush mountain trails in her time, and the pleasure never diminished. Her eagerness to explore the grounds had propelled her out of bed at first light.

Vivian hadn't exaggerated her descriptions of the pastoral splendor of the shelter's remote setting. Forested hills rolled gently around the perimeter of the grounds, dotted with fragrant, snow-spangled clusters of spruce and pine. The morning sky was cloudless, an inverted bowl of pure blue, and the weak sun glinted off the swells of snow on either side of her path.

Mac couldn't wipe the grin off her face, in spite of her chilled front teeth—the air was stinging cold. She adjusted the soft muffler around her chin, catching the faintest scent of cinnamon in the warm fabric. She'd found the long scarf draped over the doorknob to her bedroom that morning, a thoughtful gesture by one of her housemates—Abby, she assumed.

She was glad she rarely heard those invisible footsteps following her during these morning runs. It was disconcerting enough when they crept up behind her at an amble—if they ever chased Mac at full gallop she would probably freak. She hoped the spectral beastie who plagued her would make itself scarce for a while. She could usually count on weeks or even months between these ghostly stalkings.

She rounded the edge of the west wing and caught a glimpse of a coat-and-scarf-shrouded figure, hunched against the cold. She recognized Degale, who gave her a friendly wave. Little Waymon, comically rotund in his layers of snow clothes, scrambled on all fours in the frosty yard, pushing a toy truck in industrious circles. Mac loped on, past long, flat patches of ground that might have been gardens before they were blanketed in white, and then up to the main house.

Mac was still stomping snow from her sneakers when the door opened to a much warmer welcome than Cleo's offering the previous night.

"It's the waif!" Vivian Childs drew Mac into a brisk hug. She had skin the color of burnished mahogany, and the corners of her eyes crinkled with warmth behind oval glasses. Mac had liked her upon first meeting, and her instincts about women were rarely wrong.

"Hello, waif." Vivian released her, but retained a gentle hold on her shoulders. "Lord, I've never seen eyes that green, except in a cat or two. I wonder if cats drink coffee."

"This one does."

Vivian wound Mac's arm in her own and led her down into the large living room. With an abundance of windows, even the tepid sunlight bathed the space in a friendly glow. The light aroma of fresh-ground coffee drifted to Mac pleasantly.

"I hotfooted it up here this morning in hopes of beating Cleo to the percolator." Vivian steered her toward the breakfast nook in the corner, a recessed deck framed by a large bay window. Cleo sat hunched over the small table, her broad hands wrapped around a steaming mug. "Cleo's coffee is like gasoline. We use it to season the firewood."

"Morning, Cleo." Mac draped one leg over a chair.

"Mmph." Cleo's eyes were closed.

"Didn't we sleep well?"

"Mmph."

"We don't expect civilized conversation from this child until noon." Vivian lifted the coffeepot and filled their cups. "After we lace her wrists to a shower spigot for a few hours. If she tries to speak, Mac Laurie, please push a bagel in her mouth."

"Yes, ma'am." Mac hooked a sesame bagel from the basket before her. "We can cut Cleo some slack this morning, though. We had a pretty eventful night."

"Yes, I heard a harrowing account," Vivian said. "Well, I heard that Cleopatra single-handedly held off an attack by a terrorist cell. But I was able to eke out the truth that our new counselor conducted herself ably and well."

"Aw, Cleo, did you say that?" Mac nudged Cleo's arm. "You sweet ball of mush."

"I told Viv the part about you crashing on your bootie. That's my favorite part." Cleo grunted at the basket and raised a finger, and Mac slipped a bagel over it.

"Coffee! Vivian's coffee, there is a God." Abby emerged from her infirmary office, dressed in a beige sweater and blue slacks, looking impossibly bright for this hour of the morning. She was folding back her sleeves, and Mac's gaze was drawn to the subtle dance of muscle in her slender forearm. She remembered the smooth feel of Abby's arm in her hand when she'd steadied her on the stairs last night.

"We were going to let you sleep in, Counselor, after your dramatic first shift. Did you rest well?" Abby plucked Mac's denim sleeve. "You need to get a proper coat."

"I slept like a rock." Mac shucked off her jacket and unwound the muffler from her neck. "Thanks for this, by the way."

"You're welcome." Abby accepted the scarf and folded it neatly as she came around the table, then draped it on top of Cleo's head. "But I must admit it's not mine."

Mac grinned broadly. "Cleo, you sweet ball of mush."

"*Anyway.*" Cleo pulled the scarf off her head, her bloodshot eyes open at last. "Do we have an agenda today or what?"

Vivian had been sipping her coffee quietly, but Mac noticed she was studying her new team with alert interest. It was hard to place Vivian's age. She could have been forty or sixty. She looked every inch the nonprofit executive, in a simple but classy gray shirtdress, her wedding ring glinting from her gracefully folded fingers. Mac thought she looked pleased.

"We do indeed have an agenda." Abby settled in the fourth chair and withdrew a small notebook from her back pocket. "We try to gather about this time to go over the day, Mac, and we have a full one ahead."

Vivian nodded. "I understand the mother and child—is it Theresa and Robin?—are due back by noon. We need to know her husband's status by then, Cleo."

"I'm on it." Cleo was fully awake and she looked hungry now, for justice rather than bagels.

"I've got well-child checks scheduled for Degale's Waymon and Ginny's youngest." Abby drew a pen from behind her ear, and the sun caught the copper lights in her hair. "And I need to drive into town to stock our dispensary. Remember the sobriety group tonight, Cleo. Mac, you'll want to sit in on that."

"And I have an intake at nine o'clock," Vivian added. "A woman and child for Two West."

Mac's mug stopped halfway to her mouth. "You do intakes, Vivian?"

"Each and every one." Cleo refilled Vivian's cup. "Viv's smiling face is the first thing women see when they tap on Fireside's door."

"Who answered the door when you got here last night, Mac?" Vivian asked. "Abby, I hope?"

"No, Cleo."

"Lord, Lord," Vivian sighed.

"I'm still here, though." Mac's liking for Vivian rose another notch. "I've never known the director of a shelter to welcome every resident personally. They're usually off writing grants and hobnobbing with donors and such."

"Oh, I nob with the best of them, I just like to be a presence here too." Vivian touched a napkin to the corner of her lips. "Scratch is stocking Two West now, and he's hanging new curtain rods. I gave him some fresh bedding, and he found a whole slew of coloring books for the little girl."

"Scratch?" Mac raised her eyebrows. "He?"

Vivian nodded. "My husband. He's honored to be our representative example of a peace-loving man."

"Our residents know Scratch, Mac," Abby said, "and they're comfortable with him quickly. He takes charge of our vegetable gardens in the spring. He's been a farmer, and he grows the most beautiful tomatoes you've ever seen."

"A farmer, a mechanic, a pastor, and a host of other things too notorious to mention in polite company." Vivian's face softened with affection, and then she patted Mac's hand. "Well, Mac Laurie, with all the hoo-rah last night, did anyone get around to showing you your office?"

Mac perked up. "My office?"

"The twinkie just met with people in the big fir out there." Cleo jerked her chin toward the bay window. "She nourished their tree-hugging awarement. But if you really need special privileges…"

"I think we can do better than the fir." Abby rose, smiling. "This way, Ms. Laurie."

Mac had the general layout of the house down. Whatever the builder's original intent, the place served well now as their multiservice headquarters. Staff offices on the first floor, even the bedrooms upstairs, were spacious and filled with light.

Mac figured she'd have last choice of working space, so she was prepared for a storage closet of an office. Abby opened a door near the base of the staircase and waved Mac through with what, for Abby's economical gestures, qualified as a flourish.

Mac stepped over the threshold and stood transfixed. The room was fairly small, true enough. But there was a fireplace. She had her own fireplace. And in front of it, two battered armchairs, a small couch, and a worn footstool.

She drew in her breath and walked to the couch, brushing its back with her fingers. She noted an oak desk and filing cabinets in the far corner, but she drank in the area where her real work would take place.

Mac had always carried the title of counselor, or advocate; that's what shelter workers were called. She'd helped women steer through storms of pain and rage, taught stress management and coping skills, eased families through crisis. Usually in the corner of a crowded dayroom, with kids shrieking around piles of toys, or on long walks in the neighborhoods surrounding shelters. And she'd done well by her people. Whatever demons might plague Mac's personal life, she'd always known she was good at her work.

But she'd never had a private office, her own space. She felt a light prickling in her hands. Now she would have months at a time to work with these women. Long weeks when she could do more than help them with housing applications, explain welfare benefits, arrange daycare. Time enough to move beyond survival skills and watch them touch the patterns of their lives. Here, Mac could offer them the privacy to explore their choices, and the safety to attempt change and healing. She could imagine that happening here, in this room, this smaller fireside a microcosm of a more benevolent world.

"You should see your eyes," Abby said quietly. "They're shining like candlelight."

Mac slid her hands in the front pockets of her jeans and let out a long breath. "I like it here."

"We were hoping you would, Mac."

Now Mac noticed other touches, recent efforts to ready her space and make it welcoming. A bowl of crisp apples on the desk, a scented candle on a window ledge. Packets of tea and an electric kettle on a side table. The hearth laid with fragrant wood, ready for lighting, music playing softly from a small radio on a bookshelf.

"We would have hung a few pictures, but we thought you'd want to choose your own." Abby straightened a small pillow against the arm of the couch. "You don't seem to want a lot of frilliness, so we kept it fairly simple."

"You did it all this morning, didn't you?" Mac waited, but Abby didn't raise her eyes from the couch. "The apples, the candle, the other grace notes in here. You got up early to make my room friendly."

A faint blush crept up Abby's slender throat, but she met Mac's gaze. "Cleo laid the hearth before I was even out of bed. I think she's trying to atone for the grilling she gave you last night. Or perhaps she just thought it would please you."

"That sweet ball of mush," Mac murmured.

"She'll deny it, if confronted."

"Thank you, Abby." Mac touched people as naturally as she breathed, but she studied Abby a moment, never assuming touch was welcome. Her body language was receptive and relaxed. Mac stepped closer and drew her into a light hug, her hand rising to cup the back of her neck. Abby returned the embrace easily, her arms enclosing Mac's waist with a pleasant answering friendliness. Then Mac felt her go still.

Mac had held many women in her arms in the course of her work, and many children. She found that tears that needed to be shed could find release in the safety of a friendly embrace. Touch could convey encouragement or comfort more tangibly than words. Mac had been told more than once by her clients, and her friends, that her hugs were healing.

There was nothing clinical in her intent now as she held Abby, just appreciation and the beginnings of affection. Her hand, cradling the back of Abby's neck, was gentle and platonic. Abby's head rested comfortably on the curve of her shoulder. But the quality, the essence of their touch was changing. Abby was relaxing against her, warming the formality of embraces usually exchanged between women new to each other.

Mac became distinctly aware of the firm swells of Abby's breasts, pillowed beneath her own, and she swallowed. Their bodies melded perfectly, as balanced and easy as if they'd been carved together from living wood by a master artist. A muted swirl of sensual pleasure trickled through Mac, igniting a heat she hadn't known for a while.

Hallelujah, it's back, she thought. She hadn't seen her libido in so long she assumed she'd left it in Wyoming. Like her ghostly footsteps, lust had found her again. She was pleased to see it, but this was certainly not the time, the place—or the woman. She released Abby gently, and straightened.

Abby's blush had deepened, filling her cheeks with color. The blue of her eyes seemed more vivid, but she looked almost dazed. Abby blinked. The simple happiness in her delicate features faded and became confusion, and Mac half lifted her hand to her, an instinctive offer of reassurance.

"You two getting high in here or what?" Cleo stepped through the open doorway, and Abby took a small step back from Mac. "Scratch is making breakfast. This is your only notice. You're not at the table, I get yours."

Mac couldn't tell if Cleo had seen what had happened between her and Abby. She seemed unfazed. Mac was unhappy for Abby, and angry with herself. She must have revealed her sudden desire as they held each other, through some subtle shifting she wasn't even aware of. No wonder Abby was rattled.

"Reach for my eggs and you'll draw back a bloody stump." Abby's voice was a bit bright, but she threw Mac a smile before walking quickly out of the office.

Mac started to follow, but Cleo lowered her arm lazily across the doorway, blocking her path.

Cleo appraised her for a moment, her dark eyes calm. "Just checking to be sure you recognize a healthy boundary when you see one, Counselor."

Mac rested her hand on Cleo's forearm and answered her honestly. "I do, amiga."

Cleo nodded. "Bueno." She dropped her arm and sauntered toward the living room.

Mac followed, but her inherent honesty had kicked in. Abby might have sensed her growing arousal, yes. But Mac hadn't been entirely alone there. She remembered an answering heat in Abby's eyes. And with one memorable exception, her instincts about women were rarely wrong.

Mac stepped down into the living room and stopped short. Unless she was mistaken, Satan himself was carrying a platter of scrambled eggs to the breakfast nook.

Vivian was seated at a table near the entry, tapping on a laptop. She peered at Mac over her glasses. "Ah, Mac. That elderly gentleman over there is my nearest and dearest."

Satan rested the platter on the table and turned to Mac. He was as tall as she was, a rail-thin black man, his grizzled iron hair cropped short. He ambled over to her, his movements slow and relaxed, which gave him an air of courtliness. The effect was only slightly spoiled by the red cap on his head, which sported two small curved horns on either side.

"I'm William Childs, Mac." He extended the longest fingers Mac had ever seen. "Please, call me Scratch."

"Mac Laurie." Mac noticed his swollen knuckles, and took his callused hand gently. "I'm pleased to meet you, and I can't stop staring at your head."

Scratch chuckled. "Well, my head comes to you courtesy of Ms. Cleopatra Lassiter. This fine hat was her gift to me on the occasion of my last birthday. Her comment, I believe, on my past vocation as a minister of the gospel."

Mac smiled. "It seems to suit you, Scratch."

"Doesn't it?" Scratch said. "Degale laughed fit to bust when she saw me this morning. Said the Lord had finally seen fit to mark His male children with a symbol consistent with their character."

"*Her* male children," Cleo corrected from the breakfast nook. "Amen."

"Ah, Ms. Lassiter." Scratch turned back to the breakfast nook. "Your sudden piety does not distract me from the fact that you offered to help me chop the rest of the kindling after breakfast."

"Chopping? Wood chopping?" Abby stepped off the stairs from the second floor, and Mac noticed her face was freshly washed. She avoided Mac's gaze, went to Scratch, and lifted his hand. "I'd rather you not chop anything until we get this swelling down, Scratch. I'll refill your Celebrex while I'm in town."

"Now don't you pamper that man, Abby Glenn." Vivian was still typing with quick efficiency. "He'll claim mortal frailty every time I ask him to make a bed." She glanced out the bay window, and Mac saw a police cruiser pull up into the circular driveway.

"Lord, my intake's here. She's early." Vivian flapped her well-manicured fingers at Scratch. "Honey, you shoo. Last thing this woman needs to see this morning is a demon man in a devil hat."

"My lovely wife knows best." Scratch moved with new energy to the table and lifted the platter of steaming eggs. "Breakfast in the kitchen, my friends."

"Vivian?" Mac rose. "Mind if I sit in on this?"

"I don't mind if our new lady doesn't." Vivian was her way to the entry. "It's a good idea, Mac. We'll ask her."

Abby paused at the swinging door to the kitchen and looked back at Mac, and Mac felt that small, secret muscle in her sex tighten again. Abby smiled and went through the door.

Mac watched it swing shut, wondering at the sadness she had seen in Abby's smile. She might have expected a certain awkwardness between them, after that suddenly intense embrace. But a counselor had to be adept at reading silent nuance in expressions, and there had been regret in Abby's eyes, even apology. It might be important to find a few minutes alone with her later in the day, to be sure she was all right.

Then it occurred to Mac that more time alone with Abby, so soon after that odd moment, wasn't necessarily a wise call today. Not given her newly awakened and weirdly contrary hormones. Better that she focus on why she was here, on Fireside.

"Inez, meet Mac and Cleo, two of our staff." Vivian appeared in the entry, accompanied by a slender Latina woman and a girl who looked about six, almost lost in the folds of her mother's coat.

"Hi," the woman mumbled. She seemed far too young to have mothered this child, but her eyes were old and wary. She nudged the girl with her elbow. "Say hi, Lena."

"Lo," the girl whispered.

"You two come on in and have a seat." Vivian ushered them to the sofa. "We've got paperwork to do. Might as well get comfortable."

Cleo waited until they settled stiffly side by side on the couch. Then she crouched on her heels, her sturdy body oddly graceful, to meet the child's eye level. "You all look pretty cold. You a coffee drinker, Inez?"

"I could use some." Inez was fumbling through some papers in a worn backpack.

"Are you a coffee drinker, Lena?"

"Me?" The girl blinked at Cleo. "Uh-uh."

"Hm. Wonder what else we got in there." Cleo scratched her chin. "How about prune juice, you like prune juice?"

"Yuck," Lena giggled. "Don't want no prune juice!"

"You take what they got, Lena, be nice." Inez's voice was low.

"Well, we might have some hot chocolate. I was about to heat some up myself." Cleo smiled at Lena, and Mac was introduced to an entirely different woman in the sweetness of that smile. "How about it?"

"Yeah, hot chocolate." Lena beamed.

Cleo nodded and stood up. "One coffee, one cocoa, be right back."

Mac caught Vivian's eye. "Inez, would you two mind if I sat in on your talk with Vivian? I'm new here myself. I'd like to see how things work."

"Okay with me," Inez said. The little girl nodded solemnly.

Mac settled into the hickory rocking chair she already considered Abby's as Vivian brought the paperwork back to their circle. Lena looked at Mac curiously, her short legs tapping a rhythm on the cushion's edge.

"Lena." Mac rested her elbows on her knees. "Is that short for Angelina?"

"Angelina." The girl nodded.

"Pretty name."

"My mom, she calls me Lena, but my friends, all my friends call me Angel, and then my teacher, she call me Angelina, and then my daddy—"

"Hush, Lena, Jesus." Inez nudged the child again and she subsided, still jiggling her legs and smiling at Mac. Inez stared at Vivian. "Do we have a curfew here? We had a curfew, that other shelter."

"We don't do nightly bed checks here, if that's what you mean." Vivian balanced a clipboard on one elegant knee and uncapped a fountain pen. Mac appreciated her willingness to transfer her hand-written notes to the laptop later; not having that big screen between them made for a more personal approach. "Fireside is a transitional housing program, and the rules are a little different from the emergency shelter you came from."

"Good thing." Inez licked two of her fingertips and smoothed Lena's bangs off her forehead.

"But the rules we have are enforced," Vivian continued pleasantly. "Our children attend school. Our residents meet regularly with staff. No visitors are allowed on the property, as we keep our location as secret as possible—"

"Lena didn't miss a day of school all year," Inez interrupted. "She does real good in her classes. You come into our place every day? Every day I got to meet with you?"

"We'll see a lot of you this first week." Vivian nodded. "The doctor on our staff does a health screening, and you'll have case management to help with goals and resources—"

"I don't need help with goals." Inez zipped her backpack shut, a sullen sound. "I got my business organized. Lena's up on all her shots, so we really don't need a doctor, either."

"Well, you've got a fine doctor, so best use her while you can." Vivian ignored Inez's sigh. "Abby's a family physician. She can prescribe medications if there's need. At Fireside you have case management, medical care, counseling services, and legal help, all under one sturdy roof. And everything is included in your rent, no extra fees."

"We gotta pay to stay here, right?"

"Indeed," Vivian said. "Thirty percent of your income, whatever it is."

"We don't get but about four hundred bucks a month from the state." Inez still watched Vivian with hooded eyes, but she was listening carefully.

"Then your rent for a two-bedroom furnished unit, utilities included, will be about a hundred and thirty dollars a month. And we have some funding for job training, so you can look forward to kissing off welfare someday."

"You guys pay for a computer class?" Inez flicked a glance at Mac. "I was good with computers at school."

"Lots of jobs in computers, with the right training," Mac said. "You and I can check out the community college in town."

Inez's shoulders were losing a little of their stiffness. Mac noted it, but she was in no hurry to coax those shoulders soft. This young woman had cultivated her anger carefully over time. She wore it around her like a cloak. Mac believed many women could benefit from a goodly dose of righteous rage. She remembered how she'd needed her own.

It took courage for anyone to leave an abusive relationship. But Mac hadn't been able to break free until she found rage. A simple, marrow-deep fury that the woman she loved would take the gift of her trust and shatter it, repeatedly and completely.

Mac remembered the last time she saw Hattie. Mac had been leaving the hospital and found her waiting outside. Hattie was leaning against her car, tossing her keys in her hand, her face filled with the tortured regret Mac could have predicted. Mac paused when she reached her, just for a moment. She spat at the ground at Hattie's feet, and limped on. As far as Mac was concerned, the rage that Inez harbored might prove a useful ally, if channeled wisely and well.

She watched Inez's thin arm wrap around Lena as Vivian took them through the intake forms. Mac figured her morning run had eased enough of the residual stiffness in her back that she could help Inez haul her stuff to their unit when they were ready.

Then she wanted to meet the women in the east wing, if they were up. She wanted to see Waymon's truck. She had to set up a schedule for the first week, introductory sessions, a peer support group. She needed a basket of toys and art supplies for her office, for sessions with kids. The light tingling sensation filled Mac's hands again.

A full day, Abby had promised, and it looked to be one. The first of a long string of them, beneath Fireside's sturdy roof. Mac rested the crook of her arm over the back of the rocking chair and winked at Lena, as Vivian's voice lilted on.

CHAPTER FOUR

Abby finished polishing the pedestal sink in her small
infirmary, caressing the white porcelain now more
than scrubbing it. She folded the cloth and turned to regard her
gleaming workspace with a distinct sense of satisfaction. Woe
betide any germ foolhardy enough to threaten a resident on Abby
Glenn's medical turf.

A high-pitched squeal drew her to the small window that
looked out over their spacious front yard. She brushed the curtain
aside. Mac and Inez's little girl, Lena, were having a high old
time constructing a curvaceous snowwoman in the center of the
blanket of white within the circular driveway. They had packed
one snowy arm raised in friendly greeting, a cheery welcome to
anyone approaching the main house.

That the figure was female was richly evident, as Mac and
Lena were industriously patting more snow around her already
formidable breasts. Abby's gaze lingered on Mac, and she smiled.
She could be watching two eight-year-old girls at play. Mac's
cheeks were flushed from the cold, and her eyes danced as she
laughed at the size of Lena's snow-nipple.

Yet her hands were gentle around the little girl's waist,
lifting her so she could pat down the top of the snowwoman's
head. Mac was easily adult again, careful as she lowered Lena to
the ground and spoke to her, focused entirely on the needs of this

one small client. Lena nodded solemnly to whatever Mac had said, and answered her.

Abby was seeing two free spirits at play, but she was also watching a skillful professional at work. She recalled poor Jazz as being rather hapless when it came to counseling the shelter's children. She couldn't seem to get past simply sitting even her youngest clients in a chair in her office, and expecting them to open up about the traumas they'd suffered. But Abby knew Mac was conducting a therapy session before her eyes, an hour of apparent play with a child who might more easily confide her fears when she was relaxed and happy. She was beginning to appreciate what a find Vivian had conjured from Seattle.

She saw Mac brush Lena's tumbling hair off her face, and a light warmth filled her, almost a longing. Abby wondered what it would have been like to have someone like Mac in her life when she was eight years old. She couldn't imagine her own mother brushing back her hair with such easy affection. Anything she knew about tenderness in parenting she had learned from her father. She was grateful their residents' kids now had a counselor able to express simple kindness so naturally.

Abby heard a car pulling into the drive. Good, Cleo was back from taking Inez to her deposition in town. It was always nice when they managed to end their workdays at approximately the same hour. In the two weeks since Mac had joined them, they were getting better at doing that. They had started to have dinner together more often now, and it felt like a slight letdown if one of them wasn't there.

Abby turned and regarded the infirmary once more before she put it to bed for the night. Mac had her genius for finding the right physical space to tend the needs of her people, and Abby had hers. She flipped the bar of the standing scale with one finger, then took a silent inventory of the spotless jars and small instruments set out on the counter. The infirmary was orderly, well-stocked and stringently clean, but less forbidding than the traditional medical station. The fresh scent of the small pine boughs Abby had tucked on a corner shelf helped soften the smell of disinfectant, and colorful posters drew the eye away from shining, sterile surfaces.

The clinic Abby had worked in before she came to Fireside had been much larger. The equipment had been state of the art, the medical suites expansive. Certainly the pay had been more lavish. But Abby took more pride in this small healing space than any office she'd ever known, because she had earned it.

Abby hesitated, her hand hovering over the counter, examining that thought. Yes, she had earned her home here— bought and paid for it, in every way but monetarily. She needed this place. She had come here for healing, just as much as any woman who sought refuge at this shelter. She did honorable work here, with families who truly needed her help, women who could never afford the high-priced services of a private clinic. She was finally on the right path, and she intended to stay there.

Abby started as a short scream sounded from the front yard, unnerving even through the closed window. She pulled back the curtain, and at first saw nothing but the abandoned snowwoman, her arm held high in greeting. Then Abby looked past it and saw Cleo kneeling beside Lena, who lay in the snow next to Cleo's Jeep. Inez was just dropping down beside her daughter, and Mac was moving quickly toward them.

Abby switched to automatic, lifting her newly stocked medical bag out of its cupboard and walking swiftly through the living room to the front door. Even on alert, she tried not to give in to worst-case scenarios. She was almost certain she had heard the Jeep's faint backfire as its engine stopped, almost a full minute ago. It was unlikely Lena had been run down.

She stepped onto the porch, then trotted down the steps to the yard. Lena was unleashing another ear-splitting wail, which Abby considered a good sign. She had worked on enough pediatric wards to distinguish the cries of children, and this sounded more like fear and shock than sustained agony. She kicked through the snow to the group huddled beside the car.

"Hush, *mijita*, hush!" Inez's hands were trembling as she cradled Lena's face, which was splashed with blood. "I'm so sorry, angel."

Mac had crouched at Lena's other side and was holding a folded bandana to the girl's nose. She shifted quickly to make room for Abby.

"We'd just parked, and Lena ran up to say hello to her mom." Cleo spoke from behind Abby, her voice a bit timorous. She knew Cleo didn't do well with blood. "I didn't see her, and neither did Inez. When she opened the door, it smacked her in the face."

"And gave her quite a bloody nose, I see." Cold wetness sank through the knees of Abby's jeans as she knelt in the snow and lifted Inez's hands gently from Lena's face. "Did she lose consciousness?"

"No," Mac answered. "She cried out right away."

The little girl's eyes were screwed shut and her cheeks were streaked with tears, and her yawning mouth revealed a missing front tooth. Abby did a fast preliminary check and saw no other signs of injury. She had just updated Lena's medical chart last week, and knew she had no serious health conditions that might complicate a nosebleed. The blood was still trickling steadily, but it wasn't gushing, and there was no sign of fracture.

It was the shape of Lena's small body as she lay in the snow that brought it on, a brief, painful flood of memory. In those few seconds, taking in the little girl's splayed limbs, Abby remembered the boy. He hadn't been much older than Lena, and about her size, small for his age. He had been bleeding too.

Lena's screams had subsided into sobs, and Abby gave herself a quick mental shake, dispersing the past like snowdrift. She could feel Inez's anxious gaze, and she offered her a reassuring smile.

"Lena, you took a knock to your nose, and it seems you've

lost a baby tooth, but you're going to be just fine. Let's take you inside and get you warm and dry. Here, keep this under your nose."

Abby gestured to Inez, and together they helped Lena stand. Cleo bent to pick up the child, but Mac rested a hand on Cleo's arm and nodded toward Inez, who was already lifting the girl into her arms. She struggled a little, as she wasn't that much bigger than her daughter, but then cradled her tightly, crooning comfort. Cleo tipped her chin at Mac in thanks, and escorted Inez and Lena carefully through the snow toward the house.

Abby snapped her bag shut and fell into step next to Mac. "Poor Inez. She's paler than Lena."

"Cleo's paler than both of them." Mac returned Abby's smile. "You don't think we'll need to take Lena into town?"

"Not unless I see something more worrisome inside." A breeze blew a lock of Abby's hair into her eyes, and before she could lift her hand, Mac's fingers brushed it gently off her forehead. Abby kept her gaze on the ground as they walked together, wanting to remember exactly the sensation of solace she found in that brief touch.

"You all right, Doc?" Mac asked. "Back there, you looked a little rattled for a moment."

Abby shook her head dismissively. "Just remembering another patient, someone I couldn't help. A long time ago. Mac, would you mind joining us while I look at Lena? She seems comfortable with you."

"Sure, I'm there."

Inez and Cleo had Lena seated on the raised examination table in the infirmary, and Abby brought Inez a small folded towel to replace the bandana she still held to her child's nose.

"It looks like it's just about stopped, honey. Here, I'm going to put something cool on the back of your neck." Abby took out a chemical icepack and slid it beneath Lena's hair. Lena was calmer now, her sobs reduced to occasional hitches of breath.

"I didn't even see her. She was just there," Inez said softly. She looked at Abby with tear-filled eyes. "I didn't open the door very hard, I swear."

"Hey, I didn't see her either, Inez," Cleo said. "Same thing would have happened if she'd run up on my side."

"It was loose already. My tooth was." Lena's voice was high and faint, and she looked from her mother to Mac with obvious worry. "It was already gonna come out. It's okay, Mama."

"Your mom will feel better when she sees you still have that pretty smile, Lena-Angelina." Mac selected a stuffed animal from the shelf that contained Abby's kid-comforters, and tucked it into Lena's arms. "I'm glad you let her know you're not mad at her."

Like a clear river swirling over smooth rock, Abby decided as she checked the child's pupils. She had been trying to find the right phrase to describe Mac's voice for days. That low, rich timbre, flavored with the mildest of Western drawls, sounded more like music than speech.

Inez was still patting Lena's leg with a soft, nervous rhythm. "Is she gonna have a scar?"

"No, I hardly think so. There are no real cuts." Abby noted with satisfaction that the blood flow had stopped, and she measured the girl's pulse one more time. "Lena will be out building magnificent snowwomen in our front yard again in the morning."

"Hey, yeah, I saw that statue of me you built out there, Lena." Cleo tweaked the ear of the toy bear Lena cradled. "Thank you. Beautiful work. Looks just like me." Lena giggled.

Abby let Mac and Cleo engage Lena while she drew Inez aside. "I think you can take her home, Inez. She'll sleep more comfortably in her own bed. I'll stop by to check on her after dinner, if that's all right. Just soup tonight, something light. Let me get you some baby aspirin, and—"

"I'm a good mother." Inez had been playing with the small crucifix she wore around her neck, but now her fingers stilled, and she looked steadily at Abby. "I am. We been here two weeks. You guys know that."

"Inez." Abby touched her cold hand gently. "We know this was an accident. Lena has a very good mother. She's a lucky little girl."

"Okay," Inez whispered.

The setting sun cast a rosy light through the infirmary's window as Abby ushered mother and daughter out of the infirmary.

"Damn, I left all your paperwork in the Jeep, Inez." Cleo zipped up her jacket. "I'll tag along and get it for you."

Abby lowered her voice and leaned into Cleo. "Dinner by the fire?"

"Who's cooking?"

"It's Mac's turn, I believe."

Cleo grunted. "Bring the ipecac."

"Please do." Mac waved at them from the corner. "I'll mix it right in with the chili."

"C'mon, Mama, we gotta go look out there for my tooth." Lena tugged on Inez's hand. "Or I won't get my dollar!"

"See you guys after the tooth hunt." Cleo winked at Abby and followed Inez and Lena out.

Mac was stripping the white sheet of butcher paper off the examination table, smiling at Abby faintly.

"What?" Abby asked, pulling a fresh sheet from the roll secured to the head of the bed.

"I was thinking you have good hands." Mac shrugged, folding the paper. "Hands are something I pay attention to. They say a lot about a person."

"They do?" Abby didn't look up from the table. "What do mine say?" She couldn't believe she was asking this. It felt like a craven plea for some kind of compliment. But she wanted to hear Mac's answer.

"They move skillfully, with such precision, from one task

to another. But your touch can comfort a hurt kid and reassure a scared mother too. You have good hands."

Abby swallowed and tried to think of a light reply, but stopped when she saw the red streaks on Mac's wrists. "Well, you don't. I trust that's all Lena's blood?"

"Yikes." Mac looked down at her open palms in dismay. "Dang, all you need is me tracking bloodstains all over your nice, sterile infirmary."

"Step over here." Abby took Mac's elbow and steered her toward the small sink. She hesitated, then turned on the faucet and poured a large dollop of liquid antiseptic soap in her palm. "That's warm enough, stick them in."

Mac's shoulder brushed against Abby's as she came up beside her, then held her hands beneath the stream of water.

Abby spread the soap between her palms and then smoothed it over Mac's hands and wrists, a distant part of her wondering what the merry hell she was up to. Mac was fully capable of washing her own hands, and coming into contact with blood without protection was against universal precautions, but Abby didn't much care.

The warm water felt good, and so did the glide of her fingers over Mac's knuckles, rough and supple at the same time. The light veins tracing the back of Mac's hands were visible as the dried blood sluiced away, faint blue rivers beneath her skin. Mac's fingers, curled in Abby's palm, felt strong. She had good hands.

"This is the only jewelry I've seen you wear." Abby touched the simple turquoise ring on Mac's right hand.

"It's a Hopi christening ring." Mac slipped it off easily and showed Abby the small, ornate lettering etched inside the silver band.

"Kaya." Abby smiled. "Your middle name?"

Mac nodded. "It was a gift from my folks, on my eighteenth birthday. A nice connection to my roots."

"It's lovely, Mac."

Abby turned off the water, remembering the uneasy twinge that went through her before she realized the blood on Mac's hands had been Lena's, and the relief that followed. The thought of Mac bleeding disturbed her. Well, anyone's bleeding disturbed her, of course.

Mac stood quietly, accepting the paper towels Abby handed her after the last of the water swirled down the sink. Their eyes met as they each dried their hands, Mac standing close enough that the difference in their heights was obvious. Abby had to look up to meet her gaze.

"Thanks, Doc."

"You're welcome," Abby said. "From my hands to yours."

Mac grinned. "Want to help me with dinner?"

"I'm a true surgeon when it comes to nuking leftovers. Lead on."

Abby was pleased to find Cleo and Mac still sprawled in front of the snapping fireplace when she returned from checking on Lena. "Oof." She made it down the three flagstone steps to the living room, then leaned heavily on the back of the sofa. "I shall never eat again. I can't imagine having room for a single crumb for the rest of my natural life."

Cleo jerked her chin toward the kitchen. "I think there's a few black beans left in there."

"Ooh! Be right back." Abby spun and trotted toward the kitchen, enjoying Mac's chuckle. She was already forking the fragrant, spiced beans from a cup as she returned and settled into her rocking chair. "Honestly, Mac. Wonderful dinner."

"Yeah, which I resent like hell, by the way." Nestled into one corner of the sofa, Cleo frowned at Mac. "I'm a good cook, but you know what I get when I heat up some frozen taquitos from

Safeway? I get a mess of lukewarm Safeway taquitos. You got *this*." She gestured to the empty plates scattered over the coffee table.

"Jack cheese. Black olives." Mac ticked them off on her fingers. "Green chile. Bacos. Black beans and corn on the side. Olé. Adios Safeway, hola Santa Fe."

Cleo slurped from her can of soda and burped eloquently. "Ah, Gaia. That's better." She clambered out of the sofa and went to the CD player on the corner bookshelf. Abby knew what to expect. She tended toward classical tastes, but Cleo was all about the sixties, the Motowner the better. Abby wasn't sure yet what flavors of music Mac preferred; she seemed to enjoy everything. She must have a beautiful singing voice, given her river-rich alto.

Mac was a floor-sitter, Abby had noticed. Even when her back wasn't hurting her, she usually avoided the deep-cushioned armchairs and settled cross-legged on the throw rug close to the hearth. Abby watched the red light flicker over Mac's handsome features and realized each member of the household naturally gravitated now to her accustomed place for these fireside chats.

Mac lifted a small afghan from a footstool and tossed it to Abby. "How's our intrepid builder of snowwomen?"

"Lena's just fine. I left her watching cartoons with her mother." Abby draped the crocheted blanket across her knees. "Her only concern was not being able to find her baby tooth in that slush out there. Luckily, I had the foresight to take a fifty from Cleo's billfold to slip under her pillow, so all will be well in the morning."

"Where did you learn to cook like that, Macky-wai?" Cleo huffed back into the sofa, obviously not over her taquito-sulk. "Was your mom some kind of New Mexican Martha Stewart, or what?"

"She still is, matter of fact." Mac's smile was fond as she stretched out on her side. "My mom still whacks out the best green chile enchiladas I ever sank a tooth into. My dad's useless in a kitchen, and I was their only kid, so she invested all her cookery lore in me."

Mac's smile faded as she watched the flames, the Temptations crooning softly in the background. Abby wondered if all Mac's memories of her family were as happy as those cooking lessons. Abby understood well the mixed feelings involved in remembering mothers.

"Both your folks are still around, then?" Cleo asked. "That's cool. My mama's still rattling her own pans too. Turned seventy last year."

"What about you, Doc?" Mac braced her cheek on her hand, her voice mild. "Are your parents still with us?"

"My father passed away six years ago. My mother is alive." Abby tried to elaborate, but found nothing else to say.

To her relief, Mac seemed willing to accept her brevity. "You an only child too, Cleo?"

"Oh hell, no." Cleo rolled her eyes. "Four sisters. I'm the eldest. That's how I learned to cook. I grew up frying 'em all my lame-ass taquitos."

"I would have loved that. Having sisters." Abby smiled, seeing the softening in Cleo's face when she talked about her family. "It was lonely sometimes, being the only bairn. I used to make up sisters to play with."

"Psychotic even as a sprout, huh?" Cleo clicked her tongue sympathetically. "Nah, I'm kidding, I can see you with an imaginary playmate, Abby. Playing with her, dancing with her. Breaking all her little cigarettes in half."

"Hey, I had one of those little imaginary amigas too, but she didn't smoke." Mac's eyes lit up. "Ashley, her name was. She was my best buddy. We were on a road trip once. I was five or so. We stopped for gas, and Ashley didn't get back in the car when we drove off. I was sure of it. I pitched such a hellacious fit my folks turned the car around and drove back thirty miles to get her."

Abby was seeing it again, Mac's quicksilver transformation

into childlike delight. Her dark hair, shaggy at the base of her neck, held red highlights that shimmered in the fire's glow. Abby remembered the thick softness of it beneath her fingers when Mac had hugged her, the day she came to Fireside.

She had enjoyed showing Mac her office and was happy that it obviously pleased her. When Mac opened her arms, Abby had stepped into them easily. She might have been surprised at the unexpected sensations of safety and peace she felt as Mac held her. She'd definitely been surprised when her nipples tightened against Mac's chest. Abby had never made love with a woman, but she had always accepted the appeal, in intellectual terms at least. That hug had brought the whole concept home much more clearly.

Abby felt Cleo's measuring gaze, and she forced herself to look away from Mac's face. "You must have some nieces and nephews to spoil, Cleo, with all those sisters."

"An even dozen." Again, Cleo tried to look burdened, and again succeeded only in sounding proud. "I'm still trying to get their mothers to go Buddhist, so I can get out of the Christmas presents."

"I've got a feeling each of those dozen kids has a second mom in you, Cleo," Mac said. "You might be cheap with presents, but there's a nice touch of maternity in you."

"Nah, not me." The animation faded from Cleo's face. "I'm nobody's mother. If you want a kid, you have to be around to guard their little hides every minute, twenty-four seven. Too much work for me."

Abby, who regularly saw Cleo exhaust herself on behalf of other women's children, couldn't lend much credence to her claim to laziness. But their talk moved on to other things, taking the same pleasant, meandering course these unwinding sessions by the fire often followed. College adventures and favorite books. Beloved past pets and hopes for future ones. Finally Abby stretched, regretfully, and began to gather the scattered plates on the coffee table. She caught Mac watching her hands, and they shared a private smile.

Abby savored the comfortable silence as they put away the day, collecting glasses, tamping down the fire, turning off lamps. She was relaxed now, almost limp, after a couple of hours of good food and conversation.

She wished, as she followed Cleo and Mac upstairs, that she had known these two women when she was still making up imaginary sisters. Abby had been too shy as a girl to make many friends. These evenings by the fire were starting to satisfy her nostalgic craving for the adolescent slumber parties she hadn't been invited to attend.

Mac turned before going into her bedroom. "Night, Doc."

"Rest well, Counselor." Abby closed her bedroom door, then rested her palm against the smooth wood. She studied her fingers, remembering Mac's words about her hands, and knew her sleep would be deep and dreamless tonight.

CHAPTER FIVE

"Cleo, this is a den of harsh spirits." Abby sounded a little daunted. "I'm not sure I know how to behave here. I can't even use a spittoon properly."

Mac had to bend closer to hear her over the thudding jukebox. Abby was surveying the dark interior of the tavern clinically, as if examining a suspect lab specimen for parasites.

"Ah, quit bitching." Cleo held Abby's chair for her, then kicked another back from the rickety table for Mac. "This is the only joint in town that carries both your weird green tea and decent beer."

The nearly empty tavern was as odd a hybrid as Mac had seen in her travels, a truly tacky dive that was somewhat redeemed by a weary, new-age ambience. Spittoons were not in evidence, but the dozen shimmering lava lamps set around the room cast a murky blue glow into the late afternoon shadows. Not the callow, skimpy lava lamps that emerged in the 90s either, Mac noted, but the bulky, brass-based models born twenty years earlier. She liked the kitsch, but perhaps its appeal was limited. The only other patrons were a dotting of men sitting at the bar, presumably stovepipe regulars.

She wound one arm over the back of her chair and tried to ease the stiffness in her lower back. This interesting drinking establishment seemed a worthy last stop on her first real tour of Fredericksburg. Vivian had given them all the day off, and they had spent it together. Three women forced into such close habitation might be forgiven for wanting to flee for some precious alone time whenever opportunity arose. But Mac, Abby, and Cleo had tooled off in Cleo's Jeep as a cheerful matter of course, and the day had been pleasant and light.

Fredericksburg opened a new vista in Mac's varied experience. She had never lived east of the Mississippi. The place had the feel of a small college town rather than a city, still steeped in Southern tradition and rich in history. Mac loved the broad red brick sidewalks and trim green awnings of the downtown district. The three of them had explored the wealth of antique shops on Caroline Street and shared sandwiches walking along the Rappahannock River, and now her back was more than ready for de-kinking.

"Let's keep an eye on the time." Abby peered at the ring-spotted table, as if looking for a napkin to drape across her lap. "We promised Vivian we'd be back by five."

"We've got time to toast this occasion." Cleo twined her fingers behind her short-cropped head and leaned back in her chair. If the tavern was alien territory to Abby, Cleo seemed at home here. Her dark eyes scanned the men at the bar before she turned to Mac. "The taco belle, here, has been with us one full month today. With her longevity record, I figure we should celebrate now."

Mac whistled softly, tracing the glass curve of the lamp with her thumb. Had entire weeks passed since her first night here? She remembered a blur of days filled with watching women's faces, and evenings before the roaring hearth in the main room, listening to their stories. Busy, hectic days, but buoyed by the kind of excitement she had always relished in her work.

And nights, Mac recalled, which seemed to involve a great deal of keeping her gaze from lingering too long on Abby Glenn.

Their eyes met now, and the faint light from the undulating

lamp coaxed something mysterious and shining from Abby's fine features. That faint blush began to touch her face again, and she smiled and averted her gaze.

Mac cleared her throat. "Hey, did we call a plumber for East Two? Scratch and I took a plunger to the sink, but Jo says it's still—"

"Lord, Macky-wai, you're as bad as Abby-gail." Cleo cracked her knuckles, and Abby winced. "Viv is more than capable of calling out a Roto-Rooter. Will you chill?"

"All right, but we still need to find a housekeeper." Abby slipped her ever-present notebook from her back pocket and flipped through it. "We're only budgeted for a few hours a week, but that should be—"

Cleo plucked the notebook from Abby's hand. "First, I've already found a housekeeper. Second, she's not gonna have a house to clean because I will burn the damn place down unless you two can let business drop for ten minutes here."

Mac grinned as Cleo held the notebook away from Abby's snapping fingers. "Why don't we just ask one of the residents to clean the lower level a few times a week, in exchange for a reduction in rent?" she asked.

"Because the housekeeper I found needs the money more." Cleo signaled a passing server, and pointed to Abby. "Green tea for her, Killian Red for me—Counselor?"

"Corona, por favor."

Cleo pretended to shudder, then nodded at the server. She leaned her elbows on the table and lowered her voice. "This kid I have in mind is in high school in town, about to graduate. I worked with her when I did that mentoring workshop there a few weeks back. Danny needs to build her bank account to move out as soon as she can. I get the impression her daddy's too liberal with his drink and his temper."

"Is this a CPS call, Cleo?" Abby sounded concerned. "If this girl's a minor—"

"I haven't seen bruises, and she denies getting hit." Cleo

slapped at her breast pocket for her cigarettes. "Danny has that look, though."

Mac watched the lines in Cleo's forehead deepen again, and she regretted not abiding her wish to let Fireside's business rest for a while. As exciting as these last weeks had been, they'd been stressful too, especially for their resident attorney.

Cleo's legal maneuverings had succeeded in keeping Ray Lee Cooper, the man who tried to break in on Mac's first night, locked up since his arrest. A conviction for violating Terry's restraining order could net him a year behind bars. But his intrusion had been deemed "insufficiently violent"—a phrase that drove Cleo rabid—to deny him bail any longer. Only days before, they had seen Terry and her little girl on their way to another shelter in the next county.

"I'm gonna grab a smoke before my brew gets here." Cleo's chair grated against the wood floor as she pushed it back and stood, fishing her pack from her pocket. "This is one weird fucking state—let wild men with crowbars run free, but criminalize smoking indoors."

Cleo shucked the collar of her jacket higher around her neck, and Mac noted she studied the men at the bar again as she passed them on her way out.

Abby sat across the table, her hands folded gracefully on its scarred surface. Her face was slightly turned as she watched two men settle in a corner booth, and a weak sunbeam from a small stained-glass window fell across her features.

Mac's gaze traced the delicate planes of Abby's face, the taut curve of her throat. She could read the sadness in Abby even now, in the unguarded wistfulness in her hunched shoulders as she stared into the distance. Mac didn't know what memory of loss or grief pulled at Abby at times, but she did know she had survived it with her compassion intact. Abby's private pain, apparently, had only deepened her capacity to understand the pain suffered by others. She had turned her sorrow into a gift, a talent for giving solace to those in her care. Her very presence was soothing. Not that Mac found Abby's proximity particularly soothing at the moment.

Forcing her gaze away from Abby's face, Mac curled her fist into the small of her back. She knuckled the tense muscle, amused at herself. Two years with Hattie had not exactly whetted Mac's appetite for romance, and now that her long-dormant pheromones had finally kicked in, they were perversely skewed toward straight women. Her attraction to this gentle woman was growing, to a degree that was beginning to make Mac uncomfortable.

Her skin had developed a preternatural sensitivity to Abby's presence, signaling her arrival into any room with a low, tingling welcome. Abby's velvet-sheathed voice, with its mild British inflection, sent small flurries of warmth down Mac's spine. Even now, in the innocuous public milieu of this odd little tavern, Mac was keenly aware of the curves of Abby's breasts beneath her cotton shirt, their slow lift and fall against the soft fabric. She remembered their sweet fullness against her chest, the day Abby had introduced her to her office.

How long can it take Cleo to smoke one cigarette? Mac got to her feet. "Abby?"

It took Abby a moment to turn her eyes from the corner booth, but then she smiled up at Mac.

"Thought I'd make a stop." Mac nodded toward the restrooms, then hesitated, torn between the cowardly urge to get away and a more courtly reluctance to leave a lady seated alone in a bar.

"Go ahead, Counselor." Abby encircled Mac's wrist in two fingers and shook it gently. "I'll be fine."

"Thanks." She swallowed, certain Abby could detect her pounding pulse, and walked away with as much dignity as she could summon.

❖

Abby watched Mac weave through the smattering of tables, and she could easily imagine her sauntering down a red rock canyon, lithe and easy under a desert sun. There was something in the laconic grace of Mac's movements that often drew Abby's gaze. She shivered, then returned her attention to the two men seated in the corner booth.

They looked so much like her father and Michael. The same age difference, the same evident closeness, even the same silhouettes, the respectful incline of the younger man's head as he listened to the elder.

Abby was lost in memory, a sad nostalgia for her father's company, familiar now after six years' mourning. And another kind of grief, she realized, in the rueful admission that she did not miss Michael at all.

They had both known her father was dying when Abby accepted Michael's engagement ring. Phillip Glenn, a lifelong activist for social justice, had been Michael's professor and mentor through his college years. Abby no longer knew how much of their marriage had been founded on Michael's wish to honor his hero, or her own desire to atone for past sins before it was too late.

In any case, their union unraveled steadily after Phillip's death, leaving less than a pale bond of vague goodwill. Abby had failed to inspire in Michael any of the passionate loyalty he had felt for her father—or passion of any kind, for that matter. It seemed, as her mother had pointed out more than once, that Abby was simply not the kind of woman capable of arousing strong feelings in others.

She wondered, sometimes, if a life without real love was the sentence fate imposed for that long-ago night when she had betrayed her father's trust, almost fifteen years in the past. If so, she would accept without protest. Life had its checks and balances, and she had a debt to pay.

Her eyes drifted shut as that light shiver moved through her again, a touch of loneliness as familiar as her grief. But if Abby indulged in an occasional melancholy moment, she had never been inclined toward self-pity. She thanked her stars fiercely for Fireside, with its gift of ethical work. And for Cleo's friendship, rich and solid now after almost a year together in the trenches. And of course, she was learning to trust the genuine kindness she saw in Mac Laurie.

In Abby's experience, kindness and beauty hadn't always gone hand in hand, but they seemed to coexist naturally in Mac. She believed Mac was honestly oblivious to the impact her striking good looks had on others, male and female. She was classically handsome, the only words that fit Mac's unique brand of rugged beauty. If her sensual appeal could touch even Abby's reserved and arid soul, it was a wonder every resident wasn't half besotted with her.

"I believe these are your libations, ma'am."

Abby opened her eyes. A large man stood beside the table, balancing a round tray of drinks on one raised, beefy hand. The corners of his bloodshot eyes crinkled as he smiled down at her, beer fumes wafting in his wake. He lowered the tray to the table with exaggerated care.

"Stan's busy in the back. He asked me to drop these off." The man straightened, his large belly contained behind a wide belt buckle. The thin brown hair beneath his cap was streaked with gray, and he blinked down at Abby with a kind of bleary, paternal benevolence. "Hope it's all right if I make your acquaintance. I'm Samuel Sherrill. You're one of the women out to Mrs. Childs's shelter, is that right?"

Abby maintained her courteous smile. "My name is Abby Glenn, Mr. Sherrill. Do you know Vivian?"

"Oh, just by name, just by name." The man peered at the empty chairs around the table, but Abby didn't invite him to settle in. He laid his big hands on the backs of two chairs and leaned heavily, clocking the toe of his boot against the wood floor. "How long since you joined forces with Miz Lassiter out there, Miz Glenn? Cleo and I go quite a ways back."

"What say you back the hell off, Sam, quite a ways back." Cleo was suddenly standing beside Abby's chair, and she was startled by the deadly chill in her voice.

"Well now, Cleo. A pleasant hello to you too." Abashed not at all by Cleo's tone, Sherrill hooked his thumbs in his belt and grinned. Abby was grateful the small table separated the two. The bristling hostility between them was palpable.

"What brings you out on this balmy afternoon, I wonder." Sherrill appraised Cleo beneath the brim of his cap. "I'd advise you to stick pretty close to home, lawyer lady. Shouldn't stray too far from your boss's apron strings, you want her to go on covering for you."

"Thanks for the limp-dick advice, sewer man. Now take off." Cleo glanced over her shoulder, and Abby was relieved to see Mac walking toward them, her expression calm but alert.

"I just wanted to meet your nice girlfriends, here." He turned to Mac and looked her up and down with insolent slowness. "You'd be the new one out there at the shelter, ma'am, is that right?"

"My friends have better things to do than soak up your worthless bile, Sherrill. Abby, let's go." Cleo tossed a twenty on the table and pulled Abby's coat off the back of her chair, and she got to her feet obediently. She glanced at Mac, who seemed willing to follow Cleo's lead too. Her stance was relaxed, but Abby noted she had positioned herself near the table, with room to move if need be.

"You girls be sure to tell Miz Vivian I'll get that paperwork to her soon." Sherrill raised his gravelly voice slightly as Cleo herded them toward the exit. "Prison records take a while to track down, but you tell her I'm on it."

Abby turned back, but Cleo's grip on her arm was firm. She felt heads turning to follow them as they stepped out of the tavern and into the twilight of the quiet street. The air was chilly, and Abby slipped her coat on as she tried to keep up with Cleo. They had parked a few blocks away, and even Mac's long stride had to work to keep the pace.

"All right." Abby curled her arm through Cleo's, forcing her to slow a bit. "Are you going to make us ask what that was about?"

Cleo coughed harshly into her fist, her face tight and expressionless. "I think Sam Sherrill is the prick who told Ray Lee Cooper how to find his wife and kid at Fireside."

"What?" Abby struggled to shift mental gears.

"Cooper claimed he didn't know the guy who gave him directions to us." Mac thrust her hands into her front pockets as she strode beside Cleo. "Isn't that what he said?"

"That's what he said." Cleo still looked grim. She paused at a curb barely long enough to allow a car to pass, then stalked on, pulling them along in the back draft of her anger. Abby could feel her trembling. "Cooper said he was too plowed that night to remember what the guy looked like, or even where they were drinking. But he mentioned the lava lamps. I had to check to see if Sherrill hangs out at that joint."

"But how would this Sam person even know how to find Fireside?" Abby brushed her hair out of her eyes to try to see Cleo's face. "He certainly knew you, Cleo."

"Sam Sherrill is a plumbing contractor." Cleo coughed again. "He refurbished all the residents' units before Fireside opened. Remember the damn sink in East Two? The man's work is crap."

"So Sam hears Ray Lee Cooper moaning drunkenly about his wife one night at that tacky tavern," Abby said, skipping a step to keep up, "and he gives him directions to Fireside. But why would he do that, Cleo? What's your history with this man?"

"Sherrill came out on the losing end of a case I handled in DC several years back. Where the fuck did we park?" Cleo stopped, frowning at a side street. "He didn't take it kindly, and his low-life type holds grudges. To this day, Sam Sherrill would jump on any chance to chap my butt."

"Has he got something on you, Cleo?" Mac's tone was respectful, but Abby felt Cleo's arm tense again. "He made some threat about digging up prison records."

"You asking me if I've done time, Mac?" Cleo stopped abruptly and turned to Mac, annoyance sharpening her tone again. "I'm licensed to practice law in this pitiful state. You think they allow convicted felons to practice law, even in Virginia?" She reached out and pulled Mac's arm. "Now come on, my ass is freezing out—"

Abby felt Cleo jerk in surprise. Mac had grasped Cleo's wrist and was holding it, tightly, until Cleo let go of her forearm.

Mac dropped Cleo's wrist, and regarded her with an austere authority Abby had never seen in her before. She didn't look annoyed. Just focused, and dead serious.

"I don't want you to touch me when you're angry, Cleo."

Cleo stared at Mac, her mouth open. She closed it and looked at Abby, then at Mac again. "Hey, Mac." Confusion and contrition warred in her eyes. "I didn't mean…did I hurt you?"

"No, I'm fine." Mac spoke from that same formal distance. "I just don't want it to happen again. All right?"

Cleo was silent for a moment. "Absolutely," she said quietly. "Mac, I apologize."

She extended her hand, and Mac accepted it readily. With relief, Abby saw that familiar dimple appear in Mac's cheek as she smiled. They stood together silently for a while under the glow of a street lamp, until lacy white flakes began to fall.

Abby moved between Cleo and Mac, and slid her arms through theirs. "Come on," she murmured. "Let's go home."

CHAPTER SIX

*S*he liked it here okay. More than that place that was sunny *and dry all the time. More than the city where it rained all the time. It was pretty here. And even more than the pretty trees and snow, she liked the other kids who lived here.*

The little boy was her favorite! He was so cute and nice. His name was Waymon. She knew this because Waymon yelled out his name a hundred million times a day. He was maybe three or four years old. She remembered being three years old. Not very clear, but she remembered faces.

Waymon was playing with another little girl, but she didn't know her name. They were building a fort out of the snow. She wanted really bad to help, but nothing moved when she touched it, so she just watched. Then she got all upset because the little girl slipped in the snow and fell down hard!

And the little girl didn't even get scared. She just got up and covered her knee with her mittens and yelled to the big lady wrapped in the blue coat who was watching them. The big lady came over and looked at her knee and then steered the little girl toward the long building. She didn't look scared either, but then almost everybody in the world was braver than her.

Waymon's eyes were wide too, though. The lady called back to him and told him to stay there and Waymon said yes, he would.

He watched the lady take the little girl into the building and then he went back to the snow fort.

And then Waymon looked up at her and she almost fell down on the ground in surprise because he looked right at her!

"What's your name?" Waymon yelled.

She giggled because he had a cold and it came out "What's your babe?" And he laughed back.

She thought very hard. "Ashy," she called finally. That wasn't quite her name, but it was the best she could remember. She could hardly believe the little boy could see her and even hear her. None of the other kids in the other places had ever heard her before. Maybe Waymon heard her now because this place seemed more than just a place. More almost like a home. A rare bubble of joy rose in her chest. "Chase me!"

Ashy spun and ran, leaving no tracks in the snow, and Waymon emitted a delighted yelp and tottered after her, his short arms waving vigorously in his padded jacket.

It started to snow again.

Their morning staff meetings were beginning to take on the rhythms of a musical composition, one voice answering another in easy cadence. The four women sat around the table in the breakfast nook, moving methodically from one resident's file to the next, discussing medical needs and legal issues with practical efficiency.

They were becoming a team now, maybe the best Mac had ever worked with. A well-designed mobile, personally as well as professionally. Just as the separate elements of a mobile shifted together in tandem, staying balanced on changing currents of air, so the staff was learning to balance each other.

Mac sipped her tepid coffee. It was new to her, this half-sentimental rhapsodizing about her workplace. She had found something to like in every staff she'd worked with, but these women were starting to nudge her toward hyperbole. Mac wondered if she'd ever be lucky enough, in her travels, to find a team this solid again. Then she wondered why she assumed she would be traveling. She had promised herself she'd give Fireside a chance.

"Deep thoughts, Counselor?" Abby was refilling Mac's mug. Cleo and Vivian were chatting about their poker night, so Mac hadn't zoned out on any important client business.

"Oh, always." Mac rested her elbows on the table. Abby's eyes were shining and clear, and there was more color to her cheeks this morning. "Are you sleeping better these nights? You look well rested."

Abby seemed mildly startled. "How did you know I have trouble sleeping?"

"I hear you sometimes, pretty late, sneaking downstairs." Mac shrugged. "I figure you're just after my leftover taquitos."

"Ah, I hope I didn't disturb you. But yes, thank you, I've been sleeping quite well lately." Abby replaced the coffee decanter on the trivet. "I think our nightly fireside chats are better than Seconal. Two hours of good chick-talk, and I'm out like a lamp."

"I often have that effect on women." Mac grinned and nudged Abby with her shoulder. And then told herself to stop flirting.

They all turned as the front door opened.

"Ladies, I'm afraid we have a red alert." Scratch led Degale down into the living room. He sounded calm, but Mac read urgency in his protective hold on Degale's arm.

"Waymon's gone." Degale was breathing hard. "I can't find him anywhere. We was in the yard, and I was only gone a minute, I swear. Inez's girl scraped her knee—"

"Don't worry, Degale, we'll all help." Vivian rose from the table, and Mac followed her gaze out the bay window. She felt an uneasy jolt at the curtain of snow falling outside, and she stood too.

"Degale tells me she last saw Waymon just about five minutes ago." Scratch went to the closet near the entry and began pulling out jackets. "We looked around both wings and the backyard."

"I'll get my satchel." Abby moved swiftly toward her infirmary's office.

"Mac, please get the whistles from our security box," Vivian ordered. "Cleo, I want you to go through the units and call out any women who are home to help. Take them and look between the main house and the front road. Mac, let's have you and Abby cover the area out back, past the gardens."

"Yes'm." Mac jogged to the front door and opened the tin case that contained whistles, flashlights, and an emergency cell phone. She took the cell and snaked the cord of one whistle around her neck and tossed another to Cleo.

"He can't have gotten far, Degale." Mac injected as much reassurance in her tone as she could. Degale's complexion was ash gray, and she was still shivering.

"Degale, I'd like you to stay here with Vivian and Scratch to help organize this search." Abby had returned with her satchel, and apparently she shared Mac's concern. "You look a bit peaked to me."

"Fine," Degale mumbled, rubbing her face in her hands. "I know I couldn't keep up with y'all. Please, just go."

Vivian checked her wristwatch. "If we don't hear a whistle within twenty minutes, we'll call the police."

"You butter yourself a scone and sit tight." Cleo leaned over and gave Degale's cheek a smacking kiss. "We'll be right back with your boy."

At first Mac was relieved at the mild chill in the air as she followed Abby off the front deck. It wasn't terribly cold, and the new snow wasn't adding much to the white swells already carpeting the ground. But it was snowing crazy hard, a dizzying vale of flakes that obscured vision after only a few yards.

Cleo was disappearing into the white curtain rapidly as she trotted toward the west wing. "I've got my cell. Whistle when you find him, and then call Viv."

"Keep your team together, Cleo," Abby called, closing the collar of her jacket around her throat. "We don't want to lose anyone else in this soupy mess."

Cleo whistled back that she heard, but Mac had already lost sight of her, as well as the entire west wing.

"Good advice, Doc." Mac took hold of Abby's hand as they headed toward the trail that led to the open spaces behind the property. She shortened her stride to suit Abby's shorter legs, and they both stepped carefully. The path was rocky under several inches of snow, and footing was treacherous.

"Waymon's just getting over a head cold," Abby said, "and he's asthmatic. He shouldn't be out in this."

Mac could hear the worry in Abby's tone. The snow's chaotic dance was almost silent, and sound carried clearly.

"Let's give him a call." Mac was giving up on being able to see any farther down the path. "Loud, but keep your tone light. Don't sound angry."

"Waymon!"

Silence answered the chorus of their voices, and they kept walking. Faintly, Mac heard Waymon's name echoed far behind them. Cleo's team was searching the north yard.

Mac struggled to quell the first stirrings of real alarm. Kids wandered off all the time. She'd been on half a dozen lost-child quick searches in her career in shelters, and every kid had been found safe. It wasn't that cold, it hadn't been that long…

Abby let go of her hand and slid her arm around her waist. Mac didn't know if she was seeking comfort or offering it, but she was instantly grateful. Abby glanced up at her, white flakes dusting her lashes, and smiled reassuringly—beautifully. Walking shoulder to shoulder, clinging to each other, they probably looked less like an intrepid search party than a pair of stumbling, anxious parents.

"Could those be tracks?" Abby gestured at minute indentations in the snow ahead of them.

"Could be," Mac answered, but it was impossible to tell. The marks were irregular, mere nudges in the blanketed snow. "Let's give another yell."

They called Waymon again. While their voices almost seemed amplified at close range, the thick curtain of flakes buffered sound in the distance. Mac strained to hear Waymon's high, piping voice, and turned instead at the far-off sound of stamping feet. "Did you hear that?"

"What, Mac?" Abby stopped immediately. "Did he answer us?"

Mac lifted her hand for silence, and she heard the sound again. Apparently she was the only one who did. "There's something back this way."

❖

"Over HERE over HERE over HERE," Ashy screamed, *punctuating each yell with a flat-footed crash of her hard-soled shoes on the big rock. She could jump very high and stomp down very hard and loud. "Hurry UP hurry UP hurry UP!"*

She only waited until she saw the dumb woman and the blond lady finally turn around and come back. Then she jumped down off the rock and scrambled back to Waymon.

He wasn't crying when she left him, but now he was crying. Not a lot, but there were two tears rolling down his fat cheeks. She felt very bad for leaving him, but it was just for a minute. Ashy was scared. They were having so much fun until Waymon started breathing funny!

She sat down in the snow beside him under the tree. She knew he couldn't feel her, so she just talked to him until the two grown-ups finally turned the corner around the rock and saw Waymon.

❖

They reached Waymon quickly. He was sitting in the snow, leaning back against a pine, his short legs splayed. Recent tear tracks marked his cheeks, but he didn't look frightened now. Waymon was frowning, his small eyebrows furrowed, obviously having to work hard to draw breath.

"Hello, little one." Abby knelt in front of Waymon, already drawing a red-capped albuterol inhaler from her satchel. "We've used this before together, haven't we?"

Abby slid the inhaler between the boy's lips. Mac waited until they counted down and Waymon breathed in the medicine that would ease the constriction in his lungs. Then she mirrored Abby's friendly voice. "Waymon, I'm going to blow this whistle, okay? Really loud, just like at the start of a game."

Abby nodded, then shielded Waymon's ears for good measure. The albuterol needed time to work, and they didn't want to startle him.

Mac stepped a few feet away, lifted the whistle to her lips, and sent a long, piercing blast through the air. Then she fished the cell phone from her jacket pocket and keyed Fireside's main line.

"We found him. He's not far from the house." Mac spoke quickly when Vivian answered. "Looks like he's having a little trouble breathing, but Abby's had him use the inhaler. Hang on for a moment. We'll see if we need 911."

"Wonderful, Mac. We'll stand by." Mac heard Vivian repeat the message to Degale.

Mac watched Abby's face, rather than Waymon's, as the seconds ticked by. Her eyes were keen as she studied the boy and talked to him quietly. In spite of Mac's concern, there was room in her heart to wish that every lost and frightened kid in the world could be found by Abby Glenn. Her touch on Waymon's wrist was maternal as she read his pulse.

As far as Mac remembered, Waymon's history with asthma wasn't particularly severe, but she'd seen some nightmare attacks in young children before. She didn't exhale until she saw the faint lines in Abby's forehead begin to fade.

"That's better, isn't it?" Abby capped the inhaler, then slid her hands beneath Waymon's arms. "I'm going to pick you up out of this wet snow, little friend. I'll bet your bum's pretty cold."

"Bum," Waymon echoed sadly, but Mac was deeply relieved he had the air to complain.

"We need to get these wet pants off." Abby stood, cradling Waymon in her arms, and Mac whipped off her jacket.

She helped Abby ease Waymon's soaking pants and underwear off his legs, then wrapped his hips quickly in the warm bulk of her coat. The snow flurry was beginning to let up, but fat flakes still drifted around them, so they stood in a protective arc over Waymon to shield him. Mac thought he was looking better, his little body relaxed in Abby's arms.

"Ashy," Waymon said, pointing over Abby's shoulder.

Abby glanced back. "Yes, I see the tree too. Mac, grab that small blue meter from my bag, please, and we'll start back."

Mac found it, and they walked carefully back toward the main trail while Abby had Waymon blow into the peak flow meter. She read the dial, then nodded at Mac.

"I think we can tell Vivian we won't need an ambulance. He's coming back nicely."

Mac relayed the news over the cell, then looked up to see Cleo plowing toward them, followed by Jo and Tina, two residents from the west wing.

"Thanks for leaving good tracks," Cleo puffed, her breath steaming in the air. "How's the little bean?"

"Looks like he'll be fine and feisty again soon." Mac returned the high-five slap Jo offered.

"Waymon can tell us about his travels once we get him home." Abby shifted the boy in her arms.

"I'll be happy to pitch in with the Waymon-toting." Cleo took Waymon gently from Abby, freeing her to retrieve her satchel. "C'mon, little guy. Your grandma's gonna be happy to see you."

They plodded toward the house. Cleo glanced back at Mac. "Don't linger, Counselor. You're out here half naked."

Mac waved acknowledgement, then turned back to stare into the small stand of trees where they'd found Waymon. She folded her arms against the chill, hearing nothing now but the silence of the snowy woods.

"I'm sorry, Mac. I know you're far too heroic to feel the cold." Abby was still standing beside her, and she slid her arm around her waist again. "But I'm going to supply what thermal support I can, so just humor me."

"Th-thanks." Mac's teeth had begun to chatter. She let Abby turn her away from the trees, but she looked back over her shoulder again as they followed the others toward Fireside. "You believe in an afterlife, Abby?"

Abby didn't answer right away, her brow creased. "I haven't really come to any conclusions about that, Mac. Lord knows I've thought about it often enough, in my line of work. I guess I'd say that I don't have any firm beliefs in an afterlife. But I do have hopes. Why do you ask?"

"What about ghosts?" Mac stumbled a little on the uneven path, but Abby's arm held her steady. "Any thoughts on those?"

"Well." Abby brushed stray snowflakes from Mac's shoulder as they walked. "My beloved childhood nanny believed in them. She was a bit of a romantic. She thought ghosts were souls who wanted something so badly, they haunted this earthly realm forever trying to find it. It sounds like a lonely existence to me."

"Yes, it does."

"Is something wrong, Mac?" Abby stopped and looked up at her.

And there in the snow, shirtsleeved and shivering, Mac almost told her. About hearing invisible footsteps when she was in grade school, and then junior high, and her friends teasing her when they walked together and she turned to look back at nothing. She almost told Abby about a ghost following her around the country for years, as tirelessly nomadic as she. A ghost who must have stomped on a rock to call them to Waymon, because that little boy sitting under a tree surely hadn't.

"No, nothing's wrong." Mac nudged Abby on again. "Lost kids just spook me, I guess."

The house came into view, and Mac saw Degale emerge from it and step off the front deck. The cluster of women in front of them waved, and Jo unleashed a cheerful whistle through two fingers. Mac was relieved to dismiss the notion of lonely ghosts in exchange for a happier scene of reunion.

She walked very quietly through the deepest part of the snow.

The woman looked back at Ashy, but she didn't see her. She never ever saw her. She never heard her voice, either. Almost nobody could.

Maybe that was good. Look what happened when somebody finally saw her. Ashy went and got little Waymon in trouble, but she only meant to be friends.

She watched the woman walk away with the gentle blond lady with the blue eyes. Ashy liked that lady the best of all the new grown-ups. Back there in the forest, when the lady held Waymon in her arms, Ashy got really lonely for a second. She wanted to be where Waymon was, when the blond lady hugged him. She had hugged herself instead.

She liked all the woman's new friends. There was nobody mean here, like that mean lady the woman lived with for a long time back at the other place. Everybody here was nice.

But they would probably leave again, Ashy knew. The woman never stayed, even where people were nice. Ashy hadn't had a home for as long as she could remember because the woman was all she knew about home. And the woman never wanted to stay anywhere for very long. As soon as Ashy got used to a place the woman moved on. She said good-bye to all her friends and went away, and Ashy followed.

Ashy stopped as the woman and the nice blond lady got smaller as they walked away. She filled her lungs and yelled "Mac!" Then she yelled it again, as loud as she could. The woman didn't turn around.

Ashy knew the woman's name was Mac. She had known it forever. But why should she call her by her name? Mac didn't ever call her by anything. At first, it had hurt Ashy's feelings, a lot, that Mac didn't even know her name. Now she didn't care anymore. But she wasn't going to call Mac by her name until she learned some better manners.

The woman had a lot of friends here, but Ashy only had the woman, who couldn't even see her, and didn't even know her name.

She watched all the grown-ups take Waymon inside the big house. Then she sat down on the ground and cried and cried.

CHAPTER SEVEN

Mac's sessions with Degale often passed in comfortable silence.

She had no new wisdom to offer this grandmother, a survivor first of her husband's abuse, and then her son's. Degale Pettus understood interpersonal dynamics and self-empowerment, thank you. And she had talked things out enough. The silence she shared with Mac now allowed for deep contemplation, and thus was time well spent.

Tears would sometimes coast silently down Degale's seamed face during these quiet sessions, as they did tonight. Mac watched the firelight from her small hearth flicker redly across the older woman's weathered features. A windstorm was picking up outside, throwing sleet against the house like handfuls of rattling rice, but this small room was warm and safe.

Mac hadn't told Degale about her own abusive relationship. She rarely disclosed her past to clients, or even to coworkers. She was able to convince herself that her silence was evidence of sound personal boundaries, and that was partly true. But Mac had made close friends in the past five years who had never heard about Hattie, and probably never would. She still felt shame.

And she castigated herself for that shame, even tonight. Mac spent uncounted hours counseling women through their guilt over staying in violent relationships. She helped them claim their histories as testament to their ability to survive. It was pure illusion to believe that any professional working in this field was somehow immune to abuse or coercion, Mac knew that. Perhaps, after enough years had passed, telling her story would come easier.

It wasn't all that different from many Mac had heard from her clients, gender aside. Her first months with Hattie had been euphoric, filled with the passion of their shared political activism and unbelievably intense sex. Mac had been in her early twenties, and Hattie was eight years older, but Mac's love for her had been innately protective. Hattie had survived a childhood in foster care that still haunted her. It gave her a passion for changing the child welfare system, but left her angry and cynical and wary, and in the second year of their relationship, increasingly vicious.

But you didn't leave someone because she was in pain. You didn't just give up on her. Not if you wanted to spend your life as a healer. Mac believed that, at twenty-three. She weathered the rages, the glasses shattered against walls, the nights when sex was more punishment than making love. She didn't leave the first time Hattie hit her, or the second. It took an ambulance carting her to a hospital to bring her to her senses.

Degale was still silent, so Mac closed her eyes and let Hattie fill her mind, testing her image like a tongue probing a sore tooth. There was no real flash of pain. There hadn't been for some time. Emotionally, she had done most of the hard work needed to close that ugly chapter in her life. It had quelled any immediate urge to jump into other relationships, true, but Mac had hardly been a nun. She had welcomed other women briefly into her bed, along the many stops her path had taken so far. They had taught her to make love gently again, to share all the pleasures of a woman's touch that she had known she wanted since childhood.

Mac heard Degale hitch a slow, deep breath, and she opened her eyes.

"I could have lost that baby, the other day."

"That's possible," Mac said quietly. "But not very likely. You knew Waymon was gone within five minutes."

Degale nodded, but her shoulders were still slumped. "Never thought I'd be raising a grandbaby, not at my age. I sure want to do better by Waymon than I did by his daddy."

"You're working hard to make sure Waymon grows up in a loving home, with no violence. He's lucky to have you, Degale."

Degale smiled with real warmth and slid on her shawl. "You gonna drop in on our surprise party for Ginny tomorrow night, Mac?"

"I am, yeah. Looking forward to it."

"Ginny's gonna be fine down in Atlanta. Got a job waiting and family there."

"I think she'll be fine too."

"Family sure counts." Degale closed her eyes again, but the sparkle was back in them when she looked at Mac. "Thank you for your time tonight, honey."

"I enjoyed it, Degale." Mac waited while she climbed out of the sofa that sat before her office's small fireplace. "Tell Waymon I'll help him finish his snow fort before the party tomorrow."

"I'll tell him." A wave of weary affection passed over Degale's face. "You have a real nice evening."

"You too, ma'am."

After the door closed behind Degale, Mac unwound gingerly from the sofa, wincing freely now that there was no one to see her. She lifted a brass poker from the stand on the hearth and adjusted the nearly charred logs, relishing the fragrant remnants of pinesap, and then looked around the cozy room.

It was her office in full now. County stat sheets were stacked beneath her obsidian paperweight, a shiny ebony glory culled from a mine near Taos when she was a kid, hiking with her mom. Her mother had been in and out of psych wards for most of Mac's childhood, but that had been a truly nice day. She had hauled that black rock in her duffel from town to town for over a decade.

Her favorite prints were on the wall, an O'Keeffe and a Pena. Mac dismissed any notion that Georgia didn't intend to portray women's sexuality in her paintings—those liquid swirls of pink and azure sang pure celebration of a woman's most intimate pleasure.

Mac heard the faint chiming of the grandfather clock in the living room, and then a quiet tap at her door. She replaced the fireplace poker with a minor grimace, and her hand was on the doorknob when a white light washed over the wall. Cleo's Jeep was trundling down the circular gravel drive outside, the headlights flashing across her small corner window.

It would just be her and Abby tonight.

Mac swallowed. And then decided she was being ridiculous. She lived with this woman. She worked with her every day. Fate would often decree they be alone together in the same room. She opened the door.

Abby smiled up at Mac, looking pleased to see her and weary and achingly touchable. "Hey, Counselor."

"Hey, Doc." Mac said. "How went the parenting class?"

"Hah." Abby sighed and tapped her thighs. "We desperately need a child advocate. I can talk about stages of development, but I'm hardly qualified to give mothering advice. Urging our moms to watch out for lactose intolerance has limited value, after a while."

"We'll hit Vivian up for a child advocate right after Cleo lands us a housekeeper." Mac slid her hands in her jeans pockets. "Cleo took off?"

"Yes, this is her poker night with Vivian and Scratch. I believe they both owe Vivian a small fortune." Abby sobered as the sleet clattered again against the dark window. "I hope they'll send her home early, if it gets any nastier out there."

"You know they will."

"So. Do you feel up to helping me restore our main room to some order?"

Mac's back didn't feel particularly up for chair stacking this evening, but her butch sensibilities could hardly allow Abby to do the heavy lifting alone. "Lead the way."

She followed Abby down into the spacious living room, lightly scented by the wood smoke from the still-crackling fireplace. A few chairs had been added to the furniture around the hearth to accommodate Abby's class. Mac slipped her keys from her pocket and unlocked the storage closet near the stairway, then began gathering the chairs inside it.

"Did Vivian tell you we switched plumbing contractors?" Abby said as she slid her hickory rocking chair back into place.

"Sounds like a good idea."

"It is. We'd rather not have Samuel Sherrill on the premises again, for any reason."

Mac lifted another chair. "Is Vivian worried about this feud Sherrill seems to have with Cleo?"

Abby was silent for a moment. "I doubt Mr. Sherrill can tell Vivian anything about Cleo that she doesn't already know."

Mac was content to let that statement stand, vague as it was. She could share Abby's trust that Cleo had been straight with Vivian about any problems in her past. Beyond that, her history was no one's business. Still hefting the chair, Mac sidestepped a footstool, and regretted it instantly as an ominous twinge shot through her lower back.

"Degale looked peaceful as she left," Abby said from somewhere behind her. "She's done so well, Mac. I'm so glad her housing will come through in the spring. Waymon will have a nice *fenced* yard to play in."

"Me too." Mac got the words out through clenched teeth. She lowered the chair to the flagstone floor more abruptly than she intended, hoping against hope the damn spasm would ease before Abby noticed. She leaned on the chair and tried to stretch the locked muscle in her back.

"And Inez's daughter, Lena, and little Waymon have become

great buddies," Abby continued. "Their snow fort is a wonder to behold. Mac?"

This was a wicked one, the worst in a long while. Mac grit her teeth again as the searing vise clamped down to the right of her lower spine. She caught a hint of cinnamon and knew Abby was beside her.

"Hey." Abby touched Mac's shoulder, her voice low and calm. She studied Mac's face, and her stance. "Muscle spasm?"

"Yeah." Mac smiled, but it was a strained effort. "It'll pass."

Abby's hand smoothed across Mac's shoulders, over the soft fabric of her flannel shirt, and then coasted down, pausing to probe very carefully just above her belt. "That's it, I think."

"You'd be right." Mac stared straight ahead into the fire, feeling Abby's nearness like cool moonlight on her skin. She gripped the back of the chair. "I just need to walk it off."

"I never should have let you lift those chairs, Mac." Abby frowned up at her. "Look at you, you've gone pale."

Mac wasn't surprised. She fully intended to faint soon, if Abby didn't take her hand—

"Here. Stretching isn't doing it." Abby took her arm. "Lie down, Mac."

Damn. If it had been Cleo beside her, Mac well might have slung her arm over her shoulders and yelped like a pup. It hurt that much. Bleating in front of Abby was a little tougher. But Abby wasn't allowing her any gallant stoicism. Her touch was firm as she guided Mac down onto the flagstone floor in front of the hearth.

"Lie flat, please. Knees up." Abby knelt beside her, and inserted her hand carefully under Mac's back. Her fingers easily targeted the steel cable that had replaced her muscle, and began a gentle massage. "Just lie quietly a minute."

Mac's breath shook as she tried to relax. It wasn't even the pain of the spasm so much, as unexpectedly vicious as that was. It was the sudden, remembered pleasure of a woman's physical nurturing that stunned her. It had been a long time since Mac had known this particular comfort.

Abby was watching her carefully. She stroked Mac's hair lightly with her free hand. "Is it starting to let go a bit?"

"Yeah." Mac closed her eyes in relief as the wretched tightness in her lower back began to loosen beneath Abby's strong fingers. "Yes, better already."

"Was it an injury, Mac?"

"Yes. Years ago."

"You've tightened up all over to compensate." Abby slid her hand beneath Mac's hair to feel her neck, and then sat back on her heels. "You're going to be stiff as a board in the morning, I'm afraid, if we can't work some of that tension out tonight. A good massage would help the soft tissue, at least."

Mac closed her eyes again, because that's how one traditionally prepared for prayer, and she was in need of divine intervention. A hiccup of laughter almost bubbled out of her. What kind of merciful goddess would cast her prostrate in front of a roaring fireplace on a stormy night, subject to the tender ministrations of the straightest woman on the eastern seaboard?

Mac sat up carefully, suppressing a moan. "Abby, I can just take a hot shower."

"Yes, you should do that later too." And Abby took Mac's chin in her hand, and waited until she met her eyes. "Let me help you, Mac. I think we can really spare you some pain, and I'd like to do that."

"All right," Mac whispered. "Thanks."

Abby smiled. "I'll be back. Take off your shirt and stretch out." She got to her feet in one graceful movement and went to the side door that led to her infirmary.

Mac fumbled with her belt buckle. She stared at the flames and shrugged off her flannel shirt, then the undershirt beneath it, ignoring the residual ache in her back and shoulders. She lay face down on the throw rug in front of the hearth, and waited.

"Cleo swears this lavender oil can restore a sore muscle's will to live."

Mac felt Abby kneel beside her again, and then heard her indrawn breath. Cool fingers touched the small of her bare back.

"The surgeons did a decent job." Mac rested her head on her crossed hands. "My spine's in good shape."

Abby's finger traced other scars across her left side.

"I reckon I was lucky. It could have been worse."

"I gather it was bad enough." Abby brushed the raised lines lightly, as if, Mac thought, she could erase them from her skin. "A fall, Mac?"

"Yeah. I fell through a wooden banister and dropped several feet. Mostly soft tissue damage, but it took a few years to heal. I had help."

"Help healing?"

"Help falling."

Abby was quiet. Mac heard her uncap a vial and then brush her hands together. "Tell me," she said.

Mac watched the flames and gathered her courage. "Hattie was smaller than me. About your height. Mean as a snake at times. She shoved me into the banister."

Abby's hands rested briefly on Mac's shoulders, then spread the warm oil across her back in smooth strokes. Her touch on Mac's lean sides was careful, as if she were exploring new territory and wanted to learn it well.

"We'd been together two years," Mac said. "She'd gone off on me before. Hattie hit hard, but I was big enough to hold her off, for the most part. Then the 'fall.' I let my folks believe I got bucked off a horse." She smiled into the flames without humor. "That might be the only important lie I've ever told them."

"She was your first partner? This Hattie?"

"My first anything. There's been no one since."

Abby's hands were gentle but insistent, kneading warm tracks from Mac's neck to her waist, then back again. Her touch conveyed an offer of comfort more tangibly than any words, a caring connection to Mac's pain as eloquent as Degale's silence.

"You've been alone a long time, then."

Mac closed her eyes. She thought Abby might understand the kind of bone-deep loneliness that swept her at times. She was all right alone, mostly. But there had been times in Mac's life when the ghostly footsteps that followed her were her only constant friend—entire months when she'd trimmed her own hair because she knew if a woman touched her face she would weep. The length of her body relaxed against the floor, the skillful massage melting away the last of her tension.

Abby's fingers were light on her now, her nails gliding across Mac's bare shoulders, tracing liquid spirals down the length of her back. Mac felt a drop of warmth fall between her shoulder blades, and she opened her eyes.

"Doc?"

Mac sat up carefully and turned to Abby, her face only inches away. Her throat tightened. Abby's delicate features reflected a dozen fleeting emotions—compassion, sorrow, and a kind of lonely wistfulness. Another tear slid down Abby's face, and she smiled, unashamed.

It was that moment, Abby's look of simple sweetness, as far from carnal desire as a look could possibly be, that did Mac in at last.

Disengaged from her mind's command, Mac's hand rose to cradle Abby's face. The velvet softness of her cheek filled her palm.

Abby stared at her, motionless. Her gaze fell to Mac's lips, and it was Abby who moved first, leaning closer in stages, lifting her face to receive Mac's kiss.

The blending of their lips felt like something lost but essential sliding into place, a natural connection Mac had never known clicking home at last. She explored Abby's mouth tentatively at first, almost chastely, with the lightest brushing of lips and tongue. Abby lifted her hand to slide beneath Mac's hair, her fingers suddenly cold on the back of her neck, but holding her, pressing her closer.

Mac inhaled Abby's breath and returned it, a tender exchange, but now a stealthy heat began rising in her that swiftly banished any thought of chastity. It occurred to Mac that she was kissing this highly desirable woman while shirtless and bare-breasted, her nipples tightening hard against the soft fabric of Abby's sweater.

She could feel her hand tremble against Abby's face. She gave her lips a last feathering brush with her own, and then made herself lift her head.

Abby's eyes were closed. They remained that way. High color had filled her cheeks.

Dismay was making swift inroads into Mac's lust. "Abby."

Abby's shoulders lifted and fell with her breathy sigh. "My goodness."

Mac grinned.

Abby's eyes finally opened, and they were tearless and clear. Her hand slid from beneath Mac's hair and rested in her lap. Mac waited, but she didn't speak.

"There are so many reasons," Mac said at last, "I should apologize to you. Abby, I—"

"I've never felt anything like that in my life." Abby blinked, as if in wonder that she'd spoken aloud.

Mac swallowed. "I'm sorry?"

"Don't be. I'm not. I've never felt anything like that in my life." Abby seemed to think about it, and then she bent her head, the gold firelight flickering over her face. "My goodness."

She sounded bewildered, and Mac had to touch her. She lifted Abby's hand onto her knee and covered it with her own. "Listen, it was pretty intense for me too. Are you...how are you?"

And with the worst timing of the new millennium, a knock sounded at the door. Their heads whipped around in such sudden alarm it would have been funny on any other night.

Mac blew out a long breath.

Abby cleared her throat. "I don't know what to say to you, Mac. But I'll think of something."

"You're okay?"

The knock came again, a patient tap, not urgent.

Abby smiled at last. "I am, yes. But I'd rather not chat with a resident just now. Would you mind?"

"Not a problem." Mac patted Abby's hand and climbed carefully to her feet. "Stay here. I'll be right back."

"Macawai?" The twinkle had returned to Abby's eyes. "It might be cold out there."

Mac glanced down at herself. "Oh, shite." She accepted the shirt Abby handed her and put it on over her shoulders. "Thanks, Doc."

"You're welcome."

Mac couldn't move as long as Abby held her gaze, but finally she was able to make her way to the entry and the front door. With any luck, opening it would blast her with cold air and clear her mind a little.

She had to stoop to see through the small oval glass in the door, but saw nothing through its curved surface except the empty front deck, illuminated faintly by a high lamp. Snow was swirling in tight bursts of wind, scattering over the porch. Mac thought of keying the intercom, but changed her mind. No one should be out in this mess.

She slid the bolt back and pulled the door open, swept as promised by a chill gust as she stepped out onto the porch. "Hello?" she called.

"Oh. Hi." A slender figure stood wrapped in a blanket at the far side of the deck, too deep in shadows to see clearly, but it was a woman's voice. Or a girl's. She sounded young. She shuffled forward. "Is Cleo Lassiter home?"

"Cleo?" Mac squinted, trying to see the young woman's face. "No, afraid not. Why don't you come in, though? You've got to be freezing out here. My name is Mac."

"Cleo said if I came here, you guys would let me in." The girl lifted her face, and Mac's stomach did a nasty lurch.

"You're bleeding," she stammered.

"I know," the girl said politely. "I'm Danny Sherrill. Do you know when Cleo might—"

But Mac was already moving because the kid's knees started to buckle, and only a neat lunge caught her before she crumpled to the deck. Mac lifted the girl, adrenaline drowning any trace of her backache. She stared at the blood caked around a gash near her hairline and the bruises emerging on her flushed cheeks. She was out like a light.

Mac spun with the girl in her arms, kicked the door wide, and yelled for Abby.

CHAPTER EIGHT

L ie still, honey, we're almost done."
Abby's stitches were neat and even, all but invisible against the girl's hairline. The lidocaine was working well, she noted. Danny was awake, but her brow was smooth and she hadn't flinched since the needle's first touch.

Abby drew the last stitch and tied it off, then snipped the thread and laid her forceps aside. "That's the worst of it, Danny. Well done."

Danny lay still under two thermal blankets in the small infirmary adjoining Abby's office, her pale features illuminated by the bright light at the head of the raised bed. Mac sat across from Abby, holding Danny's hand.

Abby checked Danny's pulse at the throat again, then adjusted the neck of her gown to examine the thundercloud bruise emerging over the girl's collarbone. A familiar fury rose in her, directed toward the creature who inflicted these injuries, and an equally fierce compassion for Danny that was almost painful.

But Abby felt an old sense of peace too as she tended her patient. She knew what to do here, in this clean, healing space. She understood how to help. Abby trusted her training and the skills she had honed for years, and her hands moved over Danny with ease and confidence.

She feared her assurance would disappear like a snowflake on hot coals if she looked at Mac.

Danny shifted beneath the blankets, and Mac adjusted them around her slender shoulders. "You warm enough now?" Mac's rich alto sent a light shiver through Abby.

"Almost." Danny's voice was still faint, but her color was better. She was beginning to lose that frightening pallor. Abby had given her a mild analgesic earlier. That and simple exhaustion made her sluggish and sleepy.

Considering her small frame, Abby would have placed this teenager closer to fifteen than seventeen. Danny didn't seem malnourished, or unhealthy in any other way before this beating, but there was a general air of fragility about her. Spiky blond hair feathered across her forehead, and there was a tired wariness in her brown eyes.

"Did you guys carry me in here?" Danny's words were a little slurred.

"Just me, ma'am." The dimple appeared in Mac's cheek again, but Abby saw her taking in every nuance of Danny's expression. "You went down pretty fast out there."

"God," Danny sighed. "I'm sorry. This is so embarrassing."

"Miss Sherrill." Abby folded the blood pressure cuff and placed it in a drawer. "You walked here, over two miles in a near blizzard, wearing a sweatshirt and jeans and a *blanket*, and you're embarrassed that you fainted? Mac here would be comatose."

Mac flicked her a smile, and Abby almost melted into a puddle of maple syrup on the spotless tile floor. She finished taping a neat bandage over the cut on Danny's forehead. "We've called Cleo, Danny. She'll be here soon."

"Ah, shi—ah, man." Danny closed her eyes. "She'll be pissed at me."

Abby looked at Mac, puzzled. "I don't think that's likely, dear. Cleo's just going to be glad you're safe."

Mac nodded. "She told you to come here if you were ever in trouble, right?"

"Right." Danny sighed again. "She gave me bad directions, though. She said turn at the sign, but hello, what sign?" She touched one finger to her split lip. It obviously hurt her to talk.

"You'll be staying with us tonight." Abby brushed a wisp of hair off Danny's brow. "I'd like to get some food in you before we let you sleep. Do you think you can handle something light?"

Danny nodded listlessly, plucking at the blankets.

Outside, a muted grinding sound emerged over the wind, and Abby heard one car, then another pull up the gravel drive. "I believe our attorney is home. Would you two excuse me? I'll let her in."

Abby swiveled off the high stool beside the bed. Cleo hardly needed her help finding them, but she wanted to brief her before she saw Danny. Her injuries weren't serious, but her battered face made for an alarming first impression.

She closed the door to the infirmary just as Cleo stepped down into the living room, followed closely by Vivian and Scratch. She lifted a reassuring hand.

"Danny's resting, Cleo. She's not badly hurt."

Cleo blew out a breath, but her gaze never left Abby as she shucked off her parka. "How bad is not bad?"

"She has a cut on her head that required stitches, and some nasty bruises. But her vitals are stable, and she's lucid. No broken bones, no sign of internal injuries. She's been asking for you."

"You see, Cleo, Mac told us there was no need to rocket back here like a bat out of hell." Vivian unwound a long scarf from her neck and winked at Abby. "Your Danny is in very good hands."

"I believe we were rocketing along right behind her, my love." Scratch patted Abby's shoulder. "Tell us how we can be of service tonight, Dr. Glenn."

"Well, you could heat up some of that good chicken soup you brought us yesterday, Scratch," Abby said. "Danny needs something in her stomach."

"There's no ill in the world that can't be made better by the company of friends, and a fine chicken soup. You'll find me in the kitchen, ladies."

"And I plan to commandeer Cleo's office to make a few calls." Vivian rummaged in the large handbag she carried, then peered at Abby. "You look like you could use a little TLC yourself tonight, young woman. Are you all right?"

"Oh, yes." Abby smiled weakly. "I'm fine. It's just been… an eventful evening."

Cleo was already heading toward the infirmary, and Abby followed her. Cleo tapped softly on the door, then pushed it open.

Danny turned her head on the thin pillow and lifted three fingers in a small wave. Cleo went still for a moment as she took in her face, but she recovered quickly. She glanced at Mac, then walked almost casually to the bed.

"Lord, this is one colorful little high school senior." Cleo's tone was gentle, and Abby could see Danny's body relax under the blankets. "So, Danielle. How was your day?"

Danny almost smiled, but it must have hurt her lip. "It kind of sucked, really. I'll be okay, though."

"Yes, you will be." Cleo rested her hand on Danny's arm. "You hurting much?"

"Not now." Danny pointed at Abby. "She gave me some good drugs. Amy, right?"

"Abby." Abby smiled and slid onto the stool next to the bed. She checked Danny's pupils, and then her pulse. "And yes, they were good drugs indeed."

"Have you told Abby and Mac what happened?" Cleo's expression was calm, but it must have taken effort. Imagining anyone striking this girl in anger was appalling.

"You know what happened, Cleo," Danny mumbled. "My dad lost it."

Cleo nodded. "Had he been drinking?"

"Well, duh, of course he was drinking." A spark of irritation entered Danny's tone for the first time. "He wouldn't have hit me if he hadn't been drinking. He's never hurt me this bad before, ever." Danny fingered the bandage on her forehead. "And I was stupid. I pissed him off."

Cleo spoke without inflection. "How did you do that?"

Danny looked at Mac uncertainly, and Mac nodded encouragement.

"It's gonna piss you off too," Danny muttered to Cleo. She shifted in the bed, and Abby helped her turn partially onto her left side. Danny fumbled with the neck of her gown and drew the fabric down to bare the back of her right shoulder.

Abby had seen the small tattoo before, when she initially examined Danny. It was obviously a new adornment, well drawn, still slightly red. Cleo stared at the colorful design, and Mac seemed to be watching her closely.

Finally, Abby spoke. "It's lovely, Danny. Is it an iris?"

"No, it's a lily." Danny peeked up at Cleo unhappily. "I know, I promised you I'd wait until I was older. But her birthday's next week. She'd be thirty-eight."

"Lily was the name of Danny's mother." Cleo brushed a blunt finger over the tattoo with unmistakable tenderness. "Your dad saw this tonight?"

"Yeah." Danny did not elaborate.

Cleo's eyes were a study in veiled emotion. "It's real pretty, baby."

Danny's smile, split lip and all, lit up the room.

Abby turned at a polite knock on the infirmary's door. "That will be Pastor Childs, Danny, bringing you some dinner. He's one of our good friends. Do you mind if I steal Cleo and Mac for a while, so we can catch up while you eat?"

"Okay." Danny yawned, and winced. "You gave me lousy directions, Cleo."

"Sorry about that. Glad you persevered." Cleo bent and kissed the top of Danny's head. "I'll be right in the next room."

"Okay."

Cleo didn't look at Abby or Mac as she left the infirmary.

Abby adjusted Danny's blankets, then followed her. Mac's hand on her arm stopped her before she reached the door.

Mac glanced over her shoulder, as if making sure they were far enough from Danny's bed to ensure privacy. Then she looked down at Abby, whose pulse picked up considerably.

"You hanging in all right?" The soft Western twang in Mac's voice was more evident when she spoke this softly.

"I am. I suppose I'm still in crisis mode." And Abby was glad of it. She could no more begin to sort out her body's intense erotic reactions to this woman right now than solve all of Danny's problems in one night. She resisted a craving to touch Mac, and told her as much of the truth as she knew. "We're going to be all right, Mac, you and I. You've become my friend. Whatever happens, I want to hold on to that."

The relief in Mac's eyes was palpable. She smiled at Abby, then gestured to allow her to leave the room first.

❖

Cleo was in the living room by the fireplace, striking a match to the cigarette clenched in her teeth. There was a murky light in her eyes, and she lifted a warning hand when they joined her. "Look, it's either this, or I go upstairs now and get my gun and kill him tonight."

Smoking was strictly forbidden on the lower level of the main house, but Abby hardly felt inclined to protest. Cleo looked dead serious. She started to reassure her, but Mac touched her wrist and nodded toward the rocking chair. Abby followed her lead, curling into the familiar comfort of the rocker while Mac sat on the sofa.

Mac's instincts were right. Cleo wasn't ready to talk. She paced in front of the hearth, blowing smoke in tight bursts, the ticking of the grandfather clock and the gusting wind outside the only other sounds in the large room. Abby could feel Cleo's struggle for control, and her heart ached for her. She had a thousand questions for her colleague, but Cleo was her friend too, and Mac's, and they would give her time.

Finally Cleo paused in front of the fireplace, and slid back the steel mesh screen that separated the grate from the hearth. She flicked the butt of her cigarette into the waning flames. Then she bent and picked up two small logs to add to the grate, and Abby knew she was coming down off that dangerous crest of rage.

Heels tapped across the hardwood floor, and Vivian stepped down into the living room, looking as poised and immaculate as if she hadn't been pulled out of her warm house in the middle of a stormy night. She studied them alertly as she settled into a stuffed armchair.

"We were lucky. I knew the intake screener working the CPS line tonight." Vivian consulted the pad of paper in her hand. "We're licensed for under-18, so she agreed to place Danny here temporarily, under our supervision. And Fredericksburg's finest are on their way to interview Mr. Samuel Sherrill as we speak."

"Thanks, Vivian. Good to know." Mac extended one arm over the back of the sofa, and silence fell again.

"Ms. Lassiter?" Vivian's voice was kind. "I believe you have a story to tell."

Cleo still stood by the fireplace, her arms folded as she watched the flames. "You know all my stories, Viv."

"Yes, but Abby and Mac don't, and they need to. Fireside has been drawn into this now."

Cleo rubbed the back of her neck. "What do you want to know?"

Abby thought it likely that Cleo wasn't being evasive; she honestly didn't seem to know where to start. "Cleo, you said that Sam Sherrill lost a case you were involved with, years ago, when you lived in DC."

"I handled Lily's divorce and got her custody of her daughter." Cleo spoke Danny's mother's name quietly. "Danny was four at the time."

They waited while Cleo sat heavily on a wide footstool and

clasped her hands between her knees. "I was working family law, and Lily Sherrill was one of my first clients. I fell for her hard. Crappy professional boundaries, I know." Cleo looked at Mac, and the corner of her mouth lifted ruefully. "Lily and Danny moved in with me, and we were a family for five years."

Abby sat very still, not wanting to distract Cleo but wishing mightily she could touch her. This was bedrock ore, from the shadows of Cleo's deepest mine. Abby closed her eyes at her next words.

"Lily died when Danny was nine. Breast cancer. Sherrill sued for full custody, and of course he got it. He wouldn't let me see Danny again." Cleo studied her hands. "But there are ways of keeping track of a kid, if you're patient and careful. I knew Danny's teachers, and I'd park by her school to watch her on the playground. I'd see if she looked healthy, if she wore warm clothes, if she had friends. I watched her soccer games from my car, when she was older."

Cleo's grim features softened. "That scrappy little girl. Bright as a damn diamond, with all of Lily's sweet spirit, and none of her sadness. Until she lost her mom."

"And you too, Cleo," Mac added. "Did Danny ever know you were there, at those soccer games?"

"We talked, on three foolhardy occasions. Danny knew no one could know I was looking out for her, especially her dad. We've been each other's best-kept secret."

Red and gold light flooded from the renewed fire, and the logs snapped sleepily on the grate. Abby saw Mac watching Cleo with the same listening stillness she must bring to her counseling sessions.

"Two years ago, Sam Sherrill ran his business into the ground in DC," Cleo continued. "He moved Danny down here and set up that pathetic plumbing outfit on the east end of town. And soon after…" She looked at Vivian.

"Soon after," Vivian caught up the thread, "a new domestic violence shelter opened just outside Fredericksburg and advertised for a legal advocate. A certain overqualified attorney from the Beltway was willing to slice her salary in half in order to take the job." She removed her glasses and nodded at Cleo. "Fireside's women have benefited richly ever since."

"And I think Danny has too." Abby regarded Cleo with compassion. "You've been able to see her more often, now that she's older?"

"Yeah. We meet in a park near her school during her lunch hour, sometimes." Cleo shrugged. "We talk about her art class. She's a wicked sketch artist. Or the basketball player she's crushed out on. We talk about Lily. Sherrill won't allow her mother's name mentioned in his house."

Cleo's shoulders were bowed, as if the telling had drained her. "Viv's right. I should have told you guys. I was just so used to keeping Danny my private business."

Abby understood the impulse toward secrecy very well, and she held nothing against Cleo. The grandfather clock in the corner chimed midnight, and they were quiet until its melody faded.

Then Vivian folded her pad of paper and sat up. "Let's have Danny move into the guest bedroom upstairs tomorrow, if Abby deems her able. We'll need to house her in the main facility with staff, since she's still a minor. We don't know how long this placement will last, but we can make her comfortable here."

"Sounds good, Vivian." Mac brushed her fingers together, and Abby had a visceral memory of their cool touch on her face. "I'll be glad to have some time with Danny in the next few days, if she's willing."

Abby unfolded her legs from the seat of the rocker, relieved to turn to practicalities. "Vivian, you and Scratch should take that bedroom upstairs tonight. We don't want you driving home in this weather." She paused. "There's an extra roll-out cot in the storeroom. I'd like to set it up in the infirmary, to be near Danny if she needs anything." She could feel Mac's gaze on her.

"I'll sleep in there tonight." Cleo lifted herself off the footstool with effort. "Don't worry, Abby. I'll call you if Danny springs a leak or anything." She cleared her throat. "Thanks, you all. For letting Danny stay. And for taking such good care of her."

"Someone's been taking good care of Danny Sherrill for a long time." Mac stood, and without ceremony drew Cleo into a hug. Cleo hugged her back, and for a moment, she rested her head on Mac's shoulder like a tired child.

Abby felt tears rise to her eyes for the second time that night. "I'm going to go check on Danny, Cleo, and then we'll let you get settled in there."

"Thanks, Abby."

Abby looked at Mac, regret, relief, and confusion threatening to surface beneath her crisis demeanor. Mac smiled at her with sweet reassurance, and Abby was able to turn her steps toward her infirmary.

Abby knocked softly and cracked open the door, and she heard Danny's faint voice inside, talking to Scratch.

"You can tell me the truth," Danny said. "Does it look more like an iris or a lily?"

CHAPTER NINE

"Man, I been over the moon for this girl since the third grade, Mac." Jo grinned, struggling to push the wheelbarrow over the rutted ground. Her partner, Tina, rode in its deep tray, giggling, clenching the metal sides in her gloved hands. "You tell me, what did I ever do to get so lucky, that she loves me now?"

"I'll tell you what you did." Tina's voice vibrated as the thick rubber wheel rolled over a rocky patch. "You saved me from that crazy woman, Jo. And now you're gonna kill me with wheelbarrow road rage!"

Jo laughed and slowed down, her breath pluming in the chilly air. Mac could see her wiry arms trembling even through her jacket—Tina was a large woman—but they were having so much fun, neither Mac nor Abby offered to help.

She glanced at Abby, who strolled quietly next to Jo. Abby returned her gaze, and there was no denying the pleasant current of erotic tension still humming between them. Mac remembered the yielding warmth of Abby's lips against her own, and nearly walked right into a stump embedded in the trail. She sidestepped it ruefully.

She and Abby had both tried several times throughout the day to carve out a few minutes of privacy. They needed to talk. But the hours since Danny Sherrill had arrived had been unrelentingly busy.

Their latest mini-crisis involved running out of firewood at the main house. The huge fireplace in the living room was as iconic to the shelter's residents as it was to its staff. The friendly crackling of the hearth welcomed them to support groups and budgeting classes, community meetings and parenting workshops. The flames cast an aura of light and safety, symbolic of Fireside itself. An empty wood bin qualified as a crisis. Luckily, Scratch kept a standby woodpile in the back lot. Unluckily, Tina and Jo had insisted on helping with the hauling.

"Hey, the new girl who moved into the house last night?" Tina looked over her shoulder at Abby. "Is she gonna be okay? We hear she's pretty banged up."

"Yes, Danny's going to be fine," Abby said. "You'll meet her in a few days, after she's had some rest."

"Did her boyfriend go off on her?" Jo's animated face sobered, and Mac saw the muscle in her jaw stand out. "Tina says she's just a kid. Where are her folks?"

"I guess we'll let Danny tell you about it, if she wants to." Mac plucked a pinecone from a tree bordering their path, showering her sleeve with dry snow. "Thanks for asking about her though, Tina."

"Ooh, sweetie, I got a cramp in my foot, I gotta get out." Tina craned her head toward Mac and winked, and Mac chuckled. Jo was breathing heavily, and she lowered the wheelbarrow's stand to the ground with a grateful sigh.

"Here you go, darlin', careful now." Jo took Tina's hand and helped her climb out of the barrow, and Tina limped around dutifully for a moment. Their spare woodpile wasn't far, but Mac doubted Jo could have kept up her studly carriage gig much longer. Jo kissed Tina sweetly on the nose before grasping the handles again.

"Look at me, even I just figured it was a guy who hurt the new girl." Jo shook her head, wheeling the barrow along easily now. "Everybody always assumes the batterer is a guy. Like at that first shelter we went to? We had to *pretend* we were running from a man."

"What?" Abby asked. "I haven't heard this story. What happened?"

"Well, after Fran beat me up, me and Jo didn't have anywhere to go." Tina was walking carefully on the uneven ground, her smile fading. "We tried to get into a safehouse, but they wouldn't take lesbian couples."

"So we went to another shelter, and we had to lie." Jo didn't look particularly remorseful. "We said I was Tina's cousin, and Tina's husband was after us both. That's the only way they'd take us in."

"That's preposterous." Abby had stopped a few steps behind them and rested her hands on her hips. "In this day and age? Do you remember the name of that safehouse, Tina? Or what town it was in?"

"Uh-oh, we set Abby off." Jo nudged Mac companionably. "Cleo's the same way. She gets all upset for us when she hears stuff like this. Cleo's pretty cool."

"I think she is too," Mac said.

"Perhaps I'm being naïve, but I have a hard time understanding how shelters still get away with this kind of thing." Abby was frowning as she trotted to catch up. "Diversity training is mandated by every federal grant in existence. Surely programs can't claim they haven't heard of domestic violence in the lesbian community these days."

"The lesbian community claimed not to know about it, for a long time." Mac studied the tree line, remembering heated debates in advocate meetings several years in the past. "It was pretty threatening, admitting our relationships could be abusive. We were trying to convince mainstream America that our lifestyle is normal, just like theirs."

"And turns out it is, damn it," Jo sighed, and Tina laughed with her.

Abby watched Mac's pensive profile, outlined against the pewter sky, and thought of her ex-lover, Hattie. A shiver of revulsion moved through her when she remembered the pain Mac had endured. The depth of Abby's anger when she pictured Hattie surprised her.

She knew that Cleo hated, without apology, every person who had ever raised a hand against any of the residents. Her contempt for abusers, male or female, was pure and absolute. Abby understood now that Cleo saw, in every battered woman, the bruised face of Lily Sherrill.

But Abby believed that such sweeping dismissal was a luxury she couldn't afford. Often, the women they worked with still loved the partners they had been forced to escape from. They needed to be able to talk to staff about that love. Abby struggled, successfully for the most part, to remember that violent behavior was always born of suffering, and that violent people merited understanding.

But Abby didn't care about Hattie's pain and felt not the slightest urge to understand it. She looked at Mac again, her dark head inclined to hear Jo's latest yarn, a smile flickering over her full lips. The length of her and the breadth of her shoulders conveyed such strength. For a moment, Abby remembered the smooth planes of that muscular body beneath her palms so clearly her gloved fingers loosened at her sides. Then she remembered the faint lacing of scars across Mac's lower back, and she shivered again. She gave herself permission to loathe the damaged person who had put them there.

"That's gotta be it." Tina stepped off the trail and churned through the snow with determination.

Abby followed in Tina's footsteps to the green tarp-covered heap that comprised their stand-by wood. The edges of the heavy plastic sheet were weighted down by snow, and she joined Tina's struggle to pull it free.

"Bring that barrow over here, sweetie," Tina called, panting. "And we could use some help with this thing, by the—"

Tina broke off as a loosely formed snowball smacked her in the back, spraying Abby with a few stray drops. Tina turned and perched her hand on her hip. "Oh, real mature, Josephine!"

Abby heard Jo snicker behind them, but she almost had one edge free so she kept tugging. "Don't worry, Tina. I believe Jo will soon remember that she's due for a TB test next week. If my fingers are broken and twisted from lifting this tarp all alone, I'll have to punch the needle—"

Abby broke off as a similarly wet ball of slush hit her precisely on her upraised behind. She whirled to glare at Jo, and instead saw Mac brushing snow from her hands, grinning like a bandit.

"Stop smiling like that," Abby said. "You look carnivorous. Are you going to help us with this, or what?"

"Or what," Mac called back.

"Mac."

"Abby."

"Macawai Kaya Laurie."

"Yes, Dr. Glenn?"

Abby rolled her eyes and turned back to her work, which involved the foolhardy error of turning her back. The next power slushball smacked her exactly on the same buttock.

"Two!" Jo hooted and high-fived Mac.

Abby spun again. "I cannot believe you—"

Splat. Abby sputtered through the curtain of snow that showered her face. "You bloody delinquent!"

Tina was looking at Abby, her mouth open. Their gazes met, and they nodded with grim resolve. They both bent and scooped up handfuls of white slush.

"God save the queen!" Abby cried. She clenched her tongue between her teeth and let fly, hitting Mac square in the boob.

It was the War of the Roses all over again. Abby and Tina retreated quickly from the answering fusillade behind the inadequate cover of the small woodpile, while Jo and Mac upended the wheelbarrow to serve as a shield. There was a rapid-fire exchange, accompanied by harrowing battle cries. Some snowy missiles sailed satisfyingly to their targets, many did not. Finally it was Mac who crawled out from behind her shelter, her hands raised in defeat.

"War is hell," she gasped.

"Amen." Tina laughed, leaning on the woodpile for support.

"You got a mean right arm, Abby," Jo complained, shaking snow out of her long hair.

"Hear the pitiful cry of the vanquished," Abby panted. She limped over to Mac and gave her a hand up. "Look at me, Mac. You've destroyed my credibility as a feminist pacifist for all time."

"I apologize for that, ma'am." Mac brushed snow off Abby's back, but her hand stopped short of her hips. She straightened and smiled down at Abby with a gamine charm that weakened her knees.

Behind them, Jo and Tina, crabbing happily, finished hauling the tarp off the woodpile, then brought the wheelbarrow closer and started stacking it with kindling and small logs.

Abby stood close enough to Mac to feel the mild warmth of her body. They were quiet for a moment, both watching the two women tease each other as they worked. Abby marveled at the uncomplicated ease of the couple's affection, so clear in their every word and gesture. She couldn't imagine love flowing so easily to her, light and free and without complication.

"Cleo's told me stories about what it was like, growing up black, doing anti-racism work in DC," Abby said finally. "I can empathize, but I've never experienced the kind of bigotry Cleo has." She nodded toward Tina and Jo. "I've empathized with gay women too, and the hatred they have to put up with. Has it touched you much, Mac?"

"I've been luckier than some of my friends." Mac stirred the slush at their feet with the toe of her boot. "My parents accepted my coming out with a minimum of angst. I've always lived in cities that had gay-friendly pockets to nestle into. If those pockets weren't cozy enough, I just moved on." Mac cleared her throat. "You've only been able to empathize then, eh, Doc? It's never occurred to you that you might have…similar inclinations?"

"Not really, no. Well. Not until recently." Abby felt color fill her face. She checked to be sure Tina and Jo were still occupied with the woodpile, and let the crisp air cool her cheeks as she sorted her thoughts. "I didn't date much, while I was in school. I was too busy studying, and too shy to socialize very often. Dating women never even occurred to me, Mac. I never had crushes on girls…" Abby trailed off. "But to be honest, I didn't have particular crushes on any of the boys I dated, either."

"None of them?"

"Not a one." Abby blinked, puzzled. "Not my lab partner in high school. Not my dashing anatomy professor in med school. I didn't stay up nights thinking of them."

"Not even your husband?"

"Not even Michael." Abby stared at her empty ring finger. She had mentioned her marriage briefly to both Cleo and Mac. It was one of those topics she could cover fully in three sentences or less. "My mother told me, more than once, that I'm simply incapable of feeling romantic attraction, or inspiring it. I've wondered if she was right, if sexual desire just isn't part of my make-up. At least I wondered before…"

"Before?" Mac stepped closer, and her breath stirred Abby's hair.

"Before you came to Fireside." Abby made herself meet Mac's eyes. "Before you touched me for the first time, the day I showed you your office."

"Abby." Mac took Abby's hands and lowered her voice. "Sometimes I want you so much, my teeth feel soft. Do you realize that? I walk around with my hands stuffed in my pockets, to keep from touching your face. When I kissed you last night—"

"When I kissed you, Counselor." Abby knew Mac could feel the trembling in her hands. "I was the one who leaned in first, I believe."

"Abigail." Mac traced Abby's brow with one finger. "What are we going to do about this?"

"Macawai," Abby whispered, closing her eyes. "I haven't the faintest idea."

"Hey, we've got about all the wood we can push, over here," Jo called. She and Tina were pulling the tarp back over the diminished pile. "You guys ready to head in?"

Mac waved at them. "We're right behind you."

They walked quietly down the trail, side by side, letting Jo and Tina range ahead. The two residents were still absorbed in each other, pushing the loaded wheelbarrow in awkward tandem, their shoulders bumping affectionately.

"I'll need some time, Mac. May I have that?" Abby slid her hand through the crook of Mac's arm, suddenly tired to her bones. None of the men Abby had slept with had ever robbed her of sleep, but she hadn't closed her eyes once last night. "Just a few days. To think about what this might mean for me."

"Of course." Mac planted a brief kiss on the top of Abby's head. "There's no need to rush. We can walk this trail one step at a time."

But how long will we walk it together, Abby wondered. *Next year, when the snow melts again and this trail is lined with flowers, Mac, will you still be beside me?*

Abby wasn't at all certain she was brave enough to follow this path herself, not knowing where it might lead. It saddened her to admit it, but she had found a kind of insidious safety in her solitary life. Devoting all her energies to her work carried certain advantages. She hadn't had to dwell very often on her failures as a lover.

She remembered the slow fade of interest in Michael's eyes, his indifference. Abby had never been a raving beauty, and rarely anyone's first choice. But she remembered feeling hope, at the beginnings of her few romantic relationships. Hope that she could inspire the kind of devotion she wanted to feel herself. That she was worthy of love, and nothing she'd done in the past had changed that.

Now, six feet of hope was walking next to Abby, and it scared her. She was considering an entirely new world. Mac was opening a door to her membership in a family of women, with a shared history and culture, that Abby had always respected. In truth, exploring lesbian identity seemed a far less daunting prospect than...exploring this particular lesbian.

Abby was beginning to think the hope might be real this time. She could accept the possibility that the light shining in Mac's eyes might not fade. She could risk investing her heart fully, for the first time in her life—in a woman with a history of vanishing like mist on a summer morning.

The faint sun was setting behind them as the house came into view. Abby watched their linked shadows, hers and Mac's, gliding together over the path at their feet, stretching toward home.

CHAPTER TEN

I noticed you didn't hand that girl a Kleenex last night. At the support group meeting." Danny walked beside Mac through the brisk morning air, her eyes on the frozen ground. "Inez, her name is?"

"Inez, right." Mac looked down at Danny's bent head. She had been there over a week now, and joining Mac on her morning walks had become part of their routine.

"Inez cried a lot when she was talking, and the Kleenex box was right there, but you never handed her one."

"I guess I think handing somebody a tissue when they're crying might make them feel I want them to stop. I reckon Inez would have reached for one if she wanted it."

"Oh. That makes sense." Danny lifted her head and breathed in the pine-spiced air, and Mac was gratified to see the bruises on her face fading to a less vivid hue. They both turned and looked down the trail. "Are you okay back there?" Danny called.

"I'm *fine*." Puffing, Cleo was taking her sweet time catching up. "You two little gazelles just trot right on down the road. Don't worry about me."

Mac thought Cleo might be hanging back to give Danny some private time with her counselor before this ceremony. Or maybe she needed a little private preparation herself.

"She's got this hacking cough now." Danny folded her arms and frowned at Mac. "Does Abby know about that?"

"She knows."

Cleo reached them and braced her arm on Mac's shoulder, white steam puffing from her lips. "Okay. This place? You got in mind for this? It's in Virginia?"

"It's right through those trees, there." Mac cocked her head.

"Cool beans." Cleo straightened and looked at Danny. "So. You finished this picture last night?"

Danny nodded and unzipped her parka. She drew out the large tablet that contained her drawings and held it protectively in her gloveless hands. "We just need someplace pretty."

"I think the grove I told you about will do," Mac said.

"Lead on, Counselor." Cleo took Danny's elbow to steady her as they stepped off the path.

They walked together down a tree-lined trail that opened into a small clearing enclosed by tall pines. This hidden spot had been one of Mac's happiest discoveries in her first weeks at Fireside. She could imagine this smooth white space spangled with wildflowers in the spring, but even under a blanket of snow, it was beautiful. Frosted greenery lay in intricate swirls at the foot of the trees, and the pure air enveloped them in a cathedral silence.

Mac wondered if Danny would show them this drawing. She'd seen some of her sketches, and Cleo was right—Danny had a wicked artist in her. But this image was very private. It was Lily Sherrill's birthday today, and the drawing was for her.

Danny was looking around the snowy clearing. "This is perfect," she said softly.

"Yeah, Mac." Cleo's tone was hushed, as if they stood in a library, or a church. "Nice choice."

"Glad you guys like it here." Mac folded her hands and waited while Danny opened the tablet and turned several pages, and then very carefully tore out a single sheet.

Mac believed strongly in the power of ritual when it came to matters of grief. One of her clients had scattered her father's ashes in the high meadow of a mountain they both loved, rendering the entire mountain a lasting shrine. Another had dug a small reflective pool in the garden her grandmother had cherished, and lined it with stones taken from each of the places they had visited together. Danny's tattoo was a healing ritual as well, as was this drawing.

Danny studied the thick paper for a moment, then started to roll it into a cylinder. She hesitated, then unfurled the paper and handed it to Cleo. "Mac can see it too," she said. "I don't mind."

Mac went to Cleo, and together they looked down at the myriad images swimming over the page, all sketched in dark pencil, vivid lines against the cream surface. Almost every inch of the sheet was covered by small sketches, ten or more of them, angled different ways. Near the center, a mother cradled a newborn child, her devotion poignantly clear in a few deft sweeps of Danny's pencil. Mac had never seen a photo of Danny's mother, but she had no doubt who this was.

The same mother, and a larger woman with dark skin, laughing, holding the hands of a little girl in pigtails, all three on roller skates. One sketch of the two women alone, facing each other, close enough to touch, their smiling eyes filled with warmth.

And images of Danny alone—not just as a child, but in recent years—wearing a pirate costume from a play, putting on makeup in front of a mirror, waving as she drove a car. Mac watched Danny grow up in these small drawings, and realized that seeing her grow was the gift Danny was offering her mother now.

Cleo was very still, and Danny was watching her closely. There were no tears in Cleo's eyes, Mac noted, and her hands, holding the paper, were steady. But her face glowed with a quiet light, as if washed in years of memory.

"Baby," Cleo murmured. "This is perfect."

"Thank you." Danny took the paper, and rolled it carefully into a tight scroll.

Mac was tempted to try to talk Danny into hanging on to

this skillfully drawn history of her life, but she understood that parting with it sweetened the uniqueness of the gift.

Mac and Cleo waited as Danny walked slowly around the enclosed circle, holding the scroll in both hands, looking up into the snowy branches of the towering trees. She searched for a long time.

Mac leaned against Cleo and lowered her voice. "You doing all right with this?"

"Yeah. I'm cool." Cleo nudged Mac gently. "Thanks."

Finally Danny stopped, and pointed at two branches intertwined about three feet above her head.

"I think right there." Danny glanced back at Cleo. "Can you give me a lift?"

Cleo went to her. "You sure about this? What about those bruised ribs?"

"I'm sure."

Cleo put her hands around Danny's waist, bent her knees, and lifted her with effort. Danny slid the scroll into the joining of the curling limbs, tucking it securely within the gnarls of bark.

"Okay," Danny said.

Cleo lowered her to the ground slowly and released her. Danny backed up several steps, surveying the branches with a critical eye. Mac realized that the artist in Lily's daughter had chosen the ideal resting place for her birthday gift. The trees and their snow-shrouded limbs all seemed to incline slightly toward the joining of the two branches, as if in tribute to the illustrated lives they sheltered.

"I don't think the wind will blow it down," Danny said. "I twined it in there pretty well."

"Yes, you did," Mac said. "Good job."

The three of them stood side by side in the hushed clearing, gazing up into the trees, etched tracings against the blue sky. Mac was willing to stand there until sunset.

"Happy birthday," Danny whispered. She slid her drawing tablet under her arm and started back toward the trail. Cleo rested her hand on Danny's shoulder as they stepped silently through the snow.

Now it was Mac who slowed her pace, letting Cleo and Danny walk on ahead together. They were visual opposites, the middle-aged black woman and the frail adolescent, their heads inclined as they talked quietly. They were nearly back to the house when Mac heard Danny's faint laugh and saw their postures relax a little. Cleo opened Danny's drawing tablet, then turned back to yell to Mac.

"Hey, she's got some new ones!"

"Yeah?" Mac jogged to them, pleased. "Can I see?"

"Sure." Danny flipped a few pages.

Cleo grinned broadly, tapping the sheet with one finger. "Aye, look at this handsome wench, would ye now."

It was a great sketch of Cleo, uncannily and affectionately true to its subject. She was resting her chin in her hand, her dark eyes sparkling with deviltry. Mac whistled in admiration. "You caught her dead-on, Danny. Cleo, I can hear your laugh, looking at this."

"Or you can hear her cough." Danny turned a page, and both Cleo and Mac unleashed guffaws that echoed through the trees. Cleo's position in the second drawing was identical to the previous one, but now a cigarette was dangling from her lips, billowing smoke, and its drooping ash was about to set her sweatshirt on fire.

"Abby would pay you a hefty commission for this one, Danielle." Cleo coughed, still chuckling. "Look, Macawai, Danny and the Brit-twit are ganging up on me with this smoking thang."

"The curative powers of good art." Mac slapped Cleo lightly on the back. Then she turned her head, listening intently.

"Damn." Mac lowered herself to one knee and unlaced her boot. "This little rock comes out of my shoe right now. Go on, you guys. I'll see you at the house."

"Okay, Mac." Cleo closed the drawing pad and slipped her

arm around Danny's shoulders, and they continued down the trail. "I'm going to go tell Abby about the time Danny snuck one of my cigarettes when she was eight years old."

"Fine, go ahead." Danny said. "And I'll tell Abby that you just called her a Brit-twit."

Mac waited until their voices faded over a low hill before she turned and walked back a few paces. The footsteps were silent now, but they had been following, as they always did, several yards behind her. Mac closed that distance, walking slowly, her hands at her sides.

She stopped about five feet from where her ghost would be standing. She hadn't heard it bolt. She assumed it was still there.

"I have this friend." Mac spoke quietly. "Her name is Abby. She's a pretty wise person. Abby tells me ghosts are here because they're looking for something. Something they want very badly."

Mac heard her own voice in the empty air and she closed her eyes, feeling foolish. But then she opened them again and looked straight ahead, focusing on the vacant space in front of her.

"What do you want?"

She had asked the ghost that question before. Often, when she was younger. Usually, she had shouted those words in frustration. She hadn't spoken to the ghost without shouting for years. Now her voice was gentle. "It's all right. You can tell me. What do you want?"

Silence. Mac waited. A breeze blew a light drift of snow across the path, but nothing else stirred. Still, Mac waited. Then she turned and walked slowly back up the path. She was cresting the rise of the small hill when she heard the footsteps behind her again.

They followed a little closer.

CHAPTER ELEVEN

Mac dozed in the deep couch in front of the fireplace. She didn't allow herself to slip too deeply into sleep. Cleo and Abby weren't back yet, and as the only staff on-site, Mac didn't want to snooze through any late-night emergencies that might arise on the grounds. Danny was already asleep upstairs, but Mac wanted to hear her if she awoke and wandered down in search of company.

Mac smiled drowsily and dug her bare feet beneath the soft cushion. She had grown to really like this kid. Talented, funny, and every bit as diamond-bright as Cleo claimed. All of Fireside had adopted Danny in the past two weeks, staff and residents alike, especially the younger children. Danny got a kick out of playing with the little ones, and their mothers were beginning to trust her enough to pester her for babysitting services.

Mac turned her head and watched the flames. She hoped Abby would be up for a cup of tea when she got back. She wanted to tell her about Danny and Cleo, about watching them walk home together on Lily Sherrill's birthday. Abby would understand the pleasant ache that had risen in her throat. She wanted to ask Abby for her thoughts on motherhood, and about Abby's own mother, why she found it so hard to talk about her.

When it came down to it, Mac wanted to talk to Abby about damn near anything. Trivia would be fine. She would happily expound upon laundry soap for hours on end, if it meant spending those hours in her company. But she knew very well that she and Abby had more important matters to discuss, and that talk needed to happen soon.

She stared out the dark bay window over the breakfast nook, turning her silver christening ring on her finger. Maybe one day, Mac would even tell Abby about her ghost.

Was it hovering outside the dark window even now, staring in at Mac with longing? Where did it go when it wasn't following her? How old was this mystery wraith? Was it male or female? It amazed Mac, the questions she'd stopped asking decades ago, because she had decided that trying to find answers was futile.

She was hearing the ghost behind her more often now since she came to Fireside. It was almost as if it had come to know this land and liked to roam it with her. It was following more closely too. She was sure of that.

Mac heard a low rustling sound. Adrenaline shot through her, and she scrambled out of the couch. She felt like an idiot when she realized it was only Abby's key in the front door.

Cleo stepped down into the living room behind Abby and frowned at Mac, who still stood rigidly next to the couch. "Look at that guilty face, Ab. See, I told you Taco Belle was toking up in here while we were gone."

"And she didn't save any for us?" Abby smiled while Cleo helped her remove her coat. "I'm sorry, Mac, did we scare you? You look a bit wild-eyed."

"Just too much Stephen King on the brain tonight, I guess. How was the board meeting?"

"Well, we ain't drawing straws next time, sunshine," Cleo grumbled. "You're taking the next two meetings. Dry as damn dust, every minute of it."

"Any luck getting funding for a child advocate?"

"Perhaps next quarter." Abby settled into one corner of the deep couch, folding her legs gracefully beneath her. "But

Vivian was able to talk the board into paying Danny for some housekeeping, now that she's up to it."

"Hey, that's great."

"Yeah, but we have to keep it to a few hours a week." Cleo coughed, then leaned against the back of the couch and yawned. "Danny's heading back to school on Monday. She's missed a lot of classes, and she'll need study time at night if she still wants to graduate in June." She yawned again.

"We'll make sure she gets it." Mac grinned. "Aw, look, Abby, I think our sweet ball of mush here is about ready for her jammies."

"No lie." Cleo chuckled. She scratched her head with both hands. "Hokay. I'm gonna check in on Dan, and turn in." She started toward the staircase, then turned back to them. "What say you two stay up for a while? Unwind. Maybe have a nice conversation."

Mac and Abby stared at each other as Cleo's heavy tread moved up the stairs.

"Did you tell her?" Abby whispered.

"No." Mac smiled ruefully. "I just think our attorney has her wise finger on the pulse of everything that happens at Fireside, especially under this roof." She still stood next to the couch, waiting, she realized, for an invitation.

Abby provided it, patting the cushion beside her. Mac eased down, close to Abby, but not too close. They regarded each other in a silence that Mac found comfortable.

"The new PTSD group you started Tuesday night seems to be going well, Mac. Tina was telling me just this morning how helpful those breathing exercises you taught her are—"

"Abby." Mac spoke gently. "I don't think this is the conversation we're supposed to be having tonight."

"Well. No, it isn't." Abby's gaze drifted to the crackling fire.

Mac hoped like hell that she sounded at least nominally

serene and balanced, because her butch equanimity was fast deserting her. She'd thought she was ready for this conversation. She had planned what she'd say in her mind for days. In the past, Mac had carried on rational discussions with clients in the grip of manic psychosis, but tonight the sight of Abby's downcast eyes robbed her of speech.

So just as Abby had been the first to move to meet Mac's kiss those long nights ago, now she was the one to begin.

"We're not going to be able to explore this any further, Mac." Abby's gaze was tender, and Mac was the one who had to lower her eyes. "You understand why, don't you?"

It wasn't a rhetorical question. Abby wanted to know if Mac had thought it all out, and whether she agreed with her decision. Mac had, and she did. It would just hurt to hear it said aloud. It would hurt to explain it, too, and Mac could feel Abby's regret shimmering between them. "Tell me your thoughts, Doc."

Abby nodded. "First, I need you to know this about me. At this stage in my life, I couldn't possibly be sexual…I couldn't possibly make love to someone, Mac, unless I was in a committed relationship. It simply isn't in me. Perhaps it's some kind of odd British prudery. I don't know, but there you have it." Abby placed her hand on Mac's knee, a movement so spontaneous and natural it prompted no immediate shock. "Please don't think I'm talking about being frightened of touching a woman. Or of loving one. That's not what this is about."

Mac nodded. "I believe you."

"What happened between us, the other night." Abby sighed, a soft mourning breeze. "My body did respond, when you touched me. As I said, you've had that effect on me since the first day you joined us, Counselor. I suppose my libido isn't entirely dead. I can't imagine anyone being indifferent if you touched them. I mean, good Lord, woman, have you seen yourself?"

Abby gestured at Mac's body helplessly, and Mac had to smile.

"I can't tell you how I struggled with this. I have many

reasons for wanting to see what we could build together. But I keep coming up against one very good reason we shouldn't try. Mac, we came here, you and I, because of Fireside. To serve the women and kids who turn to us for help. And this chemistry between us might hurt this place. If things were to go wrong." Abby fell silent, but there had been a note of pleading in her voice, as if she wanted to will Mac to understand.

"And they might go wrong." Mac sounded a little hoarse, and she cleared her throat. "I can't be casual about making love either, Abby, to tell you the truth. And if our hearts get involved in this, and then things turned out badly…it would be very tough to share living and work space, twenty-four-seven."

"Yes. I don't see how we could do our best work with these women, if some painful tension developed between us. It would be especially unfair to Cleo, Mac."

"Yeah, I see that."

They both watched the flames snap in the fireplace.

"But I'd like to think…" Abby sounded almost timid. "That after enough time has passed, we might have another talk like this, some night. When we know each other better. Not anytime soon, maybe not for several years, but eventually. Mac, would you look at me? Is that a foolish hope?"

"Ah, Doc." Mac lifted her head and smiled at Abby, sadly. "I've never stayed anywhere for several years."

"Yes." Abby closed her eyes. "I know."

It took a few seconds for the sound of grating gravel to register, but then Mac realized a vehicle was pulling up to the main house. There was no sweep of headlights across the bay window, and she and Abby exchanged puzzled looks.

"Is it Vivian's car?" Abby turned and tried to see out the frosted glass.

"Sounded like a truck."

The faint squeal of an opening door reached them, but they didn't hear it close. Mac was already on her feet when she caught Abby's whisper.

"Mac, we didn't bolt the door."

Mac was around that sofa like lightning. But the front door opened before she was halfway to the entry, and in marched Samuel Sherrill, big as life and drunk as a lord.

CHAPTER TWELVE

Y ou tell me where my girl is."
        Abby automatically moved to block Sherrill's path to the staircase, and Mac could only hope he was too soused to draw the connection. She thought fast.

"You missed her by three hours, Sam. Danny was here, but she left to spend the night with a friend in town. Sam? Are you—"

"Danielle!" Sherrill bellowed, his bloodshot eyes darting around the room. He stumbled down the three steps leading from the entry into the living room. "Danny, you get in here, right *now*!"

"Hey, whoa!" Mac pivoted into the big man's path, her hands raised. He stopped short, but just barely. "Sam! Look at me. Danny is not here. She's not in the house, all right? Just talk to me for a minute."

"She's telling the truth, Mr. Sherrill." Behind her, Abby had managed a calm, even sympathetic tone. "Please sit down. Let us try to help."

Sherrill peered at them both, scowling, weaving slightly on his feet. Mac made a fast visual check and didn't see any weapons. Then she froze at Danny's tremulous shout from the second floor.

"Cleo, don't you do it!"

"Danny, you stay up here." Cleo's muffled voice.

Sherrill's mouth yawned open and he lunged for the staircase. Mac braced her forearms against his flabby chest and heaved back, and for a sick moment they grappled in place. Breath exploded between Mac's clenched teeth as she fought for leverage, and some of her self-defense training kicked in. His hairy hands gripped her shoulders, and she focused on peeling his pinkie fingers back to the point of pain.

Sherrill bawled in rage, and then Abby was beside her, flourishing a poker from the stand on the hearth with apparently deadly intent. "You take your bloody hands off her, you bastard!"

All three of them flinched hard when the gunshot rang out, shockingly loud in the high-ceilinged room.

Cleo stepped down off the staircase, her pistol pointed at the floor at her side. A small wisp of smoke issued from the end of its barrel. She raised the gun slowly and aimed across the room directly at Sherrill's flushed face. "Let her go, motherfucker."

The panting man's hands were still clenched in Mac's shirt. He pulled them free, staring at Cleo now with an animal cunning that seemed to burn away his intoxication. Mac stepped back immediately, grasped Abby's wrist, and got them both out of range.

"Abby, Mac, go to the kitchen and call the cops," Cleo ordered.

Mac didn't like the sound of that—Cleo's suddenly wanting them both out of the room. She touched Abby and moved past her to Cleo's side. Mac shifted close and spoke quietly, so only Cleo could hear.

"Danny's listening, *mi amiga*. You know she's standing on the second-floor landing." Mac tried to see if her words were registering, but Cleo's eyes still held that frightening, murky glow. "Think, Cleo. Don't do anything you can never take back. Don't leave Danny that kind of legacy. You hear me?"

The stark fire in Cleo's eyes faded by slow degrees. Mac saw her fury ebb toward sanity in the lowering of her gun—not entirely, she still aimed it at Sherrill, but in a more controlled stance now, off that hair-trigger edge. Then Cleo raised the gun again immediately as they heard Danny's light step on the stairs, and Mac tensed.

"You stay right there, Sherrill." Cleo spoke quietly. "If you take one step toward her, I swear to God I'll cut you down."

Mac saw Danny step into the living room, dressed in the T-shirt and shorts she slept in, tousled blond hair making her seem heartbreakingly young. Abby crossed to her and lifted her hand. Danny didn't take her wide eyes off her father, but she listened to Abby's whisper, her head inclined toward her, and nodded.

"Danielle." Sherrill stayed in place. He scrubbed his hand across his mouth. "Danny, girl. You need to come home with me."

"No," Danny said. Her voice came out whiny and sullen, but then she swallowed, and when she spoke again her tone was firm. "No, Dad. I'm not going with you. You need to get out of here."

"Danny," he whispered.

Mac looked at Sherrill and saw everything she didn't want to see. The naked pain in his face, his genuine love for his daughter, his self-hatred for hurting her, the humanity that was as much a part of him as his addictions and violence. Those things were there, or Danny wouldn't love him so much.

But Mac remembered that Sherrill had doubtless felt all those things for Danny's mother too, and his humanity hadn't stopped him from whaling on them both.

"Danny," Sherrill repeated. He rubbed his hands clumsily. "You know how sorry I am, little girl. You got to come home, sugar. I miss you so much."

Danny met Mac's gaze, and her thin shoulders straightened. She had practiced these lines a dozen times on their morning walks, and her message was succinct. "Dad, I'm never coming home. I'll never live with you again. If you don't get help, you're going to lose me entirely. Call me when you've been sober for a month."

The room was silent. Abby was still holding Danny's hand, and Mac saw her press her fingers gently. Danny squeezed back and then let go and turned toward the stairs. She took them slowly, as if very tired.

Cleo waited until they heard Danny's bedroom door close upstairs, her pistol still on Sherrill. "Abby, go ahead and make that call. Tell them to cut their damn lights this time. We don't want a repeat of cop cars scaring everybody to death."

Relief seeped through Mac. Cleo was calm now, grim but rational. She heard Abby call her name softly.

"You all right, Counselor?"

"I'm fine, Doc."

Abby nodded, and started toward the kitchen.

"You go on and make that call, *Doc*." Sherrill's words were still slurred, but the venom in them was poisonously clear. "I'm the one that needs a little protection here. The cops are gonna be real interested in seeing a convicted felon waving a handgun around. They'll cuff your ass, you black bitch."

"Shut up, Sherrill." Cleo sounded more disgusted than angry. "You've got nothing on me."

"I got a drinking buddy who remembers you real well." Sherrill rested his butt against the back of the sofa and folded his beefy arms. "Told me he heard a murderer got hired out at this place. Said this worthless hag ran over a kid several years back, when she was drunk out of her mind. And then drove off and left him to die in the street." Sherrill grinned. "Real sweet role model ol' Lily ran off with, hey? Did she know about that dead kid, Cleo? Does Danny know? You think I won't tell her?"

"There's no need, Mr. Sherrill, because you're talking about me." Abby still stood in the kitchen doorway, her face the color of ash. "You might as well get your facts straight. I didn't kill the boy, but I crippled him. He'll never walk again. I was never convicted of a crime, however, and I didn't go to prison, so your ugly threats are useless. I suggest you direct your energies to following your daughter's advice." She turned, and went through the swinging door.

Mac and Cleo stood very still.

"I don't give a fuck. I'm not leaving my Danny here." Sherrill got heavily to his feet. "Not with a crazy bulldyke and a fucking drunkard. You all brainwashed her against me. You perverts put your hands on her in the night, don't you? That's what you've always wanted, Cleo, you bl—"

Mac took three steps, drew back her fist, and punched Sherrill in the jaw, a roundhouse right with all her strength behind it.

He uttered a sharp barking sound and staggered back against the couch, then toppled over it, sprawling on the cushions.

Mac stood over him. "I'd stay down, you sorry sack of sewage. And keep your mouth shut. Open it again, and I'll shoot you myself." Her hand hurt like hell.

Behind her, Cleo whistled softly.

Whether it was Mac's threat, his aching jaw, or the continued presence of Cleo's handgun, Sherrill chose not to push it. He remained in a sodden slump on the couch, his hands dangling between his knees, breathing noisily.

Abby pushed through the door from the kitchen and took in the subdued scene. She looked at Mac, then walked over to Cleo and spoke to her quietly. Cleo nodded and lowered her gun, still holding it ready by her side.

Abby stepped behind Cleo and started massaging her shoulders, and she was still doing it when the police cruiser pulled into the front drive. An hour and several forms later, the police were gone, Sam Sherrill in tow.

CHAPTER THIRTEEN

Abby closed the door to Danny's bedroom, cushioning any sound with the heel of her hand. Cleo and Mac had both visited the girl earlier, and more than anything now, Danny needed the peace and privacy to sleep.

Abby's step was silent on the carpeted hallway that connected the private quarters of the staff. Abby paused outside Cleo's door. It was cracked open, a small light burning within. Abby hesitated. As the sole personal space any of them had, bedrooms were considered fairly sacrosanct. Cleo was especially fierce about her privacy because she was fierce about almost everything. But because Cleo was her friend, Abby knocked softly.

"Yep."

Abby peered around the door. Cleo was propped up in bed, a shoebox in her lap. Photos were scattered across her blankets.

She looked up at Abby over the gold wire-rimmed glasses she wore only for reading. "Is she down for the night?"

"Yes, I think so." Abby came into the room, but not too close to the bed, not wanting to see the photographs unless invited. "Your Danny did a fine job down there."

"Yeah, she spoke up for herself real well." Cleo lifted another photo from the shoebox.

Like Abby's, Cleo's bedroom was small. Unlike Abby's, it was a cheerful mess, paperwork and books scattered everywhere, pictures of her mother and sisters, her nieces and nephews taped haphazardly on one wall. But her furry bear slippers were paired neatly on the floor beside her bed. Abby's gaze chanced across a framed drawing on another wall, and she had to smile. It was the portrait Danny had drawn, depicting Cleo about to ignite herself with her cigarette. It might have been intended as a health advisory, but predictably Cleo had enshrined it as art.

The silence between them grew. Abby waited, braced for questions about drinking and driving and a crushed boy lying in the street. But it seemed Cleo had a more important question in mind.

"You want to see Danny's mom?" Cleo extended the picture toward Abby, smiling almost shyly.

Relieved, Abby took the small square and held it closer to the lamp beside the bed. "Ah, honey. She was lovely."

Perhaps not traditionally so. Lily Sherrill had been thin and spare, and there was a pleasant plainness to her even features. But that broad splash of a smile was all Danny, dazzling and warm. Abby would have enjoyed sitting down with this woman over a pot of good tea, and talking about their lives.

"There won't be another like her, for me."

Abby felt her smile fade. Cleo had spoken the words with such quiet finality, as if voicing a simple truth. "Really, Cleo? You don't think you'll find a partner again?"

"Lily was my wife." Cleo shrugged and took the photo back. She looked down at the image fondly. "I ain't saying I'm determined to be a widow for life, but damn, she would be a hard act to follow."

Abby stifled the impulse to argue with her. She certainly didn't believe every human being needed to be matched to a mate—she quickly suppressed an image of Mac—but she wanted so much for this stubborn, loving woman to be blessed with every gift life can offer. "I'm sorry, Cleo."

"No. I've been lucky, Ab." Cleo was still gazing down at

Lily's face, with no trace of sadness now. "We had five years together. Some people look all their lives and never find what we had. Hell, most never find it. Do you know how rare that kind of love is?"

"What you and Lily shared must have been very—"

"I'm not spewing platitudes here." Cleo lowered the photo. She removed her glasses and looked at Abby with an intensity that surprised her. "*Do* you know how rare that kind of bone-deep love is, Abby? And how incredibly fucking lucky we are, if we get even the smallest chance to find it?"

"Yes," Abby whispered. "I do know how rare love is."

"Sometimes, you've just got to be brave." The corner of Cleo's mouth lifted. "That's how Danny summed up everything she's learned in her sessions with Mac. Hey, speaking of." She slipped her glasses back on. "You got your spare medical bag up here?"

"Yes, in my room, I think." Abby struggled to refocus. "Why?"

"Mac smashed the hell out of her hand when she clocked Sherrill down there." Cleo grinned. "A sight I truly wish you hadn't missed, by the by."

"I'm just as glad I did." Abby frowned. "Is she really hurt?"

"Looked like it was swelling up to me. You might want to check it out."

"I will, after I clock her in the jaw myself for not telling me about this." Abby started toward the door, then stopped, and turned back to Cleo. "Hey. You about ready to sleep?"

"All tucked in my jammies and everything." Cleo's eyes warmed. "Good night, Abby-gail."

"Sleep well, Ms. Lassiter."

"Leave the door cracked, so I can hear Danny if she wakes up."

"Will do."

Abby went to her room and retrieved the small satchel from a closet shelf. She felt unreasonably annoyed as she made her way to Mac's door and tapped on it softly but rapidly.

"I'm awake."

Abby turned the knob. "Permission to enter?"

"Granted." Mac was sitting back against her headboard, reading, her lean form bathed in gold light from the bedside lamp. She smiled at Abby. "Is Danny se—"

"Danny's fine, she's asleep." Abby went to the bed and saw the folded washcloth resting across the knuckles of Mac's right hand. She sighed and touched the damp cloth. "This is fairly useless in terms of swelling. May I?"

Mac set her book aside. "Okay."

Abby plucked the washcloth off her hand. The knuckles looked chafed and raw, and there was definite bruising underway. "Honestly, Mac. Scoot over."

Mac's eyebrows rose, but she shifted her long legs, and Abby sat on the edge of the bed. She lifted Mac's hand and tilted it carefully beneath the light. "Move your fingers, please."

Mac obliged, slowly and with some evident pain. "Nothing's broken, Doc."

"Well, I doubt if we can know that for sure without an X-ray, but I'll have to take your word for it tonight." Abby laid the washcloth aside and opened her satchel. She tore open a pack of antibiotic cream and smoothed a small dab over the chafed skin at the base of Mac's fingers. "Cleo mentioned I might want to look in on the consequences of your sudden punching prowess. You might have told me yourself, Mac."

"I didn't want you to see this."

That startled Abby, and brought her out of the distracted irritation she couldn't explain in the first place. "What do you mean?"

"I'm not sorry I hit Sherrill. I'd do it again, given a chance to do things over." Mac shifted her bruised hand. "But it's nothing I'm proud of, either."

"Cleo said he was saying terrible things."

"Yeah." Mac shrugged. "I just don't think violence is ever an appropriate response to words, even terrible ones."

Abby rested Mac's battered hand on her knee. They sat together quietly for a while as she probed the contours of her fingers with care. She reached into her satchel, pulled out a chemical ice pack, and bent it to activate it. She draped it over Mac's knuckles, then took out a small roll of elastic bandage. Mac's gaze was on her, tender and patient.

"I wasn't much older than Danny." Abby unclipped the bandage and began winding it around Mac's hand, to provide some support and hold the ice pack in place. "I'd only had my driver's license for a year."

"Abby." Mac was a still presence beside her. Abby could feel the warmth of her shoulder against her own. "I want to listen. But don't let Sam Sherrill choose your time to talk about this."

"No, it's all right." Abby wound the bandage evenly, careful not to make it too tight. "I was eighteen. I'd been to a party. My first experience with drinking, really. I never even saw the boy. He was riding his bike through a well-marked crosswalk, at a well-lit intersection. He had a dozen reflective patches on his jacket and pants. I simply plowed straight into him. I did stop, however. Sherrill was wrong about that."

Abby fixed the small Velcro strip at the end of the bandage around Mac's wrist. "Several vertebrae were crushed. I know now that the damage couldn't have been repaired, even if the boy had had surgery instantly, but I stood over him for nearly fifteen minutes. There were no other cars. I was so wiped out I couldn't think."

Mac had an old-school wind-up clock beside her bed, one that ticked rather than blinked. Abby found its soft, continuous chant soothing. It counted off a full minute of silence.

"Help me understand." Mac covered Abby's hand with her uninjured one. "Abby, you probably couldn't think because you were in shock. And yes, you made a terrible mistake, all those years ago. But it was a mistake. And you were hardly more than a kid yourself."

"Well, the mistake kept right on happening, for a while." Abby rested her head against the headboard, avoiding Mac's gaze. "The next morning, my father hired the best legal firm in the city. The case was dismissed without even going to court. But we learned a few days later that the parents wanted to sue. So there was a meeting. Me and my father, our attorney, and the boy's father."

Abby's saliva turned bitter in her mouth. "My lawyer wanted to know why the boy had been allowed out on his bike alone at night. Apparently there had been a Child Protective Services report on the family, years before. My lawyer asked the father if he wasn't concerned that he might lose custody of his son, if he insisted on dragging out a lawsuit and all the facts came to light. There was little chance of that, but our attorney was quite good. The man certainly couldn't afford high-powered legal help, and he was frightened. We never heard from him again."

Mac twined her fingers through Abby's.

"I sat in that meeting and I watched my father's face. Social justice was his life, Mac. He devoted his career to fighting the abuse of power, and teaching others to fight it. I saw him age a decade that morning. It may have been the only dishonorable thing Phillip Glenn ever did. My mother has barely spoken to me since."

Abby realized she couldn't put off seeing Mac's face forever. She looked up, and the kindness in Mac's eyes loosened the vise in her chest.

"And now you work with women and kids who can't buy their way out of trouble," Mac said quietly. "You could be bringing in huge money working in hospitals, or in private practice. Instead, you came here."

"Yes." Abby nodded. "Penance, I suppose."

"Maybe at first. Now it's service." Mac said the word with

as much respect as Cleo had voiced the word "wife." "And you love your work, Abby."

"I do." Abby drew her hand through her hair. "The boy is a graduate student at MIT now, on scholarship. Chemical engineering. I believe he's some kind of genius. But he'll always be in a wheelchair, and he'll never father children."

Mac's long fingers were strong and warm, laced through hers. And it was staring down at that hand that returned Abby at last to the visceral connection she shared with Mac, in a way that broke through all her defenses. It was remembering how Mac's hand had trembled as she cradled her face when they kissed.

She was touching Abby's chin, tipping her face so she would look at her. Abby did, and knew she would be lost if she didn't go now. She slipped her hand free and reached for her satchel, then rose unhurriedly from the bed. "Good night, Counselor."

Abby crossed the small room, noticing its chill for the first time, and had opened the door when Mac spoke.

"Abby. Stay."

Abby gazed at the oak panels of the door in front of her. The small clock ticked off the seconds. Then she closed the door, and turned back to Mac.

Sometimes, you just had to be brave.

Mac lifted the edge of the bedcovers, and Abby slipped off her shoes and slid fully clothed beneath them. She heard herself titter—actually titter—from sheer nerves. "Is this some gallant bow to my British prudery?"

"Nah." Mac chuckled, climbing beneath the blankets herself. "It's just cold in here." She raised herself on one elbow. "*Bienvenida*, Abby Glenn. Welcome."

"Thanks," Abby whispered. Mac's handsome features were so familiar to her now, and so dear. She started to speak, but Mac rested a finger against her lips.

"You've been lying here beside me, just like this, for a lot of nights now. I've made love to you a hundred times or more, in my mind. I'd like to touch you now the way I have in my dreams, if that's all right with you."

"Yes."

Mac tucked the blankets around Abby's shoulders, to keep her warm. And at first her touch was as light and platonic as air, brushing Abby's hair off her forehead. She drew one finger down the side of her face, studying her so closely that Abby realized this was the first time they could gaze at each other, full and long, without having to look away to disguise their hearts.

Mac cupped her face again as their lips met. There was no tremor in her fingers now, they were warm and sure. The kiss deepened from a friendly brushing to a more sensual caress, and a soft sigh escaped Abby as her body melted against the sheets.

"Mph." Abby had to speak, and Mac lifted her head quickly. "Mac. Cleo and Danny and God and everyone are right down the hall."

"Abby." Mac blinked. "They're behind solid walls, and they're probably sound asleep."

"Oh. Right. No real worries, then."

Mac grinned, a flash of white in the dim gold light. She rested her hand on Abby's waist and drummed her fingers patiently, and even through her shirt, the touch sent a deep shiver through her. "Is there anything else you wish to discuss at this time, Abigail? We could talk about our feministic awarement, if you want."

Abby just smiled in response. Mac kissed her again. She shifted, sliding her bandaged hand beneath Abby so her arm supported her neck, her touch feather-light on her face. Mac's lips moved against hers in sweet exploration, tasting her, her breath smelling lightly of the winesap apples she loved. Abby felt that melting begin again, a languid ease stealing through her limbs, draining away the last vestige of tension from this frightening night.

"I'm at a little disadvantage here." Mac tapped her injured hand on the pillow. "So just let me—"

"Are you going to talk all night, Counselor?"

"Nooo, ma'am."

Her mouth moved to Abby's throat, and her hand slid beneath her sweater to push up her bra. Her rough palm cupped one breast, the nipple pebbling against it as her lips skated slowly up to Abby's chin, then back down. Abby swept her hands through Mac's thick, dark hair, cool softness spilling over her fingers. A thrilling, expectant tension was forming in her sex.

Mac moved over her like a master harpist, strumming her body awake from a long and lonely sleep. She cherished the quivering tips of her breasts with her lips and tongue, then returned to her mouth for a searching, heated kiss. When she finally parted Abby's legs and touched her center, Abby gasped and turned her head on Mac's arm, unprepared for the intensity of this first pleasure.

"Shhh, babe, be patient."

Even through her closed eyes, Abby could feel Mac watching her face, timing her expertly, the skillful swirl of her fingers in her wetness quickening, then slowing again. It was the simplest way one woman could love another, pure and somehow deeply feminine, and Abby had imagined these very sensations for long nights.

She tried to control her breathing, but then gave up the effort because she *loved* the carnal wave rising in her, almost frightening in its intimate power. It crested with unstoppable swiftness, and Mac carried her into the most exquisite physical pleasure she had ever known.

It took a while to recover. Mac stroked her body soft again while she lay there panting, and then cradled Abby's head on her shoulder.

"My goodness," Abby gasped.

"I know." Mac sounded proud, and so deservedly so Abby couldn't even tease her for it.

It had been everything she'd imagined. That's what surprised Abby most. She wasn't used to having her fantasies fulfilled to their every nuance, but then before she met Mac she hadn't fantasized much. She shivered happily and turned to Mac, draping one arm over her lean waist. "My goodness."

"I know. I'm pretty damn hot."

Abby slapped her stomach lightly and then rubbed her side with the palm of her hand. "I would like very much to make you feel like this, Macawai…"

"And you will." Mac kissed the top of her head. "Over many nights. But this was wonderful for me, and I'm more than content. We both need sleep. Will you stay?"

"I really should brush my teeth." Abby snickered as Mac started to protest, her eyes already drifting closed again. "Thank you for the sweet dreams to come."

"I thank you back, *querida*."

Abby's sleep was pure and deep. She swam awake only once, near dawn, her head still resting on Mac's shoulder. Even in the near dark she could tell that Mac was awake, motionless, staring at the ceiling.

CHAPTER FOURTEEN

"How could I tell my parents?" Tina was weeping softly, her fingers twined in those of Jo, who sat close beside her. "I spent all those years trying to convince my family that two women together is a healthy and good thing. They were just starting to accept me. How could I tell them Fran was slapping me around all the time?"

The circle was silent, a fitting response to Tina's grief. Mac kept steady watch on the eight women's faces, their body language, measuring how what they were hearing was affecting them. Abby, who was co-facilitating this group, was monitoring carefully too, and Mac knew she realized this was an important night.

Tina and Jo had been there for several months when Mac arrived. Tina was always caring and supportive in group when the other women talked about their pain, but tonight was the first time she was sharing her own.

"And we don't live in a big city. Our lesbian community's real small." Tina lifted her tear-streaked face. "Some of my friends didn't even believe me. They said women aren't like guys, we're not violent. Jo believed me, though. She's the one who convinced me that I'm a good person and I don't deserve to get hurt or be scared all the time."

The look that passed between Tina and Jo was rich with love, and Mac checked the faces around them again. Degale was

watching the two women with compassion, which surprised Mac
not at all. So were most of the others, which pleased her. Even
Inez, the traditional Catholic, was listening respectfully.

"But now, see, Jo has lost all her friends too. We can't tell
anyone where we are because they might let it slip to Fran, and
she'd come after us."

"Real friends will still be there for you, baby, even if they
can't help you right now." Degale rocked gently in the hickory
rocking chair. "Don't you give up on them yet."

"Yeah, and even if they can't help, you're the nicest girl in
this place, Tina." Danny spoke up, a rare and encouraging event.
"You'll make friends wherever you go. Jo sucks, of course, but
everyone loves you."

A ripple of warm laughter eased the room, because everyone
knew the friendship that was starting to form between Danny and
Jo allowed such kidding. Tina laughed too, and then slumped
back in her chair with a look of relief. Mac caught her eye and
winked, congratulating her on finding the courage to speak, and
Tina smiled back.

Private conversations began to emerge among the women.
Mac looked at Abby and raised her eyebrows, asking if this was
a good time to stop. Abby glanced at the grandfather clock and
nodded. They read each other's silent signals easily now. Then
Mac held Abby's gaze for just a shade too long, the few seconds
it took for the group to melt away and leave them alone in the
room. The corner of Abby's mouth lifted, and Mac knew she
could read the banked desire in her eyes.

"Okay." Mac pulled her attention to the clock as it chimed
the hour. "Thanks for some good work tonight, everybody.
Remember, we can still use some help unloading our grocery run
tomorrow. Have a nice evening."

The murmuring dismissal that followed was friendly and
relaxed, one sign of a group meeting well spent. Some of the
women helped Mac and Abby return the chairs to the storage

closet, while others collected coffee mugs to take to the kitchen. Danny was doing a great job keeping the lower level clean, and the hardwood floor gleamed with polish, but Mac appreciated everyone pitching in.

Mac stood at the bay window over the breakfast nook, letting Abby usher the last of the residents out of the house. The sun was lingering longer now as Virginia's winter faded, but judging by the rose tint in the sky, twilight was close. Mac went to the hall closet in the entry for her denim jacket.

Abby strolled over to her. "If you heard that growling during group, it was my stomach, not a lurking cougar. I thought we'd heat up that nice ham Scratch brought us Sunday."

"Sounds bueno. Sandwiches for weeks." Mac shook her hair out from under her collar. "I'm going to go spring Cleo from the kids' room, then I thought I'd take a walk."

"Dinner will be waiting when you get back." Abby touched Mac's arm. "Unless you'd like some company, on your walk? You look very thoughtful this evening."

"Good thoughts, mostly." Mac slid her arms around Abby's waist. Heated glances in group aside, they didn't share even mild expressions of affection when residents were present, and it was nice to have the privacy to do so again. "Thoughts about a certain wild woman in my bed."

"Oh, those thoughts." Abby relaxed against her. "Yes, your bed has occurred to me too. Several times, in the past few days. During the most inopportune moments, might I add."

Mac dipped her head and brushed her lips against Abby's throat. "We're getting pretty vocal in there, these nights. We might need to consider putting in some insulation, what with Cleo and Danny and God and everyone right down the hall."

Abby lifted her chin, and Mac skimmed her lips toward her ear. "Oh, let them pay admission to listen at your door. We can hang a little donation box outside your room." Abby laughed softly, then pressed against Mac's chest. Mac lifted her head and looked at her. "Thank you for the two roses I found on my desk this morning, Macawai. You have the nicest instincts for romance."

"You know, I really haven't, before now." Mac thought about this, rocking Abby slightly. She couldn't remember making many romantic gestures when she was with Hattie. So far, she and Abby were blending together as easily as the leaves of one of Abby's finer teas. "I can't say I've ever been that great with love poems and flowers and such. But something about you must be bringing out my sappier side."

"I bring out your sap?" Abby frowned. "That's your notion of a romantic line?"

"I also left wild daisies in your enema bag." Mac stopped Abby's snort of laughter with a kiss, and Abby's arms grew more snug around her waist. Mac had only intended a light peck, but the kiss stretched and grew and took on a rather sordid life of its own, and they both gasped when Mac finally raised her head.

"I think I should either go on that walk," Mac murmured, "or both of us should go upstairs for an hour, and let the ham be damned."

"Go, go." Abby tapped Mac's shoulders, and she released her. "I'd rather have your undivided attention after lights out."

"Yes'm." Mac kissed her forehead, then went to the front door.

"Hey?" Abby clasped her hands behind her and leaned back against the entry post. "You're not limited to sharing only the good thoughts, Mac."

"Hmm?"

"If anything's troubling you." Abby lifted her shoulder. "I just want you to know I'd like to listen."

"Honey, what makes you think something's bothering me?" Mac realized she was pulling open the front door even as she spoke. "I'm a little stiff after an hour on that folding chair, that's all. Everything's fine."

"Okay." Abby nodded. "It's just that you haven't slept very

well, the last few nights. Just when I've conquered my own insomnia, it seems to have claimed you. Maybe a good brisk walk will tire you out a bit."

"If it doesn't, maybe you can take care of tiring me out a bit later." Mac waited until Abby smiled, and then she winked and closed the door behind her.

Mac stepped down off the front deck and thrust her hands in her pockets against the lingering chill in the air. She wondered, as she walked toward the east wing, if there was a correct way to explain to her practical new lover that she was having dreams about a ghost.

Not nightmares, just crazy, disorienting dreamscapes, filled with noise. Mac found it impossible to describe, even to herself. She heard words in these dreams, but no voices. And either the words were nonsensical or she couldn't remember them in the morning. She didn't doubt she was tossing and turning enough to disturb Abby.

"Hi, Mac!"

"Hi, Lena-Angelina." Mac rested her hand on the little girl's head as she and Inez passed her on their way out of the playroom. Most of the kids had already been picked up by their mothers after group, but Mac could see little Waymon was still there, and he was still an unrepentant knee hugger.

Cleo folded her arms and sighed in feigned martyrdom as Degale peeled her grandson off her lower leg. "Night, Waymon."

"Bye, Cleeeee-owe!" Waymon apparently loved Cleo's name, and hooted it at every opportunity.

"Come on, little man." Degale grasped Waymon's pudgy hand. "You're gonna help me pick up the toys in your bedroom before we have supper."

"Yes!" Waymon agreed promptly, probably not fully understanding his grandmother's agenda, but an unstoppably sunny child nonetheless. Mac waved to them as she and Cleo started straightening the cluttered room.

"Well, I didn't resort to spiking their orange juice with Nyquil, but it was a close call." Cleo flipped open a toy chest and tossed a few blocks inside. "I swear, Macky-wai, we need a child advocate on this staff before these kids give me cholesterol."

Mac made sure the windows were locked as she listened to Cleo crab on, sympathetic but unconcerned, knowing the kids were in excellent hands when Cleo watched them. The three of them tried to rotate evening childcare duties to accommodate support groups or other necessary appointments, and it could be damn tiring to run herd on a room full of them at the end of a long workday.

"Abby's lighting a fire under that ham, up at the house." Mac snapped off the lights, and Cleo shook out her keys and locked the playroom. "Go dig in. But leave a few tattered shreds of pork for me, please, I'll be back soon."

"You want ham, be at the table." Cleo slipped her hoodie over her head. "You can have whatever Abby leaves of her half."

Mac watched Cleo walk toward the house. "Cleo?"

Cleo turned back to her and rolled her eyes, a wicked Danny imitation. "Yes, glutton, we'll save you some pork." Then she snickered, acknowledging Mac might have more on her mind than dinner, and waited until she joined her in the open yard. The breeze wasn't strong, but it was very cold for late March, and they both huddled with crossed arms.

Mac studied Cleo's face, and saw nothing but friendly interest. "You know what's happening between me and Abby, right?"

"You mean what's been happening since the day you moved in? Right."

Mac grinned. "I believe you warned me against this, on my first day. Professional boundaries, and all that."

"Oh, hell." Cleo turned to take in the sunset over the ridge of trees bordering the west end of their property. "Who am I to slam anyone on professional boundaries? And who knew Abby was going to turn out to be a sister? That girl didn't give off a single gay vibe for months. I'm good, I'd have noticed."

"Cleo." Mac appreciated her light tone. "We need to talk about how this thing between Abby and me might affect Fireside. And you. It already has, in small ways, just the last few weeks."

"Like how?"

"Like you leaving the house more often at night, to give us time alone."

"Just how do you know I don't have a hot mama in Fredericksburg?"

"Cleo."

"Okay." Cleo rocked on her heels beside her, looking thoughtful. "Mac, I'm not worried about Fireside, where you and Abby are concerned. We can handle whatever comes up, and Viv will keep us honest. And maybe having another healthy couple on-site can be a good thing. Vivian and Scratch have been our only role models for too long."

"Yeah?" Mac was surprised, and oddly unsettled. "What about you, though?"

"Not to worry about me, either. Or Danny." Cleo lifted one finger. "As long as we don't have to listen to you fight, if you ever do. And no coming to me with complaints about each other, either. I warn you now, I'll never take sides."

"That sounds fair." Mac felt some relief. "So, you're okay with all this?"

"I didn't say that."

"Ah." Mac waited.

"I'm not worried about Fireside, and I'm not worried about me. You know she's falling in love with you, Mac."

Mac's mouth was dry. "Yeah. I'm falling back."

"I got that." Cleo nodded. "And listen, I'm behind this hard, for you and Abby both. I think you're the best thing that could happen to each other. But I believe Abby had to call up some courage to let you and her finally happen. It took some moxie on her part. That first night together might have been easier for you. The time might come, though, when you're gonna need to show some intestinal fortitude too." She shrugged. "I care about you guys. It would be hard as hell to see either of you get hurt."

Mac couldn't form an answer, and after a moment Cleo bumped her gently with her shoulder.

"G'wan, take your walk and then come get some supper."

Mac watched until Cleo mounted the front deck, scraped her boots on the mat, and disappeared into the house.

She followed the meandering trail that wound around the rough periphery of the property. They weren't quite through with snow yet—muddy clumps of white still dotted the ground—but the season was beginning to change, to ebb toward spring. This was the only time of year that didn't thrill Mac, these sodden, rainy weeks that were sure to contain a late frost or two before lasting warmth arrived.

She listened to her boots clock against the stone path as she watched the first stars emerge overhead. Drab weather aside, Fireside's luck seemed to be holding well. They'd heard nothing from Sam Sherrill since his rude intrusion, so apparently he wasn't going to fight Danny's placement. He was out of jail on bond, but he'd made no effort to contact his daughter. Danny was back in school and catching up on her work quickly, and that wary edge had begun to leave her gaze.

Abby's blue eyes superimposed over Danny's brown ones, in Mac's mind.

Mac would never have predicted this. Not her falling for Abby, but her reaction to it. Teenagers were supposed to turn into slack-jawed imbeciles when they fell in love, but Mac was thirty fricking years old. Too old to duck behind the lockers when the cute girl came by, too young for the kind of hot flashes that went through her every time Abby walked into a room.

She was feeling all of it, every besotted emotion Mac had seen in her high school friends when they rhapsodized about their crushes. Astonished pleasure that Abby had seen fit to choose her. A constant, restless desire to be near her. An unseemly urge to announce their status to every citizen of Virginia.

But this wasn't a crush, and these feelings ran deeper. One of the strongest was the soul-satisfying pride she had in Abby. Not just as a lover, but as a doctor and a friend. Her skills, her gentleness, her brave heart. It was an honor to love this woman, and Mac knew that to her bones.

But did Abby know how strong and sure this connection was beginning to feel for Mac? Or was she only aware of her misgivings—few of which had anything to do with Abby. Mac knew she was concerned about her. She needed to do a better job in the reassurance department, because Abby's worries were groundless. Mac's probably were too.

The happy certainty was that she and Abby shared a new love that grew richer every day. They had supportive friends who cared for them both. They were of the first, lucky generation of women who had a reasonable expectation of living together openly. Surely the first generation to confide in their employer with confidence, and see that confidence justified.

Mac remembered her conversation with Vivian Childs the week before.

"Coworkers fall in love all the time, Mac. Neither of you supervises the other, so there's no ethical conflict. Of course, you and Abby will face a few unique challenges here, but we can make this work."

"That's good to hear."

"I've said all this to Abby too." Vivian smoothed her dress neatly over her knees. "Now, this relationship is bound to change the dynamics of our team a little, but I think we can minimize any negative effects. I don't want Cleo feeling like odd person out."

"We don't either," Mac said. "All three of us will watch out for that."

"Good. You three are a dynamite crew. I don't think I've ever seen a team that's meshed so well, professionally and

personally." Vivian tapped the sheaf of papers in her lap. "And this is one of the best three-month evaluations I've ever written, Mac. I'm pretty strict with first performance reviews, but yours is basically a rave."

"Thank you." Mac meant it. She had been lucky in her supervisors. She'd respected them all, but Vivian's opinion was especially important to her.

"And now that you and Fireside have gotten to know each other, it's time to look down the road a bit." Vivian crossed one elegant leg over the other. "I realize no one in this field can make any promises about longevity, Mac. Social service uses people hard, and burns them out fast. I can't ask front-line staff to sign multiyear contracts. But I want you to consider staying on here, longer than the one or two years you've been at your other jobs."

Mac shifted in her chair. "I was in Seattle for almost three years."

"You've been program-hopping, honey." Vivian's voice was kind. "And maybe that works for you, moving around the country, learning more with each new placement. I can see that as an exciting way of life. But Fireside is my baby, and I want the best for her. And the best means building a stable staff, a long-term, established team."

Mac couldn't argue with that.

"Just asking you to think outside the box." Vivian smiled. "Ponder things for a while, and we'll talk again."

Mac's mood had darkened. She felt like a petulant child now, arguing internally with Vivian, sounding whiny even in her own mind. She kicked a pinecone off the rocky trail.

It galled Mac to admit that Vivian's mild criticism was valid. She was fully aware she had been shelter-hopping. She worked through the first years of a position, honeymooning, flush with the challenge and excitement of learning a new program. Then she moved on, passing through shelters but not investing in them, not sticking around to do the tough work of helping them grow and flourish.

Mac tried to explain it to Vivian in her mind. More important, and more frightening, she tried to explain it to Abby.

They were wrong if they feared Mac just got bored easily. It wasn't boredom or disillusion or burnout that had driven her from one city to the next for the past decade. It was an inherent restlessness that Mac had been born with and still didn't understand, a sense of needing movement in order to stay afloat. And that easy mobility, that urge to wander, was her way of life now. Mac had been a nomad for so long, nothing else felt normal or safe.

Putting down roots. Falling in love. The most crucial tasks of adulthood, and she had managed to avoid both, until now, through determined effort. Her step hesitated on the stony trail. Cleo was right. If Mac wanted to change any of this, she might have to find her own intestinal fortitude.

"She's worth it," Mac whispered. "The lady's worth it."

She paused again, listening.

The steps fell silent behind her. Close behind her. Mac turned.

It was fully dark now, and Fireside's drafty back property seemed barren and wild beneath the full moon. She waited.

"I can't hear you," Mac said finally. She spoke as calmly as she would to anyone who needed Mac's help. "But I'm trying. I'm listening, and I want to understand. You keep trying too. Okay?"

Mac stood there until the chill breeze cut through her denim jacket. Then she moved on, focusing on the roof of the main house, just visible over the rise. Friendly smoke wended from one of its chimneys.

❖

"I wanna stay!" Ashy yelled again, after the woman's retreating back. "Hey! I wanna stay right HERE!"

The big dumb woman still couldn't hear her. Ashy was doing her best. It wasn't her fault if Mac still didn't even know her name. She had told her. it a gazillion chillion times now. Ashy had said what she wanted, too, as loud as she possibly could. It's not like she was asking for a box of diamonds or a real pony or something. It wouldn't be that hard.

She puffed her bangs off her forehead in exasperation, and trotted to catch up.

CHAPTER FIFTEEN

Abby realized Mac didn't really need her assistance on a simple Danny-fetching trip. But Cleo was up to her ears in phone calls when the time came to pick Danny up from school, and she had waved them both out the door—still finding ways, Abby suspected, to give her and Mac time alone.

Abby had offered her overworked colleague cheerful thanks before she hopped into the Jeep beside Mac. She had already covered a full day of examinations and paperwork, and she was more than happy to escape the confines of the main house for a while.

For the second time, she politely peeled Mac's hand from her thigh and placed it back on the steering wheel. "Here, Mac, let's try this. I'll clamp your knee in a death grip, and you'll keep both hands on the wheel, so that we shouldn't die. Will that be all right?"

"Guess it'll *have* to be. Just trying to be romantical, and all."

Abby rested her hand on Mac's knee and sat back to enjoy the scenery. Mac seemed lighter today, more herself. She must be working out whatever worries were plaguing her dreams—though Abby would still prefer she work them out aloud, with her. She silently thanked Cleo again for their unexpected time together this cloudy afternoon.

"Ooh, we should turn off there on the way back." Abby nearly nicked Mac's ear, pointing to the gated road dwindling behind them. "Want to see the farm where George Washington grew up? Where he famously told the truth about murdering the cherry tree? Before he became a man and stole all of the Colonies away from us."

"I don't know, I'm still pretty torn up about that little tree. That's a dark moment in our national conscience." Mac checked her rearview mirror, her cheek dimpling. "Sure, why not. I bet Danny hasn't seen the murder scene either. We'll stop off on the way home."

"There are several stops I'd like us to make sometime, Mac, places I haven't had a chance to show you yet. The Kenmore Gardens. And oh, the Hugh Mercer Apothecary Shop. Did you know they have live leeches there, those famous medicinal bloodsuckers of old?"

"I didn't know this." Mac sounded appropriately impressed. She removed her hand from the wheel just long enough to pat Abby's. "Sounds good to me, Doc. As long as we can sneak in tickets to a baseball game now and again."

Baseball season was almost upon them; spring was near. Abby contemplated the seasons as she watched the trees flicker by her window. Mac would be here this spring, and probably the next. Knowing that had to be enough, for now. Abby was determined to focus on moments like this, when Mac was warm and real beside her.

"Abby. We probably should finish that talk."

"Which talk is this?"

"Our first one. About what might happen to Fireside, if things don't work out between us."

Abby closed her eyes. Mac usually had a superlative sense of timing in all things, but this was not her finest hour. She turned her head on the backrest and looked at her.

"I just need to say that I would be the one to leave." Mac looked as if she knew this was a painful topic, but a necessary one. "You helped Cleo and Vivian open Fireside, Abby. And you love this town. I could see it in your eyes just now."

"I am fond of those leeches." Abby wasn't smiling. But she reminded herself she had just wished Mac would talk to her about her worries, and she needed to truly listen. "Can I ask why this is coming up right now, Mac? I thought we were doing fairly well."

"We are. I needed to say that, because I want to say this." Mac waited until Abby nodded. "Abby, I'm crazy about you. I want us to work, and so far, things are going beautifully. And that means I want to protect you, if I can. You chose this shelter as your path of redemption, I know that. You've put down roots, and you have good friends here. If disaster strikes us—and I'm seeing that as unlikely, mind you—I just wanted you to know I'd be the one to go. I won't let you lose Fireside."

"Thank you." The words sounded wooden in Abby's ears. But then she thought about them, rode with them through a mile of silence. She could feel Mac's troubled glances. The thought of losing her stunned Abby. It was easy to let that thought override any other consideration. But she did understand that this was Mac's way of taking care of her. It was true, they had never finished that first talk, and Fireside mattered deeply to Abby. Mac was promising her that whatever happened, Abby's needs would come first. She spoke the words again, and meant them this time. "Thank you, Mac."

The Jeep rumbled down the tree-lined street that housed Danny's public high school. It was a working-class neighborhood, and the vehicles lining the street were sensible economy models. On their first pass by the school to find a parking place, Abby didn't see many students milling outside; they were a little early.

"Let's get Cleo power steering for her birthday." Mac cranked the wheel slowly at the end of the street. "I do love this butch little Jeep, but—"

Abby touched the dashboard as Mac put on the brakes. "What's wrong?"

"That's Sam Sherrill's truck."

"Oh, Lord. Where?"

"Up ahead on the right." Mac backed smoothly into a no-parking zone and opened her door. "What say you stay here and keep an eye out for Danny?"

"Yes, excellent idea." Abby was already climbing out of the Jeep. "I can still keep an eye out for Danny while that ugly man beats you with his tire iron."

She trotted to keep up with Mac's stride. She recognized Sherrill's truck. The same dirty white Dodge pickup with the garish red plumbing logo on the door had been idling in the drive only a few weeks ago. Abby could see one burly arm braced on its open side window.

"Mr. Sherrill." Mac stopped just behind the driver's door and put a hand out to keep Abby well out of the man's reach. Sherrill jumped and had to crane back over his shoulder to see them. "I'd say you were about two feet away from violating a court order. What are you doing here?"

It took a moment for Sherrill to stop gaping at them. He was unshaven, but at least Abby couldn't smell liquor on him. The bruise Mac had punched into his jaw was just the faintest of circles among the whiskers. Abby wished she could see farther into the truck for anything he could use as a weapon; all she could make out was a pair of binoculars on the dashboard.

"Hey, I'm a hundred feet from the entrance." Sherrill jabbed his finger toward the school down the street. "I damn near counted off the steps. I'm not violating a fucking thing."

"Danny doesn't want to talk to you." Mac spoke succinctly. "You heard her say it."

"I wasn't gonna talk to her. I just wanted to see her." Sherrill lifted the binoculars, then dropped them again on the dash. "All this time, I don't even know how my little girl is, if she's okay."

Abby thought of Cleo, parked outside schools and soccer fields for years, unable to talk to Danny because of this man.

"Danny is fine, Mr. Sherrill. All you can accomplish here is upsetting her again. Is that what you want?"

"What I want is for that big bitch you work with to stop stealing my family." Sherrill gripped the steering wheel, and Abby could see his knuckles go white. "She thinks she can brainwash my only child into hating my guts. She can file all the fucking orders she wants—"

Abby heard a faint buzzing sound from the direction of the school, and Mac glanced over her shoulder before leaning both hands on Sherrill's open window. "Look. We're not having this conversation. Unless you think pulling out a tape measure will convince a cop not to take you to jail, move on out of here. The order is clear, you're not to come anywhere near Danny. If you're still here when she comes up that walk, she'll see you get slapped into cuffs."

Sherrill was silent, grinding his hands around the wheel, and Abby wanted to tug Mac farther away from the truck. Then he keyed the ignition sharply. "I haven't had a drink in twelve days," he spat. "You tell Danny that. You better tell her!"

Mac stepped back as he gunned the engine and lurched off in a spray of gravel and dust. Abby moved closer to her, and they watched the white truck careen down the street and around the corner, until the roaring of its motor faded.

"I reckon I could have been more diplomatic." Mac brushed dust from Abby's sleeve. "But time was a factor here."

"Danny has to know about this, doesn't she?" Abby hated seeing the light fade from Danny's eyes whenever her father was mentioned.

"Yeah. But let's tell Cleo first. She can talk to Danny after dinner."

"Hey! There you are." Danny was walking toward them, canting to one side from the weight of her backpack. "Is there some reason you guys parked in Bermuda?"

Mac was starting to come down off the tight rush of energy

that filled her the moment she saw Sherrill's truck. She shook out her hands as she went to Danny, then lifted her backpack from her shoulder. "Dang, young woman. What are you hauling in here?"

"Calculus. World history. Chemistry." Danny shuffled beside them, flexing her arm and sounding burdened. "All my cool art projects are finished. Now it's just the grind stuff I need to graduate."

Mac opened the Jeep's passenger door and let Danny crawl behind the front seats onto the narrow back bench. She stopped Abby before she could duck inside, and looked around carefully.

"You think he might come back?" Abby whispered.

Mac shook her head. "No, this just doesn't seem like the kind of street that would welcome a Gay Pride march." She saw no one paying any attention to them, and she touched Abby's wrist. "Did you hear what I said earlier, Doc? The most important thing I said?"

Abby looked puzzled. "You said a lot of important things earlier, Mac."

"The most crucial thing. I'm crazy about you, Abby." Mac bent her head and looked directly into Abby's eyes. "I'm absolutely crazy about you, Dr. Glenn."

A slow smile dawned on Abby's lips. "I'm glad to hear that, Counselor. Because I'm growing excessively fond of you too."

Mac's knees went numb. She could recognize all the subtle shades of Abby's smiles now, and this one held a touch of sweet sultriness that made her want to sweep her into her arms for some prolonged liplock, as Cleo would call it. She restrained herself with effort and gallantly held the door open for Abby.

"Hey, go around the drive, Mac!" Danny bounced lightly on the bench, craning between them to see through the windshield.

"Through here?" Mac turned into the circular drive that went past the school's entrance.

"Yeah. That's him, the big redhead in the letter sweater. Sitting on the steps. See him?"

Mac noticed Danny ducked back into a corner as they drove past the basketball player she'd had a crush on for months. Mac would have recognized him without Danny's prompts, as she had described him in loving and lavish detail on their walks.

"He has a nice face," Abby said, looking back out the window.

"Don't *stare,* Abby!" Danny yelped.

"Sorry." Abby leaned her arm on the front seat. "Is the young man with the nice face someone special, Danny?"

"No, he's just one-way special at most. He doesn't know I'm alive." Danny slumped back on the bench as Mac turned them onto the street. "He asked *Effy Lundgren* to the prom, if you can believe that."

"I can't," Abby said. "We've always hated that Effy with a passion, the little banshee."

That coaxed a smile out of Danny. "She's a slut. I'm sorry, but she is. That reminds me, though. I'm supposed to ask you guys something."

Abby looked faintly alarmed that sluttishness might bring her and Mac to Danny's mind. "You're supposed to?"

"Yeah. Cleo told me to ask you because she's tired of me asking her." Danny lowered her voice into an affectionate imitation of Cleo. "Girl, you want to know about Mac and Abby, you go ask Mac and Abby." Danny's smile turned shy. "So I'm asking."

Mac caught Abby's eye and winked.

Abby turned to face Danny more fully. "Well, I guess you've noticed we're spending a lot of time together. Living at the other end of the hallway, it would be difficult to miss."

"Well, *yeah.* You guys are real discreet and everything, but yeah."

"Your instincts are right, Dan," Mac said. She reached over

and pinched Abby's cheek, gently. "I'm sparking Miss Abby, here."

"You could say we're courting." Abby smiled at Mac, and damned if that light blush didn't color her face. Sultry one moment, bashful the next. Mac pressed on the gas, wanting to get home. They had a good hour before dinner.

"This is so cool." Danny was grinning broadly. "When did all this start?"

"We're still fairly new to each other," Abby said. "I believe our six-week anniversary is coming up."

"Darling, you remembered." Mac blinked at Abby sentimentally, and Abby slapped her knee.

"This is *so* cool," Danny said again. Her sulk about the slutty Effy Lundgren forgotten, her face glowed with a genuine and unselfish happiness for them, a side of Danny they were seeing more often lately. "So, can you be pretty out, around Fireside? Vivian seems like she'd be okay with it."

"Sure." Mac checked for cross-traffic and turned onto the highway. "As out as any couple should be, in a professional setting. We won't touch a lot around the residents, but they'll probably know we're together." She glanced at Danny in the rearview mirror. "And we can relax around folks who become friends too, like you."

"But what about in town?" Danny's smile faded. "I mean, Fredburg is a college town, but this whole state is so damn backward. Are you guys worried about getting hassled?"

"Well, neither of us are big on public displays of affection, and we'll be careful," Abby said. "And the city does have a nice Gay Pride celebration, in August. We can find cozy pockets in this town to nestle into, if we wish."

"Leeches and Gay Pride." Mac raised her eyebrow at Abby. "You do know Fredburg, Abigail. Now, when did you add gay community celebrations to your trove of local knowledge?"

"Recently," Abby admitted. "I made a point of researching them."

"Sometimes I have dreams about Cleo getting beat up." Danny was gazing out the window, tracing a circle on the glass. "She's so...*intense* about everything. If some hick homophobe got in her face, she wouldn't back down."

Mac remembered the murky light in Cleo's eyes the night she held a gun on Sam Sherrill. From the look on Abby's face, that same unnerving memory was passing through her mind. "It's hard, Danny, knowing someone might hurt the people we love. All we can do is trust Cleo to take care of herself, and remind her how important it is to all of us that she does."

"I can't even get her to stop smoking," Danny grumbled. Then she brightened a little. "I can tell she's happy about the two of you being together, though, even if she wouldn't talk to me about it. Cleo really loves you guys. I think you and Vivian and Scratch are her best friends."

"We're pretty partial to her too," Mac said.

"Cleo's always looked out for me. As well as she could, anyway. Even when my dad tried to make it impossible. When I was a kid, I was always planning to run away and live with her, if he got on my case too much." Danny shrugged. "I guess I finally did, huh?"

Mac considered this. "Seems to me that when you thought about running to Cleo as a kid, Dan, that was a kid wanting to run to a grown-up. The night you left your dad's house, you made an adult's decision. You like Cleo watching out for you because you love her. But you're taking the reins of your own life now."

"That's true, Danny," Abby said. "You're graduating from high school. Starting college."

"Only if I pass calculus." Danny's head dropped to the back of the bench, and Mac knew she was ready for less weighty topics.

She clicked the turn signal. "Hey, Danny. Want to see the farm where a little white boy murdered an innocent cherry tree?"

CHAPTER SIXTEEN

Abby drifted awake, draped across the firm cushion of Mac's body. The pleasure of these morning awakenings still felt new to her, even slightly miraculous, after two months of intimate nights. She brushed her hair off her forehead so she could see the face of her sleeping lover. Abby smiled, savoring the word, and trailed the tip of her finger lightly over Mac's full lower lip.

Mac listened, she thought, even from the reaches of dreams. During the night rounds of her hospital training, Abby had become well acquainted with the expressions of sleeping women. Most were slack and vacant, befitting restful slumber. Others were tense with some unrelenting pain or worry. Mac's face reflected neither. She looked relaxed but intent, as if even asleep she listened to the stories of others, a respectful holder of their histories.

Abby brushed her cheek against Mac's knuckles. Her good hands. She remembered their thorough exploration of her body the night before, rough and tender in turn, with a sensual clarity that made her melt inside. No lover had ever shown such creative and tireless attention to her pleasure.

She wondered, now, how she could have believed she was incapable of passion. This wise, funny woman had tapped into depths of sexuality Abby hadn't known she possessed. Mac drew ecstasy from her effortlessly, even playfully, but with a loving insistence she couldn't begin to resist. And as for Abby, she had always been a quick study. She was learning to stir Mac's desire in return, with an avid dedication she'd certainly never brought to organic chemistry.

Mac stirred beneath her. "Morning."

"Hello there."

And if Abby had her way, that would be the full tally of the day, their exchange of morning greetings. As far as she was concerned, the sun could sink below the horizon again now, and she would happily spend the next eight moonlit hours nestled in Mac's arms.

"You sleep well?" Mac yawned through most of her question, her hair a shaggy wildness on the pillow.

"I did. You, however, twitched and mumbled through the night, off and on. It was quite alluring."

Mac chuckled and rubbed her face. "I'll bet it was."

"And who is Ashley, if I might ask?"

"Who?"

"Ashley. You said that name a couple of times, among the mumbling and the twitching."

"I did?"

"You did. I heard you distinctly." Abby drummed her fingers teasingly on the blanket covering Mac's waist. "Should I worry about your bringing another woman into our bed?"

"Ashley." Mac looked puzzled as she tried to stifle a second yawn. "I never dated any Ashleys. I don't even remember being friends with an Ashley."

"Was this Ashley, who you don't remember, very attractive?"

"Wait—except for my little girl Ashley, when I was a kid."

"Your little girl? Oh! Your little imaginary amiga, I think you called her. The one your parents left behind at the gas station, and you made them go back to get her?"

"Good memory," Mac murmured. She was staring out the window.

"Well, if that's the Ashley you're dreaming about, go back and pick her up already, please." Abby smoothed her finger across the shadows beneath Mac's eyes. "It's nice that she followed you all the way out here, but I'm starting to worry a bit about these restless nights."

The alarm clock on Mac's bedside table went off, and Abby reached across her to tap its button. She'd just as soon Mac slept in another few hours, and she'd be delighted to join her. Regretfully, however, there were children to vaccinate and groceries to fetch, so she kissed Mac's shoulder and swept the bedcovers aside.

Abby was instantly cold, from the loss both of blankets and her sexy bed warmer. "If we don't hurry, Cleo will make the coffee. I dibs the last slice of that banana cake." She lifted her robe from the post of the bed and slid it on. "Mac?"

Mac was still in bed, still staring out the small window. She blinked. "Banana cake." She looked at Abby and nodded. "Sure, Doc, all yours."

"I just need to grab some shoes from my room." Abby tied the sash on her robe and went to the door. She passed Mac's desk, and her eye fell on the two thick envelopes stacked neatly on its surface.

Behind her, Abby heard Mac get up and pull open a dresser drawer. She rested a finger on the cream-colored envelopes, then picked them up and read the return addresses again.

"Something wrong, babe?"

Abby turned to her, the letters in her hand. "I'm sorry, Mac. I didn't mean to pry."

Mac paused, then finished threading her belt through the loops of her jeans. "Ah, yeah. Those just came in the other day."

Abby nodded, fingering the envelopes. The addresses were from shelter programs in Maryland and Pennsylvania. "I'd think they would accept job applications online, these days."

"I'm not applying for other jobs, Ab." Mac slipped on her worn rugby shirt and fumbled with its buttons. "I just requested general info from a few programs."

"But why?" Abby asked softly. "We have an extensive regional shelter database on disk downstairs."

Mac started to speak, then shook her head and tried again. "Abby, I wrote to those programs months ago. A lot has happened since then."

"You've been here less than four months, Mac." Abby hoped she didn't sound accusing. She was trying not to sound frightened. "I'm trying to understand why you're already scouting out other—"

"Because it's a reflex. I do it everywhere I go." Mac closed her dresser drawer with some force. "Once I settle into a job, I start looking at future prospects. Even when I plan on staying put a year or two, I want to have an exit strategy ready." She rubbed the back of her neck.

"I see." Abby lay the envelopes back on the desk, and sat again on the bed.

"Vivian's worried I might bolt too. She brought it up at my review." Mac still wasn't looking at Abby. "You'd think she'd know better. I'd never put in less than a year in a job, that wouldn't be fair to...anyone."

"A year," Abby repeated.

"I'll stay here three years, then. Five." Mac raked her fingers through her hair. "How many decades should I promise, Abby? How far into the future do you expect me to see?"

"That's a fair question, Mac, but I have one too." Abby was surprised by a mild flare of anger. "How long am I expected to wait while you think things over?"

"Abby." Mac closed her eyes. "I've always planned to stay at Fireside at least two years. That means two years for us—you and me—to grow together, to see what we can make of this thing. Why isn't that enough, for now? Why is it important that I make a decision about the rest of my life today, this week?"

"But isn't that the decision I faced?" Abby flattened her hand on the bedspread. "Do you really not understand that, Mac? When I told you I can only make love if I'm in a committed relationship, what did you hear?"

"I didn't hear that I'd be proposing marriage if we made love."

That stung, and Abby slid her hand back.

"Abby." Mac sat on the corner of the bed. "I told you I agreed with you. I didn't want casual sex either. I wanted to be sure we had something meaningful too—"

"Yes. And the night Sam Sherrill broke into this house, I decided something meaningful could exist between you and me." Abby needed some distance, and she slid off the bed and stood by the desk. "Did you think that was easy for me, Mac? I've never really opened my heart to anyone, even as a girl. So, I need you to understand this."

Abby drew a slow breath. "I've reached a time in my life when I'm ready to make a home. I've found one here, at Fireside. I plan to stay here a very long time. I'm hardly a girl anymore, Mac. I'm a mature woman, and I'm ready for a mature love. If you find you're not going to be a lasting presence in my life, I have to know that."

Mac stared at her mutely.

"Hey. Taco Belle." Cleo's voice sounded from the hallway as she rapped on Mac's bedroom door. "Come grab a Pop-Tart if you're shopping with me. Jeep leaves in ten." Her heavy step faded down the hall.

"I want you," Abby said quietly. "I want us, Mac. You need to decide what you want." She turned and opened the door. "I'll see you downstairs."

❖

When Abby stepped out onto the front porch, she saw Danny kicking the tire of Cleo's Jeep with a sullen look, her hands crammed into her back pockets. She was grateful for the distraction. That unexpected clash with Mac had left her faintly nauseated.

"Good morning, Danny. Are you joining this shopping run after all?" Abby gave Danny's tousled hair a friendly ruffle. "I thought Cleo mandated more study time for your exam tomorrow."

"She mandated. I can't go," Danny grumbled. "Cleo's a bigger butt than my dad when it comes to homework."

"Well, Cleo won't let me go, either. I'll give you a hand with those formulas later, if you want."

"Thanks." Danny smiled at Abby, and her petulance seemed to ease a little. "Hey. I meant to ask you. Are you and Mac going with us to that rally this weekend?"

"What rally is this?"

"On campus. Just a little one." Danny shrugged. "Cleo and I went to UMW the other day, to check out their art department? And we saw a flyer for this rally supporting gay marriage. This state is so fucking—sorry—so fucking backward, when it comes to gay marriage. Cleo and I thought we might go."

"That sounds like a good plan for the weekend. I'll check with Mac, but I think we'd both like to come."

"Great." Danny squinted up at her. "Do you see that happening between you and Mac someday, Abby? If that's not too personal. Do you think you guys will get married? I mean, if the neanderthals who run Virginia ever get a life and allow it?"

"Well." Abby rocked gently on her toes, her smile still in place. "It's rather early in the game to be thinking of that. Mac and I haven't even settled our debate over coffee versus tea. But I know Mac believes strongly that women should have a legal right to marry, and so do I. If we're lucky enough to stay together, and Virginia comes to its senses, we would probably consider it."

Not really the ringing endorsement Abby would have preferred to make, but Mac had emerged from the house and was joining them, that lazy saunter as distinctive as the sea green of her eyes. When she reached Abby, Mac lifted her hand and held it in her own. She searched Abby's face, her features tired and shadowed with worry, and the constriction in Abby's throat eased a little. She pressed Mac's fingers. They still had much to resolve. But the day was young. Spring had arrived. They would have time. Mac must have felt Abby's softening, and her shoulders straightened.

"Morning, Dan," Mac said.

"Danny has invited us to join her and Cleo at a gay marriage rally this weekend." Abby hoped to steer Danny back to the larger issue.

"Yeah, Sunday," Danny said. "Two o'clock. In the eastern quad, whatever the heck that is."

"I believe we're free Sunday." Mac smiled at Danny. "Sounds like you're looking forward to this."

"Kind of, yeah." Danny shrugged. "I'm not real political. But I do want to go. It feels like a nice thing to do for my mom, and Cleo."

"We need all the straight allies we can get, Danny." Mac took Danny's chin gently in her fingers. "And it's a very nice thing to do, for your mom and Cleo. Abby and I are there. Thanks for asking us."

Danny looked up at Mac, and Abby saw her fall a little in love with her tall counselor. How could she not? The girl might be straight, but she had a pulse. Mac slid her arm around Abby's waist, and Abby felt the last tension between them slip away.

Cleo came out of the house, rummaging in her canvas bag. She saw them and groaned. "Oh, please. You three look like some lesbian Norman Rockwell calendar, April or some such shit, break it up. Danielle, I believe there's some calculus in there calling your name."

"Yes, Cleopatra, your highness," Danny lisped, too softly for Cleo to hear, and Abby hid her smile. "Just don't come crying home to me when Mac throws her back out lifting those big cases of tuna without me."

Danny waved at them listlessly and meandered toward the house, and Cleo ducked into her Jeep and keyed the ignition. Abby felt Mac's lips brush her hair.

"You didn't let me apologize," Mac murmured. "I shouldn't have snapped at you like that."

"No apologies necessary, Counselor. I'm not offering any. I meant every word I said."

"I know you did. You've given me a lot to think about, *querida.*"

"Yes. But right now, I believe those big cases of tuna are calling your name."

"That tuna's real popular around here." Mac smiled. "I ought to rustle up eight or ten cases. Might need some serious lumbar therapy, when I get back."

"We'll hang you by your heels from the staircase for a few hours," Abby promised. "Perhaps a nice ice bath afterward, to address any swelling."

"Dr. Glenn, where's your dang romantic spirit?"

"I'll read you love poetry while you dangle. Sappho, if you wish."

Mac snickered, then tipped Abby's chin with one finger and kissed her again—chastely, compared to recent private, torrid offerings, but quite pleasantly nonetheless. Muted retching sounds could be heard over the rumbling of the Jeep, and they both smiled at Cleo's obvious impatience to get on the road.

"So we're okay, babe?" Mac whispered.

"We're okay. Hurry home." Abby slapped Mac's butt. "I miss you already."

"Me you back." Mac winked at her and ambled to the Jeep's passenger door.

Abby waved as Cleo accelerated around the circular drive and down the narrow road that led toward town. The turquoise ring on Mac's finger flashed in the late afternoon sunlight when she lifted her hand, and then they were gone.

Abby folded her arms, glad that she had Danny for company inside. She started to turn back to the house, then hesitated, not yet ready to relinquish the space, the column of air, where Mac had last held her.

She didn't understand it herself, this urgency to see Mac claim a lasting role in Fireside's story, and in her heart. Abby only knew that when she and Mac held each other, they both knew to their souls they were cherished. Beneath all the first blush of love, there was a certainty growing between them, a sure recognition that they had something worth fighting for here.

And that didn't mean getting through the dramatic highs and lows of a passionate beginning. Mac was her first true lover, but Abby had lived long enough and had learned enough about human nature to understand that. The true fight would come two years on, and ten and twenty years after that, the plain hard daily work two people faced if they wanted to build a life together. She could only hope Mac could find the courage for that journey.

Abby shivered and pulled the collar of her sweater closer around her throat. Perhaps some intensive lumbar therapy later tonight would help strengthen her lover's spine. She smiled at the prospect and turned to the house, trying to remember the basics of high school calculus so she could coach Danny for her test.

Mac rested her elbow on the open window and brushed her thumb across her lips, savoring that last kiss. The warmth in Abby's eyes made it possible to still the last echoes of their talk. And the task was made easier by the driving rhythms blasting from the Jeep's speakers.

"Honest, Cleo, there has been decent music recorded since 1969." Mac had to raise her voice to be heard over Creedence's wailing of "Bad Moon Rising."

Cleo ignored her, jutting her chin to the beat. She shifted

and dug a folded list out of her back pocket, peering at it between glances at the twisting road. "What, Abby has you on Similac now?"

"That's for our new mother's baby, in West Two."

"Top Ramen. Breakfast cereal. Salad greens. Ooh, look, a *leash*!" Cleo rattled the page. "How much am I gonna have to pay to find out what Abby wants with a *leash*?"

"It's for *Lena*. For the *puppy* Inez plans to give her for her *birthday*, because we found out her new apartment complex accepts *puppies*." Mac thought she'd pulled off an excellent imitation of Danny when she was in exasperation mode.

Cleo snorted cheerfully. "Right."

Mac grinned. "What snapped your frilly garters today, Cleopatra? You're in rare form."

Cleo shifted again and rummaged in her other pocket, and Mac put a steadying hand on the steering wheel. Traffic was pretty light considering the time of day, but Cleo tended to be lead-footed on the gas. Finally she pulled out a small, cream white envelope and passed it to Mac. "Looky, the school sent us three weeks' notice."

"Hey!" Mac studied the embossed message on the card. "Is this a done deal?"

"It is unless she bombs calculus tomorrow." Cleo bounced lightly in her seat, the springs beneath them creaking. "Graduation ceremony, four o'clock p.m., May thirtieth."

"That's fantastic, amiga." Mac clapped Cleo's shoulder. "This calls for a party."

"Or two. Danny turns eighteen the same week as her graduation. Guess what she's asked for."

"What?"

"A Ferrari. Guess what else. She wants a slumber party downstairs in front of the fireplace—you, me, Abby, Vivian, Mr. Vivian, everybody."

"Hey, that sounds kind of fun."

"We can set up cots for Scratch and Viv." Cleo's face softened as the pavement hummed beneath them. "You know, Macky-wai, when this time came, I thought it would be all about Lily, for me. About being sad for her, that she's not here to see Danny graduate. And that's there. But man, Mac, mostly I'm just damn happy for this kid. I'm so proud of her."

"You should be. I'm damn happy for Danny that she'll have you in the audience."

"Thanks." Cleo shrugged. "Makes me feel like a mom again."

Mac rested her elbow on the window of the Jeep and watched the countryside whistle by, remembering her own high school graduation. Her father had been there, clicking his camera at her every time she breathed. Mac still had a photo of them together, she in a blue gown, his arm around her shoulders.

Most pictures from the major events in Mac's childhood featured only her and her father. Her mother had often been hospitalized, battling a brutal, recurrent depression that no given combination of meds eased for long.

She'd been better, in the years since Mac left home; the hospitalizations were further and further apart. When Mac visited her parents' small adobe house outside Albuquerque now, her mother was the funny, gracious and loving woman she remembered from her family's best times together.

A sudden image appeared in her mind, a vision of taking Abby to New Mexico to meet her folks. Mac didn't let herself question the fantasy, she just let it evolve. Her mom would make her immortal green chile enchiladas. Abby would convince her dad to take his damn blood pressure medication. The four of them would pack a basket with leftovers and picnic by the Rio Grande.

"Hey, no fantasies about ravishing lady-doctors in my G-rated Jeep." Cleo's voice interrupted her thoughts. "Danny rides in here sometimes."

"What, are you reading minds now?"

"No trick to it, you had that sickly sweet smile plastered on your face." Cleo glanced at her as she accelerated around a slow pickup truck. "So. You taking that little talk we had a few weeks back to heart, Mac?"

Mac remembered it well. "Yeah, the night you left me no ham. I've been thinking about that talk. Abby and I were just discussing it."

"Good. Thinking's good. Discussion's good. But you did ask me for my sage opinion, and I don't believe I advised you to engage your brain. That's your hang-up sometimes, Mac, you and Abby both. You think too much." Cleo patted Mac's belt. *"Cojones."*

Mac frowned. "I should engage my *cojones*?"

"Absolutely. There comes a day when you've thought things into a stupor, and it's time to make a choice. It's usually a little scary, whenever that time comes. So when it does, hell yes, engage your *cojones*. Be brave."

"Why does that sound so easy, when you say it?" Mac rubbed her eyes. "You were right, it wasn't easy for Abby. It's not easy for—"

"Mac!"

Mac's eyes flew open to see Cleo staring hard at the rearview mirror. Her arm flashed across Mac's chest to brace her, and then a crashing impact threw them both back against the seat.

The Jeep careened wildly as Cleo cursed and fought to steady the wheel, and Mac clutched the dashboard, blanching as they slid narrowly past a honking van on their left. She whipped around to look out the back window just as Sam Sherrill's truck caught up and hit them again.

Mac gasped and absorbed the jolt, gripping the back of the seat. "It's Sherrill."

"No shit!" Cleo fought the Jeep out of a harrowing skid on the narrow road. There was a steep drop-off on their right, and they swerved perilously close to it.

Mac grit her teeth hard. "Gun it, if you can."

The big utility truck was only inches behind them again,

its front grill twisted and cracked. She could see Sherrill's face through the windshield, his teeth bared in a rictus of glee rather than hate, which spooked her even more.

"How does that fuck know *Danny* isn't in here?" Cleo hissed, leaning on the accelerator, the Jeep's motor thumping ominously now. "Tell me when he—"

"Hang on!" Mac tried to brace her as the truck smashed into them again, and this time two cars were coming in the opposite lane. Cleo wrenched the wheel to miss them, and the momentum was too much. The steep embankment that bordered the right side of the road swam sickly into Mac's view, and for ten breathless seconds they skimmed the edge of it.

Then Sherrill struck them for the last time, and his truck hurtled after the Jeep, over the crumbling edge and down.

Mac registered the first impact, a heavy detonation of airbags and steel and stone—a queasy rolling sensation, and then nothing.

CHAPTER SEVENTEEN

The chemical smell of disinfectant actually comforted Abby, as did the bright lighting and white tile of the critical care unit's hallway, which she walked calmly, as if her heart weren't about to explode from her chest. She donned the white jacket with its plastic ID badge quickly, to ward off unnecessary questions.

Mac was alive and breathing and she was here, and Abby knew how to take care of her here. She had privileges to practice at Mary Washington Hospital, and knew the staff of the Neuro unit upstairs was competent and vigilant. She had left Mac in good hands. But she had left her, because she needed to see Cleo, and every cell of Abby's body screamed to go back.

"Abby."

She stepped back and swept open the curtain to a cubicle, and saw Cleo sitting up in an elevated white bed, her left leg encased thigh to ankle in a stabilizing brace. Abby almost burst into tears, a combination of relief at seeing her and the sheer terror of the last hour, but she contained herself. Cleo looked ashen and half dazed.

"They won't tell me much about Mac." Cleo let Abby take her cold hand.

"She's still unconscious, honey." Abby examined the IV tube taped to Cleo's inner arm and checked the drip, plain glucose to keep her hydrated. "But we expect her to wake up soon. Her vitals are good. She has three broken ribs, on her right side. But she'll be all right, I'm sure of it."

"Why is she still unconscious?" Cleo hadn't softened an inch. "Abby, it's been hours."

"Well, she took a bad blow to the head. The CAT scan showed subdural bleeding, and after they operated to control it, they left a shunt in to relieve the pressure—"

"Ah, Jesus." Cleo rubbed her eyes.

"I know. But the surgeon was pleased with the results, and things look good for a complete recovery. I'm with you, though, I'll feel much better when she wakes up." Abby looked down at the brace and winced. "Can we talk about you for a moment?"

"It's broken in two places." Cleo scowled and shifted on the bed. "Guy said I was lucky I didn't need surgery to set it, they're just hairline fractures. I'm waiting for some orthopedic asshole to take a look at the x-rays."

"Are you in pain?"

"Hell, yeah, but they put something in the IV earlier that makes me not care." Cleo's eyes darkened again. "What about Danny?"

"She's home." Abby patted Cleo's arm. "Vivian and Scratch are with her."

Cleo was silent a moment. "Sam Sherrill is dead."

"Yes."

"The cop at the scene told me, but he didn't have to. I saw his truck. Cop said there were beer cans all over the cab. He was blitzed."

Abby nodded. She hadn't seen the body, but she'd spoken with the ER physician who had signed it over to the morgue, and he had been honest. Sam Sherrill's death had been neither immediate nor painless. He had bled out. Abby hoped Danny would never ask for details.

"Does she know?" Cleo asked.

"Not yet. Morning will be soon enough. You need to be there when she finds out."

"You think I'd be any better than Vivian at giving Danny this news?"

"I think Danny will need her mother with her when she hears this news."

Breath sighed out of Cleo, and she lay back against the brace of pillows. "That kid's lost too much for her tender years, Abby."

"Yes, she has. But Danny isn't alone." Abby leaned in and kissed Cleo's forehead. "I want to take a look at your x-rays. Will you be all right?"

"Fine, Ab, check the x-rays, but then get back to Mac, okay?" Cleo's tone was both stern and pleading. "And come tell me the minute she wakes up."

"You know I will. Rest easy, honey. I'll be back soon."

Night had fallen sometime in the last few disorienting hours, and the hospital had emptied of its daily commerce. Abby could hear her steps echo in the hallway before she turned into the room where Mac lay, surrounded by banks of monitors. A nurse was standing by her bed, entering data in a handheld digital chart. The look she gave Abby when she joined her was sympathetic.

"Still no response, Dr. Glenn." The nurse handed Abby the chart, and she surveyed the latest entries. She nodded.

"Keep a close watch on her readings from your station, please. I'll stay with her and do regular neuro checks."

"Can I bring you some coffee? You might be in for a long night."

"Thank you, Karen. I'd appreciate that." Abby didn't particularly want or need the caffeine; she was alert to the point of trembling rigidity. But she did need badly to be alone with her patient, and fetching coffee would accomplish that. She eased onto the high chair next to the bed.

"Hey." She reached over the railing and rested her hand on Mac's forearm. "Are you in there, Macawai? Open your eyes."

Mac's dusky lashes lay still against her cheek. Her chest lifted and fell slowly beneath the neat blanket. There was a shallow scrape at the base of her jaw, but she looked otherwise untouched by the crash, a miracle in itself. But it was unnatural, seeing this strong, vital body, always so flush with energy, hushed and motionless now, and Abby's stomach knotted.

"Mac." Abby lifted Mac's hand in her own and held it against her breast. "You're starting to scare me a little. Please, sweetheart. Look at me."

But Mac's sleep continued, deep and relentless. Abby kissed the silver turquoise ring on her finger, then held her palm to her cheek.

A few minutes later, she heard a slow step behind her.

"I'm sorry to intrude on you, Abby. That nice young nurse allowed me to bring you this." Scratch rested a steaming Styrofoam cup carefully on the table beside the bed, then lowered himself stiffly into the only other chair in the crowded room, at Mac's other side. "I'm happy to say being an ex-pastor does help me circumvent visiting hours, when it's important."

"Oh, Scratch. It's good to see you." Abby meant it. His calm demeanor loosened some of the fearful tightness in her gut. "I was going to call you again, soon. Vivian's still with Danny, at Fireside?"

"She is. She'll pass the night there with her." Scratch reached across Mac's still form and patted Abby's hand. "Danny only knows that our friends were in an accident. We passed on what you told us, that Cleo will be fine and Mac is being well looked after. Nothing about her father being involved."

"Danny's father is dead, Scratch."

"Ah." Scratch sat back in his chair and shook his grizzled

head. "Samuel Sherrill was a poor, misguided monster of a man. May the good Lord forgive him, Abby, because I just can't find that kind of grace in my heart tonight."

"I can't either, I'm afraid."

They were silent, listening to the muted beeps of the monitors.

"Well, Dr. Glenn," Scratch said finally. "I came down to sit with Miss Cleo for a while, to keep you from wearing yourself out running back and forth. What can you tell me about this child here?" Scratch rested his long fingers on Mac's smooth forehead, his touch tender as a father's.

"She's so far away, Scratch." Abby knew her worry showed in her voice, and she didn't try to hide it. "She should have responded by now. She should be awake."

"Abby, Mac's going to come back to us." Scratch spoke with certainty. "The universe has too much need of this fine young woman to let her leave us now. Do you mind if I make an entreaty along those lines, on Mac's behalf?"

"Of course not," Abby whispered. Prayer didn't come as naturally to her as it did to Scratch, but she realized she'd been making fervent, silent entreaties of her own ever since the police called Fireside.

Scratch lifted his head and closed his eyes, and his lips curved in a smile as he prayed, as if having an intimate talk with a close friend.

Abby checked Mac's pulse at the throat, and then she bowed her head, and tried to find words to describe what this woman meant to her. She wanted to explain things properly, to Scratch's God or anyone else out there who would listen, but her tears started to fall at last, and she had to be content with letting Scratch speak for them both.

❖

Mac wandered.

Judging by the fog swirling around her, she thought she must be on her early morning walk, but it was a crazy, thick fog. The trees and shrubbery on all sides were barely visible through the billowing white mist, lit a diffuse blue by the dawn light. The air was so silent she could hear her footsteps in the snow.

Had she awakened with Abby in her arms that morning? What did they have for breakfast? Mac frowned. She couldn't remember, but she wasn't hungry and she wasn't cold, and she was out here in shirtsleeves. Snow blanketed the ground, but it hadn't snowed hard in weeks. She stopped as a curving bank of trees appeared in front of her, and turned in a slow circle.

She knew where she was. This was the grassy enclosure not far from Fireside, the cushioning arc of trees that had become Mac's favorite retreat for reflection.

Her gaze fell on something above her head, an object held in place between two twining branches.

Mac stared at it, puzzled. Danny's drawing, the one she had left behind for her dead mother, had disappeared without a trace, the very next time Mac had visited this spot. She didn't know if it had been carried off by animals or blown away by a fierce wind, but in any case, it was gone...and now it was back.

Mac stepped closer. The rolled drawing hadn't just returned, it seemed perfect, untouched by these weeks in the elements. And the paper itself had changed. Mac had seen Danny tear the page from an ordinary drawing pad, but this scroll looked richer, finer, a creamy vellum held closed by a slender silk ribbon. Mac stretched on her toes and reached up to brush a finger across it. Definitely real.

She heard the sound of flowing water and turned, startled. It wasn't that water had been flowing ever since Mac walked into this strange grove, and she just became aware of it. The lapping of slow-running waves simply began out of the silence, and continued, and Mac's disorientation grew. She knew the topography of the property pretty well now. There were no streams cutting through it. They were a good two miles from the nearest river.

Mac couldn't place the direction of the sound, and she started to walk out of the grove to try to find this mysterious creek. Then she stopped abruptly.

A little girl was sitting cross-legged in the snow on the other side of the circle.

Apparently she didn't feel the cold either. She was dressed in the kind of skirt and blouse Mac's mother had made her wear to school when she was very young. She sat slumped with her chin in her hands, peering up at Mac through dark, spiky bangs. Until Mac met her eyes, and then she sat up.

They stared at each other in what seemed to be mutual astonishment.

"Hey." Mac's voice shook. "Is it you?" She took a step toward the little girl, who shot to her feet. "Whoa." Mac held up both hands. "Slow down, kid. I won't hurt you."

The child hovered, as if she still might bolt. She clutched her hands together across her chest and watched Mac warily.

If Abby had asked her to describe the little girl she had created to be her friend when she was five years old, Mac wasn't sure she could have. She honestly didn't remember if her imaginary amiga wore skirts or had bangs. But Mac had seen this child before. She knew her.

Mac took a few steps closer, then bent her knees slowly until she was crouching on her heels. She decided to disregard the fact that she had somehow slipped into another fricking dimension. And that this dimension was inhabited by a creature she had conjured whole-cloth from her own mind, twenty-five years ago. Mac focused on this creature being a small, scared child. She knew how to comfort frightened children.

She settled cross-legged into the snow, which was neither cold nor wet. Mac looked up into the blue-lit trees, feeling the *little girl's curious gaze on her face, letting her study her. She didn't speak until the hands the girl had clenched to her chest began to loosen.*

"My name is Mac." Her tone was low and friendly. "I bet you already knew that, though."

The child didn't answer, but after a moment she shuffled a few steps forward.

"We've known each other a long time," Mac continued. "But it's been a long, long time since we've talked. You've been following me around for years and years. Is that right?"

The girl nodded, looking a little like all of this should be obvious. She stood close enough that Mac could see the light spray of freckles across her nose.

"Is your name Ashley?"

A furrow appeared between the girl's eyebrows. "Kind of." She had a sad, piping voice.

"Kind of?"

The girl nodded, her wide green eyes level with Mac's, since she was seated on the ground. She was no more than five years old. She took the last few steps, and Mac could have touched her.

The child seemed fascinated with Mac's body. She reached out a timid hand and patted Mac's breast. Then she looked down at her own flat chest with a puzzled frown.

"Ashley? I think you must want something very—"

"I wanna stay here," she answered at once. She pointed to the ground with both hands in emphasis, in case Mac needed help understanding where "here" was. "I want us to stay right HERE."

"You mean at Fireside?" Mac saw the small turquoise ring on the child's finger, and the words died in her throat. She stared at the blue stone, smaller than the one in her own ring, but identical in every other way. A chill coursed down her back.

"Yes! Here. Sheesh." The child sighed explosively, possibly

in satisfaction or relief, and then turned and plunked down in Mac's lap, as naturally as a weary wolf cub nestling against its mother.

The sturdy little body was warm and real and solid.

Mac's arms slid around the girl and held her lightly. She breathed in the scent of her hair, salty and fresh and somehow deeply familiar.

"You walk too fast," the child complained.

"Sorry. I know I do," Mac murmured. She showed her the fingers of her left hand. "Look. Your ring's real pretty. I've got one almost exactly like it. Want to see?"

The girl's head nodded against her shoulder. Mac slid off her ring and handed it to her. She turned the aqua blue stone in her small hands, and traced the letters etched into the silver band.

Kaya, Mac's middle name. A Hopi word, meaning "older sister."

"Can I see yours?"

Another nod, and the child pulled her turquoise ring off her small finger. Like Mac's, it bore the distinctive etchings of a Hopi christening ring. The letters in its band were almost too tiny to read, and Mac had to squint to make them out.

Ayashe. Hopi for "little sister."

Mac shivered, cradling the child in her lap. She had not one iota of psychic ability, none. But she could still hear the slow rippling of the river. She could see it, behind the lids of her closed eyes. Not a pure, fast mountain stream, but the deep roiling of the muddy Rio Grande in high spring.

"I fell in," the little girl said. "Then you forgot."

"You fell in." Mac opened her eyes and stared sightlessly at the blue-tinged trees. "Ashley. Ayashe. Did you drown?"

"And then you forgot."

A dozen glass tumblers clicked into place in Mac's mind.

Her mother, immobilized by depression throughout Mac's childhood, especially on milestone occasions like her birthday, her graduation. Pictures of a young Mac on the walls of her family home, but only of Mac, alone. All traces of a brief life locked away, hidden out of a grieving mother's sight. Even the mention of the lost child unendurable. Her younger sister.

"No." Mac rested her lips in the child's soft hair. "You're five years old. I would have remembered a little sister who was five years old."

The girl craned her neck to look up at her, apparently puzzled. "Well. We were the same size, til you forgot. Then just you kept getting bigger. I stayed like this."

"Okay." Mac thought this out. It wasn't easy, because she wasn't feeling especially logical. "You died when you were younger than this. But you kept growing as long as I remembered you. Until I forgot."

"I guess." The girl squirmed in Mac's lap, getting more comfortable. "I want to stay, Mac."

Mac felt Ayashe relax bonelessly against her, still clutching Mac's ring.

Mac had no conscious memory of a younger sister, or a family outing by the Rio Grande that had ended in tragedy. But she was holding a very real small girl, who was following her big sister around because that's what little sisters did when they were lost and lonely.

She and Ayashe were a fine pair of ghosts. It made an effortless kind of sense.

She had wandered as ceaselessly as her sister's spirit, seeking peace and never finding it. Seeking comfort from an immeasurable loss she had never understood, and never properly mourned. Mac had only sensed, in a deep and shadowed corner of her mind, that unguarded love was answered by mysterious and painful separation. She had spent her youth traveling, searching for healing in some nebulous future, unaware that her true grief lay in her past.

And in all those years, Mac had never been able to see this ghost. She had never heard her voice. She still didn't understand the dynamics of this eerie morning, or how the living and the dead came to meet in this uncanny grove. But Mac was beginning to understand why this reunion was possible now, for the first time since Ayashe died, a quarter century ago.

The sound of the flowing river was fading, and in its place a faint, muted crackling rose around them. Mac closed her eyes and saw the tendrils of flame rising in the hearth, flickering redly on the backs of her lids. She squeezed Ayashe carefully. "You see the fireplace?"

"Uh-huh. It feels nice."

The warmth of the flames reached Mac too, then.

She had tested Fireside in every way possible since her arrival. And in every way, it had met her challenge. The richness of the work she'd found here. The growing depth of her friendships. The beauty of her surroundings. And in Abby, the dawn of a genuine and passionate love.

Mac couldn't have seen Ayashe before. She couldn't have touched her. She needed Fireside to ground her, to promise a lasting safety Mac could trust, if she was to give her little sister what she wanted.

Mac stroked Ayashe's hair, her throat suddenly dry and parched. Over the crackling of the fire, she realized she was hearing Abby's voice. It was too low, too far away to distinguish words, but it was Abby's voice. Mac would have recognized the light music of her tone through a raging typhoon.

She opened her eyes and saw her, standing a few yards away. Abby appeared imperfectly and briefly, just a few shining seconds of her, and she did nothing spectacular during her visit. She just stood with her hands clasped behind her, looking down at Mac. Her eyes were filled with longing and patience and faith.

"What do you want?" Abby asked softly. She smiled at Mac and faded away.

Mac remembered the night she came to Fireside. She remembered seeing the house for the first time, and thinking healing could begin in such a place. A faint echo of Cleo's belly *laugh reached her, and she pictured Danny's face. She thought about Abby. She thought about having* cojones.

Sometimes, you just had to be brave. She made a decision.

Mac wrapped Ayashe's small fingers securely around her turquoise ring, and held them gently. "Hey. You awake?"

"Uh-huh."

"I want you to do me a favor," Mac whispered into the child's hair. "Hold on to my ring. Keep it with you all the time."

"Okay." The little girl's eyes were drifting closed.

"I'm going to make you a promise. I want you to remember my promise, every time you look at my ring."

"Okay."

"We can stay, Ayashe. We've found a home here."

"Okay," the girl sighed. "Good. That's good, Mac."

Ayashe slept in her arms. Mac held her for a long time, until a new sound began to filter out of the sounding trees. It was a faint, odd beeping noise, and with it, Mac heard again the murmur of a much-loved voice.

❖

"Mac? Open your eyes, sweetheart."

Mac swam up out of a foggy mire, her surfacing less ethereal and more leaden with every passing second. She cracked open one eye, and then closed it immediately as a ray of sunlight dazzled her.

"Come on. Show me those baby greens, now."

Abby's soft voice, rich with feeling.

Mac filled her lungs slowly, which made her side hurt, but then she opened her eyes again, and this time a bleary image of Abby's lovely features appeared above her. "Hi," she whispered. Her throat was gravel dry.

"Good morning." Abby's cool fingers brushed her face. "Do you know me, Mac?"

"My sex slave."

Abby smiled, and the tears in her eyes spilled over. She ignored them, and held a tumbler with a bending straw to Mac's lips. "One sip. Hold it in your mouth, and swallow slowly, please."

Mac savored the benediction of cool wetness on her tongue, then looked around, groggy. The beeps she'd been hearing apparently came from the machines surrounding the bed.

"Do you know where you are, love?"

Suddenly Mac did, and she gripped the blanket. "Cleo?"

"She's all right, Mac." Abby lowered the railing of the bed and sat carefully beside her. "She has a broken leg, but it should heal well. She's on another floor in this hospital, and Scratch is with her. Mostly, she's been worried about you." Abby stroked her forehead. "She hasn't been alone in that."

"Ah, I'm sorry." And Mac was, she could see the circles beneath Abby's eyes. "Have you been here all night?" She tried to lift her arm to touch her face, but stopped when that distant pain gripped her side again.

"Take it easy, Counselor." Abby eased her arm down. "You have a concussion and a few broken ribs. I'm afraid they're going to smart for a while."

"I remember the road, and Cleo yelling. Not much else."

"We'll fill you in on the details, when you're more alert. What's important is you and Cleo will both be fine."

Mac was already sleepy again—the juice in her IV must be powerful juju. She forced her eyes open. "I need to call my parents."

"You can do that. As soon as you can stay awake long enough. We'll let them know you're safe."

"Abby?"

"Hmm?"

"Can we go home soon?"

"As soon as we know I can take care of you there, yes." She felt Abby's lips touch her forehead. "Rest, honey. I'll be right here."

"Okay." Mac brushed her thumb against her finger to be sure, and she was right. Her ring was no longer there.

Just before she drifted off, she heard Abby whisper, "Thank you."

CHAPTER EIGHTEEN

I s she awake?"

Abby was checking Mac's IV, and she hadn't heard Danny enter the room. She was pushing Cleo in a wheelchair, her blue-casted leg extended on the foot brace.

"Well, hello." Abby kept her voice low. Mac had been dozing off and on since early afternoon, but now she seemed to be sleeping in earnest. She saw the growing alarm on Danny's face as she looked at Mac. "It's all right, Danny, she's just napping. She's come around very well since last night."

Danny let go of the wheelchair and walked slowly around Mac's bed, studying the IV line in her arm, the shallow scrape on her jaw. "Cleo says she has broken ribs."

"Yes. Her left side."

Abby noticed Danny's pallor as she pulled a chair closer to Mac's bed and sat down. "We're going to keep her here for a couple of days, to keep an eye on her concussion and make sure she's on the mend. But as I told Cleo this morning, Danny, Mac's going to be fine. She'll be home soon."

Danny nodded, staring at Mac's still face.

Abby folded her arms and sidled to Cleo. Her cast looked well placed, but her face was drawn and tired. "How are you this evening?"

"Ready to get out of here. I've been sprung." Cleo lifted a fistful of papers, but she hadn't taken her eyes off Mac. Abby took the sheets from her and studied them, and found the discharge instructions sound enough.

"How's your pain? Any nausea from the meds?"

"Pain's bearable, no nausea." Cleo dropped her voice another notch. "Danny knows. We talked this morning."

Abby nodded. She could have guessed Danny had heard about her father just by looking at her. She rested her hand for a moment on Cleo's head, then pushed her chair closer to Mac's bed. "Is Scratch downstairs?"

"Yeah, he brought Danny in, and he'll take us both back. Viv's still holding down the fort." Cleo reached through the bed's railing and brushed her finger across Mac's hand. "Did she eat anything?"

"Yes, a full course of tasty liquid protein." Abby gestured to the IV bag. "It'll have to do until she can sit up and handle some solids."

"Hell, let Mac take that bag and trot it down to Safeway. She'd bring it back loaded with enough condiments to make a gourmet feast." The humor in Cleo's tone faded. "Danny?"

There were no tears in Danny's eyes, but she was looking at Cleo with a wrenching bleakness. "He was so terrible to you, Cleo. All my life, he was so awful. It never mattered to him that I loved you."

Abby sat quietly in the only remaining chair. She and Cleo must have learned something from Mac and her listening silences; neither of them spoke.

"But I loved him too." Danny sounded suddenly half her age. "Do you think I'm stupid, to still love him? Does it make you mad?"

"Danny." Cleo rested her fingers on the bed's thin pillow. "Of course not, baby."

Danny played with the edge of Mac's blanket, and the only sound in the cramped room was the beeping of the monitors. Abby saw Mac's eyelashes flutter and knew she was surfacing.

She monitored the shallow rise and fall of her breasts beneath the blanket.

"I'm sorry, Cleo," Danny said. "For all of it."

Cleo glanced at Abby before looking back at Danny, her brow furrowed. "And just what are you apologizing for, Danielle?"

"You could have died yesterday. Mac could have too. She almost did." Danny touched Mac's wrist, fleetingly. "The only reason my dad took after you guys was because of me."

"Uh-huh," Cleo said slowly. "And now you're thinking you're somehow responsible for yesterday, for what your father did?"

"It's true." Danny shrugged, and the attempted adolescent casualness of that gesture hurt Abby's heart. "It wouldn't have happened, if I never came to Fireside. He came after me there too. I put the whole place in danger."

"Abby." Cleo sat back in the wheelchair, looking mystified. "Get that ice bucket. Dump it on Mac. Wake her up so she can talk some sense into this child."

Abby only smiled, even through the tightness in her throat. She'd been watching Mac's breathing, and knew she was awake. But Mac had stopped Cleo from picking little Lena up out of the snow, the day she'd had her nosebleed. She had known then that Inez, Lena's mother, should be the only one to cradle her injured child. Mac didn't stir, her lashes still against her cheek. Abby understood that Cleo had a wounded daughter too, and it was her words Danny needed to hear now.

"You listening to me, Danny?" Cleo's voice was low and calm.

"Yeah."

"Okay. I know how much you're hurting, baby. You had an awful shock today. But I think you're losing track of something that's real important." Cleo paused until Danny met her gaze. "You did love your dad. You tried to take care of him. You cooked for him, you nursed him when he was hungover. Sometimes, in that house, it was more like you were the adult, and he was the child. But that wasn't the way of it, Danny."

Cleo's brow was smooth now. "My troubles with your father began when you were three years old, honey. He was a grown-up man even then. And every day, for the last fifteen years, Sam made his own decisions. Bad ones, lots of them, but they were his to make. You have to let your daddy be a man, now. Let him be responsible for his choices, like all adults have to be. Don't you take on any blame that isn't rightfully yours."

Danny's expression didn't change, but she nodded. At least she had taken the words in.

The charge nurse tapped on the door, bringing a fresh unit of saline. By the time Abby had accepted it and thanked her, Mac's eyes were open and Danny's face had lightened considerably.

"Hey, Danny." Mac sounded drowsy but not too sedated. She turned her head on the pillow and offered Cleo a solemn peace sign in greeting.

"Yo, Counselor." Cleo smiled. "Think you've had enough beauty sleep for now?"

"Oh, yeah." Mac flicked a finger at Cleo's leg. "How's the drumstick?"

"Itches like hell already. How's the beanie?"

Mac's bleary gaze moved past Cleo and focused on Abby. "Better than ever."

"Do you need anything, Mac?" Danny still whispered, as if she were afraid of startling her.

Mac lifted her arm enough to point. "Pass me that water, Dan?"

"Sure." Danny's hands hovered over the tray beside Mac's bed until she found the canister.

"Let me slide by, Cleo." Abby was heartened by Mac's recovery so far, but that didn't mean she was willing to trust it entirely. She measured Mac's pulse as she sipped from the bending straw. She was still pale, and her ordinarily rich voice was rather thin, but Abby could allow this brief visit. Mac had been concerned about both Danny and Cleo, and time with them would do her good. Time together was doing all four of them good.

Abby brushed one finger across Mac's eyebrow, and Mac smiled at her.

"Mac, how many fingers am I holding up?" Cleo sounded worried.

Mac didn't even look. "She's flipping me off, right?" She said to Danny.

Danny glanced at Cleo. "Of course."

Danny's smile was brief but genuine, and Abby remembered that about grief. The first numb hours after a loss could give way to ephemeral moments of connection, small islands of light.

"You look pretty tired, Ab," Cleo said. "They need to pull a cot in here for you or something."

"I'll find a bed and sleep for a while, after my patient nods off again." Abby thought she might even be telling the truth. She was exhausted, and beginning to trust that she could leave Mac's side for a few hours without calamity.

Abby didn't really track the conversation that followed; the sound of their voices was company enough. Danny didn't mention her father again, and neither did they. They didn't discuss Mac's injuries any further, or Cleo's leg. It didn't feel as if these topics hovered unspoken in the small room—they just rested for a while.

Cleo complained about the dreadful hospital lunch forced upon her before she was discharged. Mac asked about Vivian's birthday the following week. There was some quiet laughter, nothing raucous.

Then Abby noticed Mac's lips held a shade less color, and knew it was time to stop. "I think we'd best let Mac rest now. She has to fall asleep before the nurse can wake her up to take her blood pressure."

Cleo snorted. "If it's that cute redhead with the tattoos who worked on my floor last night, Mac won't mind that."

"Well, if it's she, I'll be checking her pressure myself." Abby touched Danny's shoulder. "I'll come home for a few hours in the morning. I'll see you both then."

"Okay. Get some sleep, Abby." Danny put her arms around Abby's waist, the first time she had initiated a hug. "Cleo? I just thought of something. How the heck are we going to get you up all those stairs to your room?"

Cleo groaned. "I know, I've been imagining that."

Danny frowned. "Maybe Scratch and I can rig up some kind of sling—"

"No," Abby said loudly. "Cleo, the bed in the infirmary will be just fine for you tonight. Danny, I'd appreciate it if you'd sleep on the cot down there, to keep an eye on her."

"Sure, of course." Danny took the handles of the wheelchair again. She looked over Cleo's head at Mac, and her face fell a little. "Good night, Mac."

"Night, Danny."

"I'll be back to see you tomorrow." Danny hesitated. "I hope you can sleep. Stay off your left side."

"I will. Hey, Dan?" Mac lifted her head. "When you come tomorrow, can you bring that copy of *Da Vinci Code* you loaned me? It's on my bedside table."

"Sure, I'll remember." The shadows left Danny's eyes. She tapped on Cleo's head. "You ready?"

"Yep, back it up."

There was no room to turn the wheelchair in the cramped quarters, so Danny pulled Cleo carefully toward the door. Cleo lifted her hand and forked her fingers in the Vulcan *live long and prosper* sign at Abby and Mac.

Abby listened to the rubber squeak of the chair's wheels as it dwindled down the hall. She went around the bed to exchange the saline unit for dextrose. "I happen to know you finished *The Da Vinci Code* well over a week ago."

"Well. Thought I'd ask that cute redheaded nurse to read the good parts to me." Mac shifted in the bed and closed her eyes. "Danny's having a hard time."

"Yes, she is." Abby lowered the bed's railing and sat carefully at its edge. She held the backs of her fingers to Mac's cool cheek. "Among other things, she's quite worried about you. The best thing you can do for Danny is heal fast, and come home."

"Yes'm."

Abby touched a button on the headboard, and the light illuminating the bed dimmed.

"You could stretch out right here with me, Doc." Mac was beginning to slur her words. "The lady lover always does that in the movies, climbs into the hospital bed with the wounded hero."

"Yes, I've seen those movies." Abby stroked Mac's hair off her forehead. "But the lady lovers usually aren't doctors who understand that it's less than wise to knock loose an intravenous line."

"Ah, where's your...dang romantic spirit..."

Abby watched Mac's eyes drift closed, and her breathing grew deep and even. Abby did understand practical precautions. She promised herself she would be both practical and cautious. She stretched out carefully on the narrow bed next to Mac, against her right side, minding the IV line. She rested her head on Mac's shoulder.

And was asleep in seconds.

CHAPTER NINETEEN

I can take the pain, wench."

"Perhaps, but you still can't take the basket." Abby shifted the hamper higher, then slid her arm around Mac's waist again. "Honestly, is this marathon hike really necessary for your first outing? Fractured ribs take a long time to heal."

"Women of the desert heal quickly. We must, as the deadly scorpion is our main source of food."

"Nice try, mighty Amazon of the desert." Abby snickered. "But I'm still concerned about your ribs."

"My ribs have had more than two weeks to heal." Mac kissed the top of her head. "I'm too sore to walk without the bodily support of a beautiful woman, though. Also, I shouldn't carry heavy baskets for a while."

"That's true enough." Abby had pulled rank when they began this twilight jaunt. She carried the basket, or they stayed home. She didn't mind its light weight, as long as Mac's arm was draped across her shoulders. But that arm was draping rather heavily, and Abby knew her physical support was helpful. In spite of her bravado, Mac's side was still hurting her. "Honey, it's beautiful out here. But how far is our mystery destination?"

"Not far now."

The scattered yells of the kids playing in the open yard had long since faded behind them. They had passed the flat plains of the gardens Scratch had begun to prepare only this week; it was still too early for planting summer vegetables. Mac had chosen an unusually warm twilight for her first venture outside since the accident, and Abby relished the spring breeze on her face as they stepped off the trail.

"I'm embarrassed that I've lived here a full year and I've never explored this far." Abby ducked and followed Mac beneath overhanging evergreen branches, and they emerged into a small grassy meadow, enclosed by towering trees and carpeted in wildflowers. "Oh, Mac. It's lovely here."

Mac straightened, and Abby knew she was pulling in breath carefully before she spoke. "Welcome to my cool fort, Abby. I brought Danny and Cleo here once. I wanted to share it with you too."

"Lord." Abby turned in a circle, gazing at the colorful blossoms, then up at the treetops. "I know very well that twenty women and kids are sitting down to their suppers, right over that hill out there. But I'd swear you and I were alone in the world in this place. Thank you, for sharing your fort with me."

Mac nodded toward a low rock that sat in the earth near a thick bank of leafy hedges. "Let's set up over thar."

"Yes, m'lady." Abby approved of Mac's chosen landing zone; she could sit fairly comfortably on the ground, with the rock to lean against for support. Abby opened the basket and shook out a small blanket on the grass. Then she extended her braced forearm, and Mac grasped it and lowered herself to the blanket, a routine made familiar by weeks of team-driven recuperation. Abby eyed Mac's face surreptitiously as she unpacked the basket. She seemed fine; she was catching her breath quickly.

"Man, I missed the sky." Mac rested her head against the stone. "Too many days inside on my back."

"I know it's been hard for you." Abby lifted a thermos from the basket and twisted its lid. She took an appreciative whiff of the fragrant steam rising from the tea. "Mac." She sniffed again. "Is this Twinings?"

"Yeah, Twinings Prince of Wales."

"Macawai." Abby sat back on her heels. "Where, in all the vast tea dens of *Fredericksburg*, did you find Twinings Prince of Wales?"

"Actually, in the vast dens of the Internet." The dimple appeared in Mac's cheek. "You said some time ago this tea was one of your favorite memories of your years in England."

"Ah, you sweet ball of mush." Abby kissed Mac soundly on the cheek. She rested her forehead on her shoulder, touched not just by the gift, but by how typical it was of Mac's thoughtfulness. Many lovers might have preferred a bottle of chilled wine for an early evening tryst like this. But Abby would never again touch alcohol, in any form—so Mac brought along her favorite tea instead. She felt blessed. "Thank you, dear."

She poured the lightly scented brew into the plastic cup, and wrapped Mac's hand around it, her touch lingering on the empty space on her forefinger. "I'm so sorry your favorite ring was lost, Mac. I could have sworn you were wearing it at the hospital. I wish I'd paid better attention."

"You had other things on your mind, Doc." Mac took a sip and swirled the liquid in her mouth in a scholarly manner.

"Yes, split heads and whatnot." Abby accepted the cup and savored the tea, transported briefly back to the history-rich streets of London she had walked as a girl. But she didn't linger there long, as tonight she much preferred a certain small circle of trees in northeast Virginia. She saw Mac studying her ringless finger, and she traced her lower lip with her thumb. "That's a mysterious smile, Counselor. Do you have a story to tell me?"

"Part of a story. I'll tell you the whole thing, someday." Mac rested her chin on her knuckles. "You remember that long call I made to New Mexico, the day I got home?"

"I do. You talked to your parents."

"My dad, mostly. He knew I was okay, I just wanted to fill him in."

"I'm glad you did. It must have been frightening for them, being so far away and knowing you were injured."

"It was." Mac nodded. "It's scary to think you almost lost a daughter, especially if you've already lost one. It seems I had a twin, Doc."

"A what?" Abby set the cup down on the blanket.

"A twin sister. She died when we were both three."

"Mac." Abby lifted Mac's hand onto her knee. "You've always said you were an only child. You didn't know about this?"

"Well. I've suspected it for a while." Mac smiled at the ground. "But my dad confirmed it."

"What did he tell you?"

"About her death? Just that Ayashe drowned during a family day trip, a picnic by the Rio Grande. My mother had to be hospitalized after the funeral. And twice more, the next year. My dad and her doctors finally decided they had to put away any reminder of what happened—any reminder of Ayashe. So, she just disappeared from our lives."

"Ayashe." Abby watched Mac's face, amazed that she could relate all of this so calmly. She felt slightly queasy herself. "My God, Mac. All of a sudden, your entire history has changed. Are you angry that your parents kept this from you?"

"I'm not sure angry is the word. I guess I understand my dad's reasoning. But I told him I felt cheated, yeah. Robbed of knowing a member of my family. He was obviously still so conflicted about the whole thing, I didn't dump on him for it." Mac shrugged. "Guess I'm culpable in the family secret myself. I agreed not to tell Mom that I know."

Abby studied Mac's loved features, imagining her twin if she'd lived. Another woman with red streaks in her dark hair, with Mac's deep laugh. "And you don't have any memories at all, of this little girl?"

Mac shook her head, playing with Abby's fingers. "Looking back, I remember small flashes. Not of Ayashe, but of some big turmoil in my family when I was very young. My mother crying all the time. Never wanting to play with me. I reckon it was about that time I made up a little girl to play with."

"Ashley." A shiver worked up Abby's back. "Oh, honey. You did remember her, didn't you? Are you all right with all this?"

"Yeah. I really am. I remember her again now." Mac lifted Abby's hand and kissed it. "I'll tell you more Ashley stories, someday. After I've had time to digest this all a bit."

"I'll look forward to that." Abby fingered the sleeve of Mac's soft linen shirt. She didn't know how to respond to nebulous promises of someday because she didn't know how many of those there would be. She tried to resolve, again, not to dwell on an unreadable future. Mac was here now. She had come close enough to losing her forever to savor every day they had left.

"And tomorrow, she is a woman."

It took Abby a moment to realize Mac meant Danny. "Yes, a red-letter day for Fireside, in many ways. We meet our new child advocate tomorrow, and Danny turns eighteen. And she graduates next week."

"Our brave papoose."

Abby smiled. "She is brave, Mac, isn't she?"

The teachers at Danny's high school had been universally supportive. No one would have faulted Danny if she'd fallen apart these last weeks. The pressures of final exams and term papers could easily have defeated a young woman who had lost her father so suddenly, to a violent death. But even grieving and filled with the ambivalent shock of this loss, Danny had finished her senior projects. She would graduate with the rest of her class, and several voices would be there to cheer when she crossed the stage—Mac, Abby, Cleo, Vivian, Scratch—and Degale and Jo and Tina, Danny's Fireside family.

"Wait," Mac whispered. "I think I saw one."

"One what?" The last of the light was leaving the sky, and Abby couldn't see much of anything.

"Just watch. There."

And after a few seconds Abby saw it too, a tiny, sleepy blink of light deep in the hedges nearest them. It glowed briefly, a pale shimmering in the dark leaves, and then faded.

"Isn't that one?" Mac's tone was hushed and delighted.

"It is! They're quite early this year."

Cleo had tried to describe fireflies to Mac on a few occasions, and Mac had smiled politely and asked Abby to order antipsychotic meds. Apparently lightning bugs were unheard of west of the Mississippi, and Mac pretended to insist they were figments of Cleo's fevered imagination. Now more of them were appearing in the depths of the thick greenery, small lamps blinking for several seconds at a time, subtle flashes of green and gold.

"Looky," Mac breathed.

Abby rested her head on her shoulder again and watched the circle around them come gradually alive with the tiny flickering lights. Mac was seeing them for the first time, and she was thrilled to share this with her. Fireflies usually appeared weeks later, in full summer rather than spring, but Abby could believe they came early to this place. Every firefly ever born might have emerged into the world through this magical ring of trees. Perhaps their gentle light was generated here, in a space that felt timeless and somehow sacred, even to Abby's practical sensibilities.

"All right. Perfect." Mac kissed Abby's forehead. "Excuse me, ma'am."

Abby lifted her head, and Mac shifted and started to get up.

"What do you need, honey? I can find it."

"I believe that's true." Mac lifted Abby's hand and rested it on her raised knee. She knelt in the grass before her a little stiffly, given her sore side, but with an air of chivalrous dignity. She covered Abby's hand with her own. "I have something to say to you."

"All right." Abby sat back against the stone, both bracing herself and preparing to listen with an open heart. "Tell me."

Mac watched the faint stars overhead, as if to summon her thoughts. "I've been wandering for a while, Abby. A long time." Her shoulder lifted. "And I think it was traveling I had to do. I have no regrets. But as I've told you, things have changed for me here, at Fireside. And the honor of being with you has been a big part of that."

Abby sat still. The light of the fireflies was too distant to reach Mac, but their lovely luminescence still seemed to flicker over the strong planes of her face.

"I want to stay with you, Abby, if you'll have me. I want to wake up with you every morning, for the rest of my life. You're my home. I love you, and I want you to be my wife." Mac paused, and Abby was grateful for the chance to absorb the gut-deep resonance of those words. "I'm willing to work very hard, *querida*, all of my days, to keep this good for us both."

Abby lifted Mac's hand and kissed it. She started to speak, but Mac shook her head.

"Say anything you want, honey, but I'm not looking for an answer tonight. I just had the desire to tell you what's in my heart."

Abby had the same desire, but decided she didn't need words to express it. She drew Mac closer and their lips met. The kiss began lightly and then deepened, and Abby explored Mac's face with her fingertips, as if she'd never seen her before. She lost awareness even of the beauty of the twinkling lights around them, and reveled instead in the private pleasure of their touch.

Mac was stiff, and even cushioned by the blanket the hard ground was unforgiving, so there was nothing tempestuous in their joining that memorable night. They made love gently, generously, their slow dance witnessed only by wildflowers, and illuminated by fireflies and starlight.

❖

A full moon was rising by the time Fireside came into view again. Mac tried not to lean too heavily on Abby, but she wasn't overly worried about burdening her diminutive lover. She knew Abby was strong.

Their walk home held that rich, comfortable silence that fell only when everything important had been said. But even before they reached the residents' wings, the heavy thump of bass could be heard from the lit windows of the main house. They stopped and grinned at each other as they recognized the Beatles' *White Album*.

"Thank God, Cleo has commandeered the stereo for a while." Abby chuckled. "I was afraid we were in for an all-Fergie night."

"We still could be." Mac scratched Abby's back lightly. "Maybe Danny's being generous right now, but it's her party, she can call the tunes until dawn." She looked back over her shoulder, and felt an unexpected, sweet wistfulness at the emptiness of the trail.

"Did you hear something?"

"Nope." Mac pressed Abby's shoulders gently. "Not a thing. Let's go party."

❖

Cleo glanced at Mac and Abby as they stepped down into the living room, and then threw a dark glare at Danny. "Danielle, I told you that music was too loud and you're disturbing the residents. You turn it down right now."

Danny just snickered, since Cleo was the one standing by the CD player and was doubtless the one who had jacked "Mother Nature's Son" too high in the first place. "You guys took long enough," she said to Mac. "We ran out of cider already. Scratch is in the kitchen brewing more."

"In the meantime, I've discovered some wonderful tea."

Abby touched Mac's face and then started toward the kitchen. "You'll have to try it, Danny, it's sort of the Beatles of teas."

"Cool beans." Danny was seated on the floor next to the rocking chair where Vivian held reign, both of them flipping through the stack of DVDs on her lap. Mac was relieved to see ⸻ ʳ in the girl's face again. The mood cast by this ⸻ already warm and friendly, and there were no ⸻ s for the first time in weeks.

⸻ uated to a neon-blue walking cast, and was ⸻ olidly over to the deep couch. She sank into ⸻ a sigh, her one furry bear slipper extended in ⸻ vas your first sojourn into the outside world,

⸻ lk." Mac smiled down at Cleo's cast and ⸻ work of art, you know. We should cut off ⸻ on the wall."

⸻ ter canvas, Danny had made do with white ⸻ lastic shell of Cleo's walking cast, which was covered entirely with intricate swirls, patterns and symbols. Cleo lifted the thick boot onto a small footstool with a satisfied grunt. "I already promised Danny she could cut off my leg for the portfolio she's sending to the art department at UMW in town. I figure if she includes decorated body parts from all of us, she's in for that scholarship."

"From your mouth to God's ears, Cleo." Vivian rocked gently, peering down at a DVD cover. "You do have a true artistic talent, Danielle. That school would be insane not to jump on you."

"I don't even know where I'll be living next fall." A crease appeared in Danny's forehead. "Or how I'd get to the campus, if I get the scholarship, from wherever I'll be."

"Let's take one pressing issue at a time." Cleo looked at Mac and closed one eye slowly.

"Is it out there?" Mac whispered.

Cleo nodded, with a smug smile.

The solution to Danny's transportation problems was parked on the circular drive out front, concealed by the darkness. Not a Ferrari, quite a far cry from it, but it was adorable, a blue Volkswagen Beetle hatchback, of used vintage but classy trim. And its engine ran like a fine watch, Scratch had seen to that. A gift from them all. It awaited Danny's discovery the next morning, its small windshield bedecked with a huge festive bow.

"Our victuals, women." Abby backed out of the kitchen, carrying a platter laden with bowls of popcorn and pretzels. Scratch followed, bearing a lighter tray of steaming tea and fragrant cider.

"Hot doggy." Danny went up on her knees and accepted a brimming bowl of popcorn from Abby. Mac grinned, wondering if Danny and Cleo knew they were starting to share each other's catch phrases. The simple happiness on Danny's face went straight to Mac's heart. Not many high school seniors would consider a non-alcoholic slumber party with older adults the height of celebration, but time with the people who loved her was what Danny needed and wanted most. Family time.

"Thank you, dear heart." Vivian took a cup from Scratch and tilted her face so he could kiss her cheek. "Danny here was just expressing curiosity about her living arrangements next fall."

"Ah, I'm pleased to be back in time for this discussion." Scratch settled into the stuffed recliner next to the sofa, and laid his large hand on Mac's knee. He arched one grayed eyebrow at her inquiringly, and Mac nodded assurance she was feeling fine. Scratch patted her knee and sat back. Mac loved these nonverbal conversations that served as affectionate shorthand between people who knew each other well. She was growing fluent with everyone in this room. Abby sank into the sofa between her and Cleo, and Mac took her hand as naturally as drawing her next breath.

"Next fall nothing, I don't know where I'll be living next week." Danny's smile was fading again. "You guys have that

Mac smiled. She bent her head and kissed her, and that familiar sensation of coming home filled her again, light and certain.

"I love you," Abby whispered.

"I love you back."

And then, of course, there was a knock at the front door.

"Damn, is it really that loud?" Cleo looked guilty as she pivoted away from the fireplace and limped toward the CD player. "Busted."

"Probably just someone locked out of their unit." Mac made herself get out of the couch, wincing at the ache in her side but grinning when she felt Abby's proprietary pat on her butt. She cupped Abby's chin. "Be right back."

"I'll be here."

"See if they have marshmallows," Danny called from the fireplace as Mac headed for the entry.

"Also chocolate bars," Cleo added. "We want s'mores."

"Perfect," Mac agreed. An evening that began with fireflies, continued with toasted marshmallows, and would end with dawn rising on a living room filled with sleeping family suited her just fine.

She strolled to the front door, unbolted it, and pulled it open.

A young woman with sandy hair lowered her balled fist quickly and took a step back. She looked a bit travel-worn. She blinked up at Mac, and folded her arms.

"Is this Fireside?"

"It is. My name is Mac."

"The police officer said I could come here."

"Yes, you can." Mac smiled. She stepped back from the door. "Come on in, and meet my friends. I believe they're building a fire."

About the Author

Cate Culpepper is a 2005 and 2007 Golden Crown Literary Award winner in the Sci-Fi/Fantasy category, and a 2008 recipient of the Alice B. Readers' Choice Award. She is the author of the Tristaine series, which includes *Tristaine: The Clinic*, *Battle for Tristaine*, *Tristaine Rises*, and *Queens of Tristaine*. Cate lives in Seattle, where she supervises a transitional living program for homeless young gay adults. She's currently working on a paranormal suspense novel set in the desert Southwest.

Books Available From Bold Strokes Books

The Middle of Somewhere by Clifford Henderson. Eadie T. Pratt sets out on a road trip in search of a new life and ends up in the middle of somewhere she never expected. (978-1-60282-047-0)

Paybacks by Gabrielle Goldsby. Cameron Howard wants to avoid her old nemesis Mackenzie Brandt but their high school reunion brings up more than just memories. (978-1-60282-046-3)

Uncross My Heart by Andrews & Austin. When a radio talk show diva sets out to interview a female priest, the two women end up at odds and neither heaven nor earth is safe from their feelings. (978-1-60282-045-6)

Fireside by Cate Culpepper. Mac, a therapist, and Abby, a nurse, fall in love against the backdrop of friendship, healing, and defending one's own within the Fireside shelter. (978-1-60282-044-9)

Green Eyed Monster by Gill McKnight. Mickey Rapowski believes her former boss has cheated her out of a small fortune, so she kidnaps the girlfriend and demands compensation—just a straightforward abduction that goes so wrong when Mickey falls for her captive. (978-1-60282-042-5)

Blind Faith by Diane and Jacob Anderson-Minshall. When private investigator Yoshi Yakamota and the Blind Eye Detective Agency are hired to find a woman's missing sister, the assignment seems fairly mundane—but in the detective business, the ordinary can quickly become deadly. (978-1-60282-041-8)

A Pirate's Heart by Catherine Friend. When rare book librarian Emma Boyd searches for a long-lost treasure map, she learns the hard way that pirates still exist in today's world—some modern pirates steal maps, others steal hearts. (978-1-60282-040-1)

Trails Merge by Rachel Spangler. Parker Riley escapes the high-powered world of politics to Campbell Carson's ski resort—and their mutual attraction produces anything but smooth running. (978-1-60282-039-5)

Dreams of Bali by C.J. Harte. Madison Barnes worships work, power, and success, and she's never allowed anyone to interfere—that is, until she runs into Karlie Henderson Stockard. Eclipse EBook (978-1-60282-070-8)

The Limits of Justice by John Morgan Wilson. Benjamin Justice and reporter Alexandra Templeton search for a killer in a mysterious compound in the remote California desert. (978-1-60282-060-9)

Designed for Love by Erin Dutton. Jillian Sealy and Wil Johnson don't much like each other, but they do have to work together—and what they desire most is not what either of them had planned. (978-1-60282-038-8)

Calling the Dead by Ali Vali. Six months after Hurricane Katrina, NOLA Detective Sept Savoie is a cop who thinks making a relationship work is harder than catching a serial killer—but her current case may prove her wrong. (978-1-60282-037-1)

Dark Garden by Jennifer Fulton. Vienna Blake and Mason Cavender are sworn enemies—who can't resist each other. Something has to give. (978-1-60282-036-4)

Shots Fired by MJ Williamz. Kyla and Echo seem to have the perfect relationship and the perfect life until someone shoots at Kyla—and Echo is the most likely suspect. (978-1-60282-035-7)

truelesbianlove.com by Carsen Taite. Mackenzie Lewis and Dr. Jordan Wagner have very different ideas about love, but they discover that truelesbianlove is closer than a click away. Eclipse EBook (978-1-60282-069-2)

Justice at Risk by John Morgan Wilson. Benjamin Justice's blind date leads to a rare opportunity for legitimate work, but a reckless risk changes his life forever. (978-1-60282-059-3)

Run to Me by Lisa Girolami. Burned by the four-letter word called love, the only thing Beth Standish wants to do is run for—or maybe from—her life. (978-1-60282-034-0)

Split the Aces by Jove Belle. In the neon glare of Sin City, two women ride a wave of passion that threatens to consume them in a world of fast money and fast times. (978-1-60282-033-3)

Uncharted Passage by Julie Cannon. Two women on a vacation that turns deadly face down one of nature's most ruthless killers—and find themselves falling in love. (978-1-60282-032-6)

Night Call by Radclyffe. All medevac helicopter pilot Jett McNally wants to do is fly and forget about the horror and heartbreak she left behind in the Middle East, but anesthesiologist Tristan Holmes has other plans. (978-1-60282-031-9)

I Dare You by Larkin Rose. Stripper by night, corporate raider by day, Kelsey's only looking for sex and power, until she meets a woman who stirs her heart and her body. (978-1-60282-030-2)

Truth Behind the Mask by Lesley Davis. Erith Baylor is drawn to Sentinel Pagan Osborne's quiet strength, but the secrets between them strain duty and family ties. (978-1-60282-029-6)

Lake Effect Snow by C.P. Rowlands. News correspondent Annie T. Booker and FBI Agent Sarah Moore struggle to stay one step ahead of disaster as Annie's life becomes the war zone she once reported on. Eclipse EBook (978-1-60282-068-5)

Revision of Justice by John Morgan Wilson. Murder shifts into high gear, propelling Benjamin Justice into a raging fire that consumes the Hollywood Hills, burning steadily toward the famous Hollywood Sign—and the identity of a cold-blooded killer. (978-1-60282-058-6)

Cooper's Deale by KI Thompson. Two would-be lovers and a decidedly inopportune murder spell trouble for Addy Cooper, no matter which way the cards fall. (978-1-60282-028-9)

Romantic Interludes 1: Discovery ed. by Radclyffe and Stacia Seaman. An anthology of sensual, erotic contemporary love stories from the best-selling Bold Strokes authors. (978-1-60282-027-2)

A Guarded Heart by Jennifer Fulton. The last place FBI Special Agent Pat Roussel expects to find herself is assigned to an illicit private security gig baby-sitting a celebrity. (Ebook) (978-1-60282-067-8)

Saving Grace by Jennifer Fulton. Champion swimmer Dawn Beaumont, injured in a car crash she caused, flees to Moon Island, where scientist Grace Ramsay welcomes her. (Ebook) (978-1-60282-066-1)

The Sacred Shore by Jennifer Fulton. Successful tech industry survivor Merris Randall does not believe in love at first sight until she meets Olivia Pearce. (Ebook) (978-1-60282-065-4)

Passion Bay by Jennifer Fulton. Two women from different ends of the earth meet in paradise. Author's expanded edition. (Ebook) (978-1-60282-064-7)

Never Wake by Gabrielle Goldsby. After a brutal attack, Emma Webster becomes a self-sentenced prisoner inside her condo—until the world outside her window goes silent. (Ebook) (978-1-60282-063-0)

Remember Tomorrow by Gabrielle Goldsby. Cees Bannigan and Arieanna Simon find that a successful relationship rests in remembering the mistakes of the past. (978-1-60282-026-5)

The Caretaker's Daughter by Gabrielle Goldsby. Against the backdrop of a nineteenth-century English country estate, two women struggle to find love. (Ebook) (978-1-60282-062-3)

Simple Justice by John Morgan Wilson. When a pretty-boy cokehead is murdered, former LA reporter Benjamin Justice and his reluctant new partner, Alexandra Templeton, must unveil the real killer. (978-1-60282-057-9)

Remember Tomorrow by Gabrielle Goldsby. Cees Bannigan and Arieanna Simon find that a successful relationship rests in remembering the mistakes of the past. (978-1-60282-026-5)

Put Away Wet by Susan Smith. Jocelyn "Joey" Fellows has just been savagely dumped—when she posts an online personal ad, she discovers more than just the great sex she expected. (978-1-60282-025-8)

Homecoming by Nell Stark. Sarah Storm loses everything that matters—family, future dreams, and love—will her new "straight" roommate cause Sarah to take a chance at happiness? (978-1-60282-024-1)

The Three by Meghan O'Brien. A daring, provocative exploration of love and sexuality. Two lovers, Elin and Kael, struggle to survive in a postapocalyptic world. (Ebook) (978-1-60282-056-2)

Falling Star by Gill McKnight. Solley Rayner hopes a few weeks with her family will help heal her shattered dreams, but she hasn't counted on meeting a woman who stirs her heart. (978-1-60282-023-4)

Lethal Affairs by Kim Baldwin and Xenia Alexiou. Elite operative Domino is no stranger to peril, but her investigation of journalist Hayley Ward will test more than her skills. (978-1-60282-022-7)

A Place to Rest by Erin Dutton. Sawyer Drake doesn't know what she wants from life until she meets Jori Diamantina—only trouble is, Jori doesn't seem to share her desire. (978-1-60282-021-0)

Warrior's Valor by Gun Brooke. Dwyn Izsontro and Emeron D'Artansis must put aside personal animosity and unwelcome attraction to defeat an enemy of the Protector of the Realm. (978-1-60282-020-3)

Finding Home by Georgia Beers. Take two polar-opposite women with an attraction for one another they're trying desperately to ignore, throw in a far-too-observant dog, and then sit back and enjoy the romance. (978-1-60282-019-7)

Word of Honor by Radclyffe. All Secret Service Agent Cameron Roberts and First Daughter Blair Powell want is a small intimate wedding, but the paparazzi and a domestic terrorist have other plans. (978-1-60282-018-0)

Hotel Liaison by JLee Meyer. Two women searching through a secret past discover that their brief hotel liaison is only the beginning. Will they risk their careers—and their hearts—to follow through on their desires? (978-1-60282-017-3)

Love on Location by Lisa Girolami. Hollywood film producer Kate Nyland and artist Dawn Brock discover that love doesn't always follow the script. (978-1-60282-016-6)

Edge of Darkness by Jove Belle. Investigator Diana Collins charges at life with an irreverent comment and a right hook, but even those may not protect her heart from a charming villain. (978-1-60282-015-9)

Thirteen Hours by Meghan O'Brien. Workaholic Dana Watts's life takes a sudden turn when an unexpected interruption arrives in the form of the most beautiful breasts she has ever seen—stripper Laurel Stanley's. (978-1-60282-014-2)

In Deep Waters 2 by Radclyffe and Karin Kallmaker. All bets are off when two award winning-authors deal the cards of love and passion… and every hand is a winner. (978-1-60282-013-5)

Pink by Jennifer Harris. An irrepressible heroine frolics, frets, and navigates through the "what ifs" of her life: all the unexpected turns of fortune, fame, and karma. (978-1-60282-043-2)

Deal with the Devil by Ali Vali. New Orleans crime boss Cain Casey brings her fury down on the men who threatened her family, and blood and bullets fly. (978-1-60282-012-8)

Naked Heart by Jennifer Fulton. When a sexy ex-CIA agent sets out to seduce and entrap a powerful CEO, there's more to this plan than meets the eye…or the flogger. (978-1-60282-011-1)

Heart of the Matter by KI Thompson. TV newscaster Kate Foster is Professor Ellen Webster's dream girl, but Kate doesn't know Ellen exists…until an accident changes everything. (978-1-60282-010-4)

Heartland by Julie Cannon. When political strategist Rachel Stanton and dude ranch owner Shivley McCoy collide on an empty country road, fate intervenes. (978-1-60282-009-8)

Shadow of the Knife by Jane Fletcher. Militia Rookie Ellen Mittal has no idea just how complex and dangerous her life is about to become. A Celaeno series adventure romance. (978-1-60282-008-1)

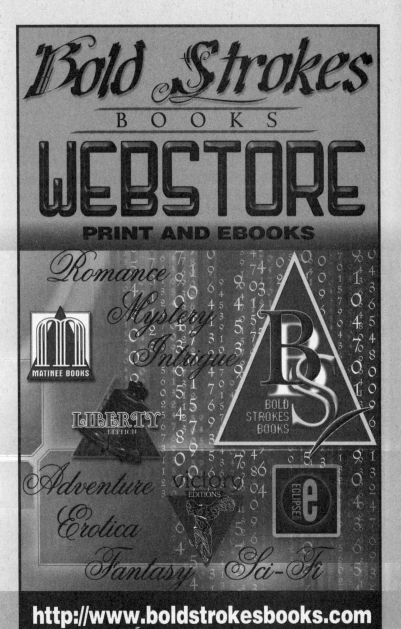